Advance Praise for *Twine*

"Dorriah Rogers's memoir is equal parts heart-wrenching and miraculous. The very fact that Rogers survived and thrived against all odds is a beautiful testament to the power of resiliency and finding inner strength."

—Ann Garvin, USA TODAY
bestselling author of *I Like You Just Fine When You're Not Around*

t w i n e

A MEMOIR

DORRIAH ROGERS

PERMUTED
PRESS

A PERMUTED PRESS BOOK
ISBN: 978-1-68261-867-7
ISBN (eBook): 978-1-68261-868-4

Twine:
A Memoir
© 2019 by Dorriah Rogers
All Rights Reserved

Cover Design by Cody Corcoran
Author Photo by Joanna DeGeneres

PERMUTED
PRESS

Permuted Press, LLC
New York • Nashville
permutedpress.com

Published in the United States of America

For Tricia Bevan: who said, over the course of seventeen years: *keep writing, it's what you do.*

*"When entering a labyrinth,
don't forget your ball of twine."*

—*Joseph Campbell*

Contents

Prologue

How does it get like this? Really, how does it ever get like this? There are reality TV shows now all about the allure of dysfunctional families and broken homes. Car crash affairs complete with pathetic characters and the sympathetic noddings of professionals. But those shows only slip a finger into the oily stink of it. They show the end result, not the *process*. Who even gives a shit what they think?

What I want to know is whether it is a slow march, seasons passing through and around each other, or rather sudden, harsh and complete in the blink of an eye. I can't tell. Even though I lived it, am forever living it, I just cannot tell. Then there's the synonymous irony of that statement. I cannot tell for many other reasons as well. The secrets have been harbored for a lifetime. Rotten and skeletal ships pushed against broken cliffs. So much shame. Not to mention the fact that telling this story proves that I killed my mom.

The truth of this is an infected sore, too turgid not to pop, too rancid to ignore. There will be repercussions and they will be significant.

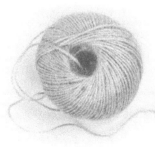

Blinders

My name is Dorriah Allesandra Burke and this is my story. It is a story that requires telling, simply because I have no choice. Even if that choice is solely within my own mind. To the world I am a middle-aged single mother of a teenage daughter, educated, professional, a scientist, strong-willed, good, maybe sometimes great, at what I do. My bills get paid, my credit score is solid, my carpet is vacuumed. My friends think I have my shit together. But that is about as real as Facebook and the perfect existence that all of us post. I am far from perfect. In fact, I am just shy of insane.

My story starts with my mother, as all family stories should.

This last visit she is a clawed skeleton. Her hair swirls about her head like tiny wisps of smoke. She is there behind those deep blue eyes. I see her. She sees me. She pulls up from the depths of her entrapment and her mind is sharp and focused. According to her, he is trying to convince me she has lost her mind so he can put her in a home.

"Do you want to go to a home?" I ask.

"No," she replies emphatically. "Never."

"But isn't he still mean to you?"

She looks down, away. "Yes."

I don't know what to say to this. The deep precision of it remains. My father's rage towards her, towards us, has been more of a constant than atoms and food. The nuclear energy of his anger. It hasn't changed. Not one bit. Despite the fact that she is bedridden from recent hip surgery, has all the symptoms of Alzheimer's. Despite the fact that he is ancient and smells like ruined dirt, it has never changed. I saw it just minutes ago, and I did nothing about it. He is, and always will be, the father of my childhood.

I gave her fuzzy socks for Christmas. The kind with the knotted soft cotton, happy pastels tied with silk ribbon. At that point she wasn't quite sure what they were, but I asked if she wanted to try them on anyway. She just shook her head no.

"Jesus, Anne, c'mon," he says from the other side of the room. "Give me those."

"I'm fine," she replies, her hand waving in front of her face. I can see every vein and bone. The nails are yellowed and too long. *I should cut them.*

He comes to the bed and throws back the comforter. Dog hair and dirt cascade down the other side. I am hoping the covers underneath will be better. They are. This somehow makes me feel like maybe it's not so bad. That she will get up. *Walk away.*

He is pulling at the ribbon, not really untying it so much as controlling its exit. His motions are staccato. Even the ribbon is afraid of him.

"Put these on," he orders. As he pulls back the flannel sheet I can see she is wearing white sweat socks, probably his. It is my moment to spy on her, to see her physical condition underneath. *I haven't been here yet. I've been too afraid. Will I see bedsores, infection, worse?* Her muscles sag away from the bone like sails in a listless wind.

She pulls away from him, turning to her side, almost fetal. "I don't want to."

He grabs her foot and yanks it towards him. Yanks it. She winces. She hasn't walked without assistance in months, hasn't gotten out of bed since her last hip surgery. She is not old, still in her seventies, yet her body is withered and atrophied, the whiteness of it almost painful, her toes twisted and cramped.

"Here," he says. He tugs the first sock over her foot. Whether she pulls from him or her leg twitches involuntarily from the awkward position doesn't matter. He jerks it back while she yelps.

"Your mother," he looks at me, "she's something else. You'd think I'd have a moment to myself. But no, after taking care of her and working for the week, I'm just exhausted." He chuckles and shakes his head as I watch silently. This dance is timeless.

She clearly doesn't want the socks or him to touch her, but he keeps talking. I can't hear him. All I can see are the legs and the control and the fear. And this is him being as nice as he's ever been in my entire life.

How the fuck do I justify this? Is it because she isn't covered in filth or smell like urine? Or maybe she does and I can't smell it through the rotted carpet and cat piss. Because she has a pulse? There are exposed wires everywhere, an obvious fire trap. Cardboard covers the window. I cannot and will not bring my young daughter to this infected place. She will never see this. I scream in my head for my mother to die in her sleep. When she nods off after the sock debacle, I pray for her to stop breathing. Merry Christmas.

So we sit, the three of us, my bed-ridden mother, my scowling father, and myself, for dinner. What should be my parents, my daughter, Delaney, my long-absent brother and I sitting around a festive table, is not. I haven't eaten in this house in over two decades. He has made Lobster Thermidor, fruit salad, and green beans. I am amused both by the portions and the menu. *How the hell can I feel amused in this house of horrors? What is wrong with me?* So many incongruities, so much I have no idea how to deal with or respond to. The food is good. I guess he can still cook with the one burner plate that is left of the kitchen. The serving sizes are for old people, but it suits me. One tiny piece of lobster and a bite of salad and I'm good. I think back to the days of large portions for big people. I think of the fact that I am sitting in this bedroom at a tiny table set up next to my mother's bed in the one room of the house that is habitable and he is so proud of himself and the dinner he has made and the fact that he cleaned the room for this dinner and it took him three days and everything is just perfect and he can't *won't* see the grime and cat shit along the baseboards and the dog hair that balls in six-inch-deep bunches at the walls and the dust that covers the books that haven't been touched along the headboard for years and the exposed plywood of the floors where the rot has broken through because he has *cleaned* it which means the piles of clothes have been thrown in the hallway where you can't walk through anyway and the spider webs fall in your goddamn hair.

Happy Holidays

That's the thing about Christmas. So fraught with emotions and expectations, supplanted by baggage and apathy. A day I have loathed for most of my life. This last Christmas was no different—simply a bizarre cabaret of lobster and socks—surrounded by filth and misery. I can only liken dinner in that disconsolate bedroom to sitting in a movie theater watching a horror film, screaming, yet no one onscreen can hear you. The actors simply continue on about their screenplay, oblivious to any audience. But I have always screamed like that, silently, into a darkened echo chamber, knowing the reel will continue to play forward.

Despite my loathing, I try with everything I have to make holidays and celebrations as enjoyable as possible for my daughter. I gave up some years ago on anything approaching routine when it came to my parents' involvement in her holidays, instead skillfully maneuvering around them and their participation. Her holidays now involve a very small hand-selected group of people, my complete and undivided attention, and a confidence in what is likely to happen. I did not bring her to my parents' house this last lobster Christmas, and because my mother is recovering from hip surgery, she will not be traveling to our house even for a brief visit. At least not until she gets up and around. *Another ridiculous fantasy I play in my head.* I have learned over the years that long dinners that include my parents will always *always* end up with my father holding court describing his endless adventures and accomplishments to anyone within earshot, while my mother sits next to him steadily advancing on staggeringly drunk. My daughter will not factor into their evening at all.

I came to this realization when Delaney was about four. Throughout her infant years I had harbored high hopes that my mom would bond closely with her, in some way replacing her dysfunctional bond with my father. I saw glimmers of this on those days she would come to my house to spend time with the baby on her own, but these moments were rare and fleeting, as on most occasions when my father was around and her demeanor and focus changed. Delaney's fourth Christmas was the end of my attempts to forge any real connection.

It began as so many holiday dinners did—Delaney flushed with excitement, my hope and dread equally aligned, and my parents showing up with a side dish of green beans, a cardboard box filled with odd gift selections, old Halloween candy, and several bottles of wine. This particular Christmas I was still married to Delaney's father, and together with his two daughters from a previous marriage, his ex-wife and her boyfriend, and my mother-in-law, we made a full house.

"Hi Gramma!" exclaimed Delaney as she ran to my mom. "Did you bring me any presents?"

My mom laughed and reached down to smooth the hair away from her face. "Of course, honey."

Delaney hugged her knees and ran back to play with her half-sisters. She never even made eye contact with my father. Like dogs, most kids knew to submit without question or avoid him entirely.

"Here, Dorriah, you can take these," said my father, handing me the box of gifts. Dog hair coated the bottom and it smelled like mold.

"Sure."

"I'm going to pour the wine," he announced. "Anyone want a glass?"

Everyone declined, as he knew they would, and thus began the three-bottle journey he and my mother would navigate for the remainder of the afternoon. How he avoided a DUI every year escaped me.

I spent the next hour or so preparing dinner with the sounds of kids playing and adults talking in the background. If I ignored my father's dominance of the conversation, I could almost imagine that it was idyllic, that I had created a warm and nurturing environment for my daughter, and my charitable inclusion of my husband's ex-wife demonstrated sublime holiday spirit. It was these small minutes that I worked very hard to achieve, minutes that Delaney could remember when she got older, summing up her childhood in short benevolent sentences like "I love Christmas" or "I was such a happy kid." Now that she is older, I am fairly certain those are not sentences she would ever say.

As that afternoon slipped away into a balmy California dusk, we gathered around the tree to open presents. My parents got Delaney a battery-animated velociraptor, both wildly inappropriate for a four-year-old girl, and a gift that utterly terrified her. It took me about thirty minutes to calm her down, and she stopped crying only when it joined the pile of other entirely useless gifts in the hall closet.

Once gifts were opened, the adults sat around the dining table for dessert while the three girls played with their toys. As usual, my father regaled everyone with outlandish tales of his bravery and accomplishment, never once stopping to engage in the normal back-and-forth of adult conversation. He talked nonstop, barely pausing between bites of food, bits of pie flying from his mouth as he continued. I could sense that my husband's ex-wife and her boyfriend were becoming weary of his verbal onslaught, yet I was helpless to stop him. It was Delaney that caught my attention.

"Gramma," she said, wandering up to my mom, tugging at her pants leg. "Come play with me."

My mother absentmindedly smiled down at her as she poured another glass of wine. Her eyes were glazed, but she was far from the fall-down drunk she could become.

"Please, Gramma."

"In a minute, honey," my mother replied dismissively.

Delaney wandered back to her pile of toys while I watched my mother sit silently beside my father as he talked ad nauseam. She never once offered an opinion or uttered a word, even though these same stories had been retold so many times that she could have recited them verbatim. After about ten minutes, Delaney came back.

"Ready now, Gramma?" she asked. "Want to play Barbie with me?"

I stared hard, waiting to see what my mother would do. She had an opportunity here to slip away from my father's barrage, perhaps claiming the need to use the bathroom, or just getting up and following Delaney to the living room.

She chose neither. Instead she smiled down at her four-year-old granddaughter and said nothing. Delaney finally wandered away, visibly confused.

For the rest of that night I watched my mother closely. She never did get up to play with Delaney. She never left my father's side, instead polishing off a bottle-and-a-half of wine and sitting mutely in the same position for hours. She reminded me almost eerily of a Stepford wife, practically Pavlovian in her response to my father's voice and the red wine. From that dinner on, I gave up any hope that she was capable of making choices beyond those that made her numb.

When I was young, around Delaney's age or a bit older, Christmas was a slightly—although not much—different affair. Parts of it were absurdly normal while other elements defied description. As children, my brother John and I clung to the normal, and danced it out the door with new bikes and roller skates to play with our friends. We left the absurdity behind, where we hoped it would stay, cloistered and locked behind shuttered windows. Despite our naïve efforts, it oftentimes leaked, leaving us both mystified and mortified at the consequences.

For many years my family spent Christmas Eve at my Aunt JoAnn's house, an expansive San Fernando Valley tract home with a steep staircase to the front door and sweeping views. The yard consisted of golf ball-sized white rocks and minimal ground cover, and the houses were perched on an irrationally steep incline. All of my extended family would join, upwards of thirty or forty people, aunts milling about the kitchen pulling out trays of food, cousins getting under-foot, while I would load my fingertips with black olives and try to spy on my older cousins smoking pot downstairs. These were joyous and fun occasions, filled with laughter and drinking, my grandmother Allesandra always keeping a sharp eye on the goings-on.

Because there were so many kids, we made a haul, our arms stuffed with gifts by the time we left, our bellies full of turkey, ham, prime rib, and inevitably, loads of fudge and peppermint bark. Because we were so young at the time, John and I neither noticed nor cared about the drama sur-rounding the older cousins and adults. This was left for the muted arguments on the wide balcony, and the occasional non-attendance by various insulted family members. All we knew was the food was great, we got a lot of presents, and for the most part, our father ignored us.

Our extended family had a gaggle of cousins ranging in age from toddlers to older cousins in their twenties. Cliques formed in various portions of the house, with the younger kids primarily running around outside and the older cous-ins plotting downstairs and locking the little kids out of the room. I always tried to wrangle my way into the older cousin clique, but it never worked, since my brother and I were part of the youngest generation of our family. When I was about four and although I don't remember it exactly, little did the adults arguing upstairs know at the time, my eldest cousin Bill spent the Christmas of 1968 trying to convince my older cousins to join him in finding out more about this enthrall-ing guy he had met, who had the best weed around. He told my teenage cousins that he had never met a more charismatic and interesting person, and that he was blown away by how easily this guy attracted women.

I found out many years later that most of my cousins thought the whole thing sounded stupid, and just listened to be polite. Afterwards, they all concurred that Bill was nuts and that they had no interest in joining him. It was my cousin Dave, Bill's brother, who decided that maybe it might be a good idea to convince him that this guy sounded sketchy and should be avoided. Dave said that there was just something weird about how Bill talked about him, and it made him uneasy.

Eight months later, the infamous Sharon Tate and LaBianca family were brutally murdered a few miles away, sending shockwaves through our community. Headlines screamed of their deaths with glamorous photos of the very pregnant Sharon Tate and images of the wholesome LaBianca family, all of whom had been butchered in their homes. It turned out that Bill had been hanging out with Charles Manson and the Manson Family in their commune in the hills about fifteen minutes from my Aunt JoAnn's house. By telling his brother to avoid that "charismatic and interesting" man he had crossed paths with, Dave likely saved Bill from a lifetime in jail. Our family talked about that dodge for many decades.

When it was time to leave Aunt JoAnn's, John and I would hide in the upstairs bathroom together. Not because we didn't want to leave—well maybe it was—but mostly because we knew that, on our way out, our mother would topple into the sweetheart ivy along the sidewalk in front of my aunt's house. She did it every single year, and every single year it embarrassed us both to the point of tears. Unfailingly, over the course of the evening, she would drink herself to oblivion, my father would drag her out of the house, my grandmother would watch in dismay, and our mother would fall in a sodden heap into the ivy. And every single time my father would scream at her the entire forty-five-minute drive home.

The next morning was Christmas. Forgotten was the mess of just a few hours earlier—stockings were stuffed with rock candy and licorice, and we were expected to behave as though nothing had happened the night before. My mother would pull herself together to open presents, my father would light the fireplace, my grandparents Allesandra and Alphonse would join a couple hours later, and the mid-morning would be spent outside riding a new Schwinn or tentatively testing a new skateboard. These were the best hours of the entire holiday—John and I riding whatever new toy around our cul-de-sac, joined by other kids on the block similarly showing off their goods.

Every Christmas morning around eleven or so we would sit down to a breakfast of Swedish crepes and sausage, and every Christmas morning John and I would wolf down our food and run outside to keep playing as long as possible, understanding full well that the eleven a.m. mimosas and early departure of our grandparents meant a drunken mother far earlier than usual. The best we could hope for was for her to pass out in the house. The most likely scenario involved a raging fight, broken gifts, and the two of us slinking back into the house to avoid detection.

A Decision

At forty years old, I've just survived my second divorce and my parents have been married for forty-eight years. What got me here is no different from the other half of couples who can't figure it out. I just do it serially. I am a self-labeled emotional moron. The sad thing is, nothing feels better after self-admission. It's kind of like alcoholism. You own it, you therapize it, but in the end, all you are is a drunk. I should know.

In my head I have a golden opportunity to change things, to have a new start. I am taking my child and I am moving. Out of state, out of here, out of my own warped mind. I can remove myself from the undeniably drab holidays and the endless insanity. I can stop watching my mother's steep descent into oblivion. I can get Delaney away from her drug-addled father. I can move to Georgia, far from California—*the other side of the world*—and get away. I have friends there and a chance for a new beginning. Away from the impossibility of my parents and this latest divorce. It will change everything, of this I am convinced. But the ties around my head are bound deep. They cut well into the brain tissue, layers of tight, thin rope that have been there for so many years that the gray matter has grown around it, absorbed it. Against that backdrop of escape lies another patina. The vast dichotomy of my choices. I can see both so clearly: Georgia and my beautiful new house on the pristine lake, my daughter adjusted and happy, surrounded by friends and healthy support. And in the other, I stay behind and move backwards into time, care for my sick mother, repeat the endless cycle. Into the house of my upbringing, into an unlivable place—at the invitation and insistence of my father—given the untenable responsibility of caring for my aging parents.

What would seem like such a simple decision is most decidedly not. It is bound with guilt and fear and disgust and revulsion. It is swathed in the cloth of blood and beatings, insanity and pain. So much of me and who I have become is placed squarely in the middle of these two options. Choose Door Number One and I save my daughter and her future but lose my parents, my past, and any hope of mental redemption. Choose Door Number Two and I will die inside myself, my daughter will survive for some period of time, but the past will be repaired by my martyrdom.

Living in limbo sucks and I hate it. I've always thought I was pretty good at making decisions, just never the right ones. My confidence wavers, not in the stuff of life that whirls around me—job, bills, going, doing—but more the struggle within myself to emotionally commit. The allure of Georgia is strong, so many new things, so many start-overs. I ignore the fact that I have only visited a few times, that I know little of the people or the culture, that I am a born-and-bred Californian, the pull is strong, something so very *other* than my story. I begin to lean in that direction, begin to justify my absence from my mother's illness with internal conversations about monthly flights back and forth.

My parents were always wildly disparate in their levels of commitment, my dad stubborn, fierce, and mean with it, my mother lackluster and shadowy. He was overly committed in everything he did, almost mythical. The only problem lay in the fact that his commitment was entirely to himself, never to those around him. Not following through was viewed as more of a failure than an allegiance to a poor choice. We saw his *commitment* to us in ways both small and large, with teeth equally proportional.

Lost behind books and alcohol, my mother fell far from us. She lived not so much in the dusk of his commitment, but beneath it—below. Hers was a murky existence, and whether she really tried to save us is subject to interpretation. Those luminous blue eyes that peer at me now from the skull that was once her face are hard to read. I have told her about Georgia and she is supportive. I do not mention it further to my father. He has convinced himself that I will build a guest house on their property and raise my daughter alongside their crazy.

Of one thing I am clear: my mother has committed her dying memories to denial. I leave our conversations oftentimes shaking my head, immediately calling my brother to see if maybe I am the one hallucinating. He says I am not, that my memories are intact and parallel with his own. Slowly, I realize I have spent the first forty years of my life feeling sorry for her. Thinking she fell victim to a horrendous man and stupefying circumstance. Recently, I have realized a different truth.

As children, John and I went through all of the motions that accompany a suburban upbringing: public school, soccer, track, basketball, piano lessons, Sunday school with Grandmother Allesandra. But there was always a stickiness to it, and no matter how hard we shook our fingers, it stayed.

I was about seven or eight when my mom would come to soccer practices. My dad, of course, was the All-American, hero/coach/champion/god of my brother's team. To hear him tell it, at six years old they were headed to the Nationals and he played every position. Despite playing soccer and running track like my brother, when it came to sports, I just wasn't as *talented* as John. Determined, yes; talented, no.

I was also just becoming aware of the two mothers I lived with—the one who read all day and gave us a snack when we got home from school, and the one who drank until she fell asleep at the dinner table at night. My practices this season were at night.

She waved at me from the bleachers. I was wearing my long socks and shin-guards with a checkered miniskirt and blue t-shirt. I had my cocoa-butter stick and was rubbing my lips fanatically. Especially when I saw the silver flask flash from her coat pocket.

"Hey, pay attention," yelled my coach as the ball whizzed past.

He was a nice man, largely bearded and tall. He had two daughters on the team, Laura and Amy. I smeared another layer on my lips and took off after the ball. As I did, I could see my mom drinking from the flask again. She sat on the top row, which I knew would be bad. The other parents stood along the sidelines. Even then I wondered why she never talked to anybody, never hung out with the other kids' moms. Sure seemed like most of the kids in school had moms that *participated*. Mine just read.

"Is that your mom?" asked Laura.

"Who?" I asked, knowing full well where she was looking.

"That lady in the stands."

"Um, yeah, that's her."

"Can you ask her if you can come over after the game this Saturday?" Laura smiled at me.

This will be hard. I really want to go to her house, but I know my mom will embarrass me if I ask her, and she won't remember me asking and...I will have to ask my dad anyway.

"Sure."

Right then her dad called an end to practice. Laura ran over to him, jumping and tugging at his sleeve.

"Can she come over, Dad, can she?"

Her dad smiled down at her. "Fine by me, honey. Just need to talk to her mom."

God. Here I was hoping I could just scuttle away to the parking lot, holding her up by the elbow.

I walked over to the bleachers. My mom was hunched down in her jacket. Her eyes were hazy and unfocused.

"It's time to go, Mom."

"Okay, honey," she smiled. I wanted the surface of that answer so badly. Like a chocolate-dipped strawberry, followed by a sweet aftertaste, not rotten with lies. I wanted her to just walk neatly down the steps and join me in a regular conversation with my coach. Instead she half-stepped, half-tumbled her way down, bleary and drunk again.

My coach and his daughters were waiting at the bottom.

"Hi, I'm Jim Hammond," my coach said. "I've seen you sitting here from time to time and thought I should introduce myself. Laura here wants to know if your daughter can come home with us after the game Saturday?"

My mother blinked her slow, glazed blink. Her answer was time-released, inappropriate, and mortifying to my seven-year-old self.

"Well, thank you for being such a great coach," she slurred. She smiled and took my arm. We began to hobble across the wet grass, both my shoes and heart sodden.

As I turned to look back at Laura, I could see her dad kneeling before her, his hands on her shoulders. I realized much later how he must have explained to her how the *otherness* of some people cannot be entirely understood, how it was healthier for people like them to avoid people like us, and that she should be extra nice to me at practice but it was just *best* for us not to play together.

How her liver even functions is lost on me. When she drinks now it is a gloomy affair—like this last visit, when she can barely hold the glass and the liquor sloshes on her blankets. I watched her nurse it, slurp at it like a suckling pig. Its hold on her is universal and will transcend her death. I can only watch as my disgust and jealousy grow. She has always chosen this—not my life, my brother's, her friends, not even the birth of her only grandchild.

Her choices over my lifetime influence my decision to stay or leave. I know that even if I stay, she will not be present. I also understand that my father's insistence that we will somehow forge a functioning family is an apparition, no more real than a foggy mist on a photograph. It baffles me how delusional this fantasy has become, as though if I build a home on their ten acres of property that somehow the past will be erased. He brings up the topic every time I see them, and I refuse to comment. His idea to use decayed garage doors for barn panels so Delaney can get a horse, his excitement over the prospect of a guest house nestled sixty feet from their crumbling home, surrounded by five large dogs and mud, repels me. Yet, oddly and irrationally, and in utter sync with the lunacy of my life, I hire an architect and ask for some guest house mock-ups. I actually consider it.

A few weeks later, I visit her again. I want to talk about my divorce, how my potential move to Georgia is based on what is best for Delaney, not me. I want to explain that what I am doing is right, is justified. I tell her that I truly believe Delaney will be better off away from her father, that custody and visitation will be problematic, that she needs consistency and calm. I tell her homes, education, everything is less expensive in the South, as a single mom I will have access to babysitters and a better quality of life. She listens intently, as she always does.

I time my visit so that my father will not be home. I already know his opinion. I want hers. But she doesn't offer much, simply telling me I have to do what is right for me. I waffle and describe how Delaney will be nearby if I stay, that once she is walking she can help me with her while I work, my mind hopeful with images of the two of them hand-in-hand, heads bent deep in a book. I ask her if she will be okay if I leave, if she wants me to stay. Her answer is simple.

"Oh honey, I will be fine."

I hear my father slam the kitchen door downstairs. Within minutes he is up the stairs and into the bedroom, two bourbon drinks with ice clinking in his hand. My mom is still on Percocet from the surgery, and I know this combination is not a good idea. I say nothing. He barely acknowledges my presence. She takes the drink and immediately swallows half.

It doesn't take long before she slops to the side of the pillow and I tell myself the glass will spill. She is already asleep and I am wholly awake. I stare at the cut-crystal tumbler in a room of filth and rank and I wonder if I am fixable. Or if I can only be fixed if I in turn repair the vast brokenness before me. Do I stay in this house and care for her and reinvent our history? I know she is beneath that defeated body—some piece of her must *know*. Can she even hear me if I just explain to her how important this is? That to be complete requires her presence? I find myself enraged by her inattention, her lack of commitment to my future, her *stupor*. I want her to give me the right answer, not pass out drunk. Her mouth is open and she snores softly. I remove the glass and put it gently on the table.

Brick by Brick

I first wanted to kill something when I was fourteen. The entire family was planting avocado trees on the ten acres of land we had just purchased with my mom's inheritance from her uncle. He had died in a fiery crash outside Barstow, drunk and passed out at the wheel, so the story goes. He was the lifelong drunk, my mom his favorite lifelong drunk niece.

I clearly remember wishing to blow the brains out of my asshole brother. If I had had a gun at that moment it would have happened, no doubt in my mind. I hated him with every pore of my being and the fact that he kept taking my *stuff* drove me nuts. This time it was a silver belt my Uncle Bob had made for me. It was hand-forged, decorated with scalloped edges and black etchings. I hadn't noticed it missing until I saw something silver winking from my idiot brother's black Stetson.

"What is that on your hat?"

"Nothing," John answered, turning to load baby trees on the wheelbarrow.

But I knew, *I knew.* "Fucker," I hissed. "Is that my belt?"

"Big deal," he says, taking the hat off, pushing his sweaty hair back, and slowly inspecting my belt.

"You broke it to make a hat band?"

"So what? You weren't using it." He gives me his slow, lazy grin, the one that all my girlfriends find so *luxurious.*

I am so mad by now I could spit. Complaining to my parents never does jack-all, except get us both beat. He knows it and I know it.

"I. Hate. Your. Guts." Every word is sawing through my teeth with serrated edges. My hands are shaking. It is my first experience with literally seeing red. The filmy haze across my eyes pulses in time with my heart.

He just chuckles and walks away. I stare at the long back of him. He is growing daily. At thirteen he is over six feet tall and has curly black hair and blue-green eyes. He is awkward and clumsy and his knees look like grapefruits trapped on a peach tree stem. I cannot protect him anymore. He has always been fair game for the fists of my father, but the schoolyard bullies now let him be. Why he chooses to torment me is lost on me. I can see only the redness of my loathing.

I turn and head down the hill, gopher pole in my hand. If I can't kill him, then I will kill something else. As I'm walking, I realize the oddness of what I am doing. I am walking around with a hand-fashioned metal pole designed to poke holes in gopher hills. The idea behind it is to fill the holes with poisoned bait, which the gophers eat, and within hours it dissolves their insides. They die so the baby trees won't. But none of this really adds up to me.

My parents have purchased acres of lush California real estate with terraced hillsides. The avocado boom is just taking off and neighbors all around us are madly planting trees as well. The climate is perfect and fruit trees are prodigious in the region. Thousands of acres of lemons, oranges, limes, and avocados surround us. Farmland and suburban sprawl is just now carving its way through, city transfers spending money to become gentlemen farmers.

My father's grand plan is to build a custom home and live off the harvest of the land. They have sold their tract home and we now live in a single-wide trailer on the property. Me, my brother, my parents, two dogs, two cats, and three parrots.

We haul miniature Haas and Bacon avocado trees in a U-Haul trailer every day for a week. They are in Swiss cheese-like boxes, tiny buds reaching through the holes. We have something of a system going: John and I haul the trees out of the trailer into the wheelbarrow and carry them to my mom, who digs a hole while my dad lays the black drip irrigation hosing. My cousin follows behind and hand-waters each newly planted tree. I'm a teenager, what do I know about agriculture? But something just seems off. All around us I see the way our neighbors are planting trees. It isn't like us. They have Calavo trucks on their land, dispersing trees, migrant workers digging holes, clearing the land, laying hose. I don't understand why we are doing this ourselves. It is hard work, dirty and exhausting. Ticks and chiggers fill our socks and pantlegs. At the end of each day, we have planted maybe ten trees to their thirty. Their planting patterns are geometric and follow the terracing of the hillsides. Ours is erratic and the water lines run uphill. Looking back now it seems my entire life has been running uphill.

It's like the bricks. A ton of effort for no pay-off. The home I grew up in for the first twelve years of my life is now past, its rooms home to a fresh new family. No longer are those hallways haunted with the echoes of screams and crying, kidney punches and broken glass. Green shag has been replaced with a woven buttercream yellow and gardeners descend on the backyard before we have finished moving out. But those bricks had been in a pile on the side of the house for the entire decade-plus we lived there. Close to five hundred bricks. They were to be used for planters, said my father, and there they sat, gathering moss and black widows. No planters were ever built.

Hell if we didn't move those godawful bricks with us to the new land. Brick by foul brick, they were loaded into the rental truck. Then unloaded twenty miles away. John and I were given too-big gloves and instructions to move them for another heady project at the new property. That pile scared the living shit out of us. We had avoided it for twelve years and now were faced with *dismantling* it, spider-by-fucking-spider.

"What do we do?" asks my little brother. John's bright seafoam-green eyes are scared and his jeans are too short.

I just stare, first at him then at the bricks. They are coated with a white layer of dust and broken brick. The skin feels tight around my elbows.

"What do we do?" he asks again.

"Start, I guess." I answer. There is no saying no or discussion at our house. Open your mouth, you get hit or yelled at or both.

I can hear my mom walking outside and loading a box. She is in the front of the house, and through the side gate, I can see her long legs in blue capris and white tennies. She is wearing a blue bandana and a UCLA sweatshirt. As she walks up the pathway, I call, "Mom."

It's not loud and it's not soft, but I know she hears me. My brother sidles up next to me and we stare out the gate, gloves loose and dangling from our hands. She turns her head but doesn't break her stride. A small jerk of her head is our answer. *No, not now, leave it be.*

We know better than to push, so we turn back to the bricks. John is the first to grab one, then another. I follow him, grabbing from the outside in, knowing full well that the hideous nest will stir from the *inside.* Nobody bothered to ask whether it was appropriate or even safe for little kids to scrounge inside the leavings of poisonous spiders and snakes. How, about an hour after a bite, a black widow's neurotoxin spreads through your lymphatic system (much more quickly with a child's rapid heartbeat) while your abdomen contracts into solid muscle and you sweat and vomit profusely. Nobody checked on our well-being or whether our sleeves were tucked into the gloves or even if we wore closed-toe shoes. Nobody bothered with how rattlesnakes bite quickly to protect their homes, their venom hemotoxic, destroying tissue, degenerating organs and causing disrupted blood clotting with some degree of permanent scarring very likely in the event of a venomous bite; how, combined with delayed or ineffective treatment, it can lead to the loss of a limb or death.

John and I cried and yelped our way through that pile for the better part of a day, our faces stained in fear and red grime. Plenty of close calls, one grandmother of a black widow, red hourglass full, not even bothering to scuttle away. One gopher snake and hundreds of small, white nests later, we were done. The unloading of bricks that night was completed in a fugue. We were so tired by then nothing mattered. My brother sobbed quietly in his sleep that night, his hands like raw hamburger because he couldn't keep the gloves on.

I have hated that pile of bricks for my entire life. Thirty-three years later they still sit, unmoved, in the same exact spot in the same exact configuration where they were unloaded by spider-crazed children. That pile is my sentry, my guardian of crazy, sent by the Sirens.

Customary

There are times when I battle a sadness so wicked it comes at me inside out. It's as though I cannot escape myself, my skin, my being. It most often happens when I see something that makes me think of what should be normal. Like a Christmas card, one with a mom and a dad and their kids, maybe even a retriever sitting at their feet. You know they have their own internal fights, disagreements, bad manners, whispers of divorce. But spread over that like a collective veil is a normality that balances everything out. You can figure that the dad probably watches the occasional porn on the internet, mom bitches at the kids to clean their rooms and nips at the Xanax bottle when it's just *too much,* and little Sarah just vaped with her gaggle of ridiculous friends.

But you can also count on them to follow some code of conduct, traditions, consistency, that most people live by. When I see those cards sent by well-meaning friends, they can't know that my soul bleeds, one ounce at a time, for a childhood gone insanely wrong. A lifetime filled with malice and psychosis, not bittersweet empty-nesting, annual vacations to warm places, quickly repaired arguments, a gentle hug from your mom.

Ours was a childhood of void and *not,* followed by terror and the occasional longing for something we had no means to identify. The memories start very, very early and may not even be entirely accurate. One of the most fascinating aspects of it is the absolute and complete denial on behalf of *both* parents that any of it ever occurred.

In his latest reinvention of self, my father shared with me his one run-in with my brother. After my mom's hip surgery, we had gone to the Verizon store to buy cell phones for both of my parents. My mom was having trouble with the phone at home and he thought a cell phone would be better somehow. He had asked for my help to set them up because he wasn't sure how the whole thing worked. *Or just maybe the landline hasn't worked for the last year because the rats have finally eaten through the wires. Did you know even your cat lives in fear?*

"Oh, I remember that," my father says as we walk across the parking lot. I hold my daughter's hand. I hate parking lots.

"It was high school, right after a basketball game."

What the hell is he talking about now? My daughter is trying to jump into my arms full of phone bags and purse. She had been a pill the entire time we were in the store, disappearing, hiding behind counters, touching new computers.

"He mouthed off after a game, I think. All I had to do was pop him in the mouth. Just once. That shut him up. Never had any more trouble."

Now I know what he's referring to. It was about my daughter's behavior in the store, and I had muttered something about how hard she was to discipline, but how I *never* hit. I guess I somehow wondered what his response would be, like a cricket taunting a chameleon. Just going to the Verizon store together was weird. We didn't *do* those things.

But something had shifted in the last couple months. He was acting differently.

My head goes back to his words. *Wait a minute. Are you serious?* There is absolutely no way to reply.

"She's a handful, that one," he nods towards my five-year-old baby girl who is now resting her head on my shoulder. Her gaze at him is steady, but cautious. "Better get her under control now or you'll have trouble."

I cannot be having this conversation. He is outside his mind, scatter-fucked crazy gourd man from hell. Don't you dare even think about how you might handle her or what you might do to get her in control. You hit him once? Really?

You almost killed him. Let's see, Dad, how about the time you threw the pitchfork at his head? Or maybe when you kicked him with your fancy cowboy boots so hard in the groin that he screamed like a girl and then you wouldn't let Mom pick him up for the day. I remember him lying in the dirt, snot sand-caked around his mouth and eyes and nose and crying, crying, crying until he ran out of tears. He was six, you fucker. One year older than this tiny body of bones I'm holding in my arms.

The hatred I felt for you, myself for not saving him. How I was seven, not a big girl yet. Or later how Mom got so wildly drunk that she couldn't walk and I was the one who got him from the yard while you glared in disgust at my weakness. I rushed him past you, past her, deep into her gin and unaware of our passing, two insignificant ghosts disappearing down the hallway. All I could do, all I knew to do, was brush the dirt and ruin from his face with a pale green towel, the darkening of purple already trailing down his thigh.

Later, you were yelling at her. Words I knew were bad and mean. Her voice came to us, slurred and pitiful, as my brother and I huddled for the thousandth time at the foot of his bed.

"Stop it, just stop." We heard sounds that children should not hear. Her protests became weaker, we covered our ears. We stifled our sobbing because discovery means more beating. But even with covered ears, the sounds of fists and flesh and muffled screams were unmistakable.

And as I carry my daughter across the pavement, my skin crawls and my eyes sting. I cannot breathe. I cannot hear. I cannot see. How could I help this man buy a phone? *Does blood transcend evil?*

Over the years I have learned that I run ahead of my sadness by doing. And the prospect of this cross-country move is making me so very sad. I respond with longer hours at work and frantic chores at home. I have spent years being good at using my mind, the one place I can go that requires no interaction other than my own. First at school, and later with my profession. I am a consultant now, parlaying my science education into the opportunity to solve environmental issues for others, and then later solving just about any business issue I came across. I have a knack for this world and my business thrives. I found over time that I made for a poor employee, better suited to running my own shop, loathe to follow directions from others, confident in my ability to go it alone. I favor intellectual pursuits over emotional ones, finding solace in the clarity and perfection of numbers and data, avoiding the unknowable of the interpersonal. Once I am utterly exhausted and run to ground, however, the sadness still creeps up, licks its tongue at my ear and settles in next to me. Those are the times that I know I simply cannot be a good parent or accomplish anything worthwhile. I do not question myself, nor do I run a tally of my pros and cons; it is simply a deep understanding. You can only run so long.

John is entirely lost now. A giant of a man, he is only seven at heart, crying and grasping at his manhood with bloodied fingers and a broken soul. His sadness is beer and a string of disappointments, wives and children, jobs and disillusion. He is in his forties now as well, living in Oregon, as far from our childhood home as he can get while remaining on the west coast. He has worked primarily in construction his entire life, starting with roofing and later, finish carpentry. He is skilled at his trade, just not at reliability, consistency, managing his temper—things his employers need him to do to keep his job. As a result, he job-hops with frequency.

We enter each other's lives like moths, shedding one chrysalis for another, the memories our flame. I believe we test our stronghold on reality every so often, checking to make sure that whatever we have become is no worse than what we came from.

"He wants you to do what?" he asks on our last call.

"Move in with them," I answer.

There is silence. I don't fill it.

"How is Mom?"

"Same."

"I tried, you know. The last time I came down." I can hear him smoking. There are children in the background. They are not his own.

"I know."

"He wouldn't let me. I spent three days trying to repair the electricals. I cleaned the garage. The bees were so bad I couldn't finish."

"Yeah." I know he came down for a while between break-ups. Jobless, homeless. His plan was to stay with them for some time, try to clean some, repair thirty years of neglect. Get the kitchen to be functional. He had to wear a gas mask while he worked. He lasted three days.

"So you gonna move in?"

I laugh a strangled noise. From somewhere in Oregon he begins to laugh with me. With tears streaming down our faces, we laugh so hard for the next few minutes neither of us can talk.

It is my father who calls this time. He wants to know if he can drop off Delaney's Valentine's Day gift. It is April. This is another of their oddities. They will not spend any time with my daughter, barely know her in fact. But my father will always drop off a gift. And it will always be late. When he brings the cardboard box full of Trader Joe's chocolate, it isn't even Valentine's chocolate. There are several bags of foiled Christmas kisses that he probably found in a drawer somewhere. There is cat litter stuck to the bottom of the box. He declines my offer to come inside—*please don't come inside*—and I say thanks as Delaney hides behind my leg. He gives me an update on my mom and how he plans to get her downstairs to lift some weights.

When he leaves I throw the candy away like I always do.

It is a flawed combination that pushes me to my final decision. I have been granted custody of Delaney; the judge has allowed me to move with her to Georgia due to her father's drug problems and my job allows me to travel. My friends in Georgia have agreed to help, and Delaney and I will move into their small pool house while I get settled. In my mind I concoct a fantasy of a fantastic new husband delighted by my baby girl, a huge house on a pristine lake, and weekend barbeques surrounded by fabulous friends. The fact that all of this resides in my imagination does little to sway me from packing my belongings in Pods and flying with Delaney to Atlanta, where together with our dog and our cat, we will share one tiny room.

I visit my mom the day before our flight. She is reading a book propped up in bed, her glasses resting on the tip of her nose. She looks up as I enter.

"Hi, Mom. How're you feeling?"

"I'm fine, honey."

I don't really know what to say. I've said everything I need to say. I can't bring Delaney to say goodbye because the dirt and the filth are too pervasive to leave her unattended. I will bring her once my mom is up and around. *We can fly back for a visit when she is better, can walk to a clean booth in a clean restaurant.*

"You leave in the morning?" she asks.

I nod.

"I've got something for you."

She hands me a small box from the drawer beside her. It is a pale pink, etched with gold filigree. Inside, the lining is frayed, its contents hidden.

"This is for Delaney...and you, I suppose."

I push aside the thin, tattered fabric to see an antique garnet necklace, intricate and ornate, the kind that drapes around the neck and chest.

"It was your great-grandmother's. It was her favorite."

It's a lovely piece of jewelry, yet nothing I can ever imagine wearing, perhaps only to a costume party or mystery dinner theater. I smile anyway.

"Thanks."

She offers nothing further and I find myself unable to say anything at all. I wave an odd, jerky wave and leave. We do not say goodbye and there are no hugs or tears. There never are.

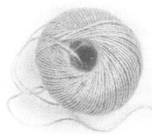

32° N 83° W

I have always thought I was good at reading people but have been proven woefully wrong on multiple occasions. I find that I assume the best in people despite almost always experiencing the worst. I've done this for much of my life, affecting this shiny, over-the-top optimism in the face of significant evidence to the contrary, persistent in my desire to avoid cynicism...or its kissing cousin, reality. And I persist in this delusion, constantly granting lengths of rope when I've already been hanging for some time.

I arrive in my new hometown on a cold January afternoon. It is about forty degrees outside the airport and I immediately understand this will be far different from anything I have known in my warm birthplace. The drive from the airport to our new room in the pool house is long, but Delaney is excited, gazing out the window of the car at the miles and miles of trees that line the highway. Our car is surrounded by semi-trucks, blaring their air horns and driving in the fast lane, for miles blocking any chance at passing. My nerves are rattled by the time I arrive in our new hometown just outside Chattanooga.

My friend, Diana, and her family greet us with smiles and hugs, a platter of local barbeque, incredible buttermilk biscuits, and a group of her friends. It is Southern hospitality at its finest, and I instantly feel better, as though my arduous trip and agonizing decision have been worthwhile. I spend that first evening relaxing in Diana's living room, nestled beneath a blanket, a fire in the hearth. As I doze, I can hear Delaney playing loudly with Diana's teenage children, and I am appreciative of their patience and attention.

Over the next few days, Diana and I discuss the logistics of the next several months, how she will watch Delaney when I need to travel for my job, how the two of us, along with our cat and dog, will live in the pool house until I can find a place of our own, how I will help her as much as I can. I intend to stay in the pool house the least amount of time possible, as I understand how quickly friendships can wear thin upon close proximity and intimate knowledge. I have known Diana for many years; she is a long-time friend from college, and we have maintained this distant friendship for decades. Moving here, I took a chance. I knew her but didn't *know* her. I knew of our yearly cross-country summer visits with well-behaved children and amusement park outings, I knew of Facebook postings complete with smiling kids on perfect vacations, occasional phone calls to catch up, and one husband exchanged for another. I had never lived near her *and certainly not with her* since we were twenty.

Unlike me, Diana had never truly lived on her own. During college, her parents always lived within minutes, and she immediately got married after graduation. She had a very close, loving relationship with her parents and leaned heavily on them. Over her lifetime they moved several times to live close by. Even now, they lived right next door to her. For over twenty years, I had been both confounded by, and jealous of, her family dynamic, and despite Diana's mother's insistence that I call her "Mom," I never was able. Oddly, it felt as though I was betraying my own mother, despite her obvious indifference and the fact she would have never known.

Diana had two kids with her first husband, met her second husband while married, cheated on her first husband, married the second, had a third kid, and now lived a fairly nondescript life in a nice house in rural Georgia—close enough to Atlanta and Chattanooga to get out of the sticks, but far enough away to own acres of land and a pool house on a modest income. Hers was a happy and healthy family, blended and adjusted, a good place for a broken little family like ours to land. It would be perfect. I could get back on my feet emotionally and financially, and Delaney could forge healthy new friendships and be absorbed into a flourishing extended family.

I guess I should have known things would not go that easily. After only two weeks of school, Delaney came home crying, saying the other kids were picking on her, bullying her. When I asked her for specifics she could only give me vague reasons with shadowy perpetrators. I decided to chalk it up to kids being kids. She was the new kid, she needed to find her way, not have her overbearing mother show up and paint more of a target on her back.

A few weeks later, I received a call from a teacher at her school.

"Miss Burke? This is Holly Wainscott. I'm a teacher here at Lion's Creek Elementary. I'd like to talk to you about Delaney."

Ah fuck. What now? Fear and anger arm wrestled in my head. *What happened? Is she hurt? Are those little shits picking on her?*

"Sure, Holly. What's going on?"

"Well, I understand Delaney is having a bit of trouble. I think I can help."

Holly went on to explain that at Lion's Creek most of the kids had grown up together, they had known each other since early on, that their parents attended the same churches, married the same people, lived very similar lives, with little in the way of expectations or exposure to the larger world around them. It was a tiny rural community, where the high school had day care for expectant students, where some mothers were in and out of rehab for meth addiction, where outsiders were treated with a healthy measure of distance and distrust. Holly went on to explain how she herself was a product of this environment, having divorced her husband and remarrying another man. Her ex-husband then remarried her current husband's ex-wife. They had six kids between the various pairings and weekends were a blur of kids, half-siblings and step-kids, an indecipherable kaleidoscope of cousins.

Holly and I decided to meet in person to go over my options on how to assimilate Delaney in a way where she could both fit in and not get sucker-punched during lunch. The meeting did not go as I expected. Holly was a bright, funny, irreverent woman, intellectually curious, emotionally adept and a teacher to be reckoned with. My vision of an unkempt, grammar school lifer dissipated the minute I met her. She was tiny, quick, fit. A mop of curls covered her head and she spoke in a clear, decisive voice. I liked her. A lot. I had been unable to really relate to anyone in my new community for the entire first few months and Holly was the first person I truly connected with. The fact that we both shared a history of breast cancer drew us even closer, and our relationship eventually became a friendship. One where we would watch each other's kids, share dinners and complain about the various side-effects of past chemotherapy, all the while simultaneously knocking-on-wood at our good fortune for surviving.

Our solution for Delaney involved Holly moving Delaney to her classroom, taking over as Delaney's teacher altogether, informing Holly's kids—who also attended Lion's Creek—that Delaney was now one of their own, and to attend a few Sundays with Holly and her family at church, sitting alongside them to be seen as part of the community. Holly understood most of this was for show, but she also understood that without it, neither Delaney nor I stood a river rat's chance in hell of making it in this place. For Delaney, school got much better, and quickly, with Holly's popular daughter, Addison, now propped up as her buddy.

Holly was also the person who enabled me to navigate the vastly different social norms of my new environment. Georgia was an entirely unique beast from the California I was accustomed to. This was a place where your value was placed on your community connections and your church affiliation. Gone were my days of passing neighborly acquaintances, Sunday gym workouts and a focus on work and the world at large. These were people who had assimilated with each other for generations, who felt that knowing each other's intimate business was simply the currency with which you paid your obligations. My aloofness and preference for personal privacy was offensive to them and did not win me many fans.

I first experienced this when I tried to buy a house. At the suggestion of Diana, I went to the local bank to talk about financing for a home. I had found a place I liked, a beautiful house above a lake, surrounded by trees, populated with Canadian geese, Tiger Swallowtail butterflies, and wild river otters. It was bucolic, serene, and exactly what I wanted for Delaney. And I was right. She loved that place, spending hours down by the lake with our dog, Riley, catching lightening bugs in jars on the front lawn and smearing red Georgia clay all over the porch. The house and property were much bigger than what we were used to in California, and I found myself falling behind on taking care of the yard. This was far from a ten-by-twenty-foot patch of brown California lawn; this was hundreds of yards of thick, lush grass that grew about an inch or two every single day. I started to feel overwhelmed and inadequate, not to mention unable to find anyone to help me keep up the property. I didn't know the local teenagers; all of my neighbors tended their own yards and I could not find a service. Things grew so fast and became overgrown so quickly I found myself spending hours trying to keep the path to the lake free of thorny blackberries and the lawn from growing up and over the mailbox. There was just so much *moisture,* so much *life,* verdant acres filled with vibrant layers of green, enormous Luna moths hidden in the leaves, rabbit kits bouncing across the grass, cicadas signing their arias at night. It was both beautiful and exasperating.

It was over the next year that I realized that my land was also home to a lot of bugs. A lot. A horde of nasty-assed, stinging bugs, the kind that made me scream and run in the house fairly often. My neighbors thought I was flat-out insane, and Riley would bark madly every time I ran. I knew Delaney was becoming used to it when I saw her carrying a pocket full of frogs into the house, followed by a handful of crickets for their lunch. She didn't even flinch. If there is such a thing as squeamish proud, I guess I was. I was the *only* person who jogged within a ten-mile radius. The only season I was actually able to run was fall, since summer was so hot and humid I would gasp for oxygen after about a half-mile, my lungs sodden, winter was so cold my bones ached, and spring sprung those disgusting bugs. I was even asked at one point, as I ran along one desolate country road, if I was okay, and whether I was running *from* something. The folks in the Chevy Impala simply could not grasp I was doing this by choice.

The purchase of that house and the ensuing banking fiasco was an adventure I will never forget. I had purchased multiple homes over my lifetime and thought this transaction would be no different. A simple *here are my bona fides, my deposit, let's enter escrow, give me my loan* and we're done. Not so much. Mr. Mark Thompson, Vice President of First Georgia Bank of the Union, had other ideas. Apparently, he didn't know me well enough, wasn't satisfied with Diana's introduction, and was highly suspicious of my lack of a husband and co-signer. Mr. Thompson decided that he needed to do *further due diligence* on this single, overly educated, clearly unremorseful—*insouciant even*—divorcee-from-California-of-all-godforsaken-places. He clearly did not like me, my lifestyle, or my choices. What should have been a straightforward process turned into one of the most bizarre financial circuses I have ever performed in. I was the gymnast for the high-wire act, yet I had no training and my circus barker insisted I needed to do a back flip. I felt as though I had entered an episode of *The Twilight Zone*. In order to qualify for the house, I had to submit *five* letters of recommendation from local residents, six years of past tax returns, proof-of-income letters from both my current and past bosses, and original birth certificates for both me and Delaney. It was utterly absurd. Even after I was granted the loan—after four months of waiting and answering increasingly obscure and irrational requests, six in-person meetings and at a rate double that of the feds—Mr. Mark Thompson began driving by my house and emailing me that I needed to take better care of my yard. He also sent follow-up emails every single month to remind me to pay my mortgage. What. The. Hell. As I described all of this to Holly and Diana, they simply laughed and said, "Welcome to the South."

Having grown up and attended school in California, I had been exposed to a hodgepodge of skin colors, backgrounds, and religions. It was not at all unusual to have a circle of friends that included Hispanics, African Americans, Asians, whites, Protestants, Catholics, Mormons, straights, gays, purples and plaids. None of it mattered. I had never really experienced any significant racism, misogyny, homophobia, or bigotry. These were SAT words to me and general concepts, but not living, breathing organisms. I had watched the Los Angeles riots on TV growing up, but even those were so far removed from my high school and my friends that they did not resonate. My father at times would rant about this or that, but in the end, he coached each of his athletes the same, no matter their skin color, gender or upbringing.

My slowly dawning realization that each of these things was alive and well in some parts of the South was extraordinary. One of the very first questions from a new acquaintance would be, "Which church do you attend?" And they did not mean it in the "Which denomination do you belong to?" They meant it as in, "Which building on which street corner of the white Southern Baptist church do you attend?" This was a real thing. When I replied I did not attend church, the response was always the same: a slight, but perceptible narrowing of the eyes and small step back, a forced smile and zero social invitations thereafter. I learned the very hard way that my ambivalence towards religion was not remotely considered acceptable in these here parts.

My second supremely eye-opening moment occurred when I met Diana's close friend, Terry. Terry was married to Vince, and together they had two sons. Terry and her family were fixtures at all of Diana's gatherings, everyone knew them, and they were sewn deeply into the fabric of the town's history. Both Terry and Vince were fourth-generation Southerners, complete with thick drawls and a love of fried pickles. I found Terry to be funny and smart, fun to be around, and her boys a good influence on Delaney. Diana and I would host parties throughout the spring and summer, where Terry and her family would attend, and the kids would spend hours in the pool. Terry's boys were fantastic with Delaney—they were smart kids, and I liked them both.

The thing about it though: both Vince and the older son were gay. It was so blatantly obvious to me *and anyone with a beating heart* that I found myself utterly flummoxed. In my previous world, this would not be a big deal. But here in the South it was clearly a *very big deal*. When I questioned

Diana about it, she shushed me, saying, "We don't talk about that here." I was confused. Diana had also grown up in California, why the obfuscation? But she would not discuss it with me whatsoever, her complicity and her absorption into this culture and these people complete. As a result, everyone continued with the theater that Vince was a happily married church man and the older son had a girlfriend at college. Ignored were the blatant unexplained absences and penchant for haute couture. I had no dog in the hunt, so I let it be.

Over time, I began to realize that my opinions were not all that popular, my outlook on life was not in sync with the majority, and my status as an outsider was likely to be long-term. I really thought I might be able to overcome it with time, but my ability to adapt was wearing thin. This was especially true when I was called into Lion's Creek Elementary a second time. This time it was the principal that wanted to see me.

"Miss Burke? I'm Loretta Etchison."

I had learned early on that women in the South preferred not to shake hands, so I simply smiled and sat down in the chair across from her desk.

"Nice to finally meet you, Miss Etchison."

Ms. Etchison busied herself with tidying some folders on her desk. As she swung her head around to the credenza behind her in search of a manila folder, the chain on her glasses *with tiny little white pearls* swung in a slow arc. I felt like she was stalling.

I began to wiggle my ankle. I could already sense I was not going to like what was to come out of her mouth.

She turned back to me, sans folder.

"Well, Miss Burke, this may not be an easy topic, but I feel it is in your child's best interest to discuss it with you."

Shit.

"It seems a couple of our parents have brought it to my attention, that well, they are worried about your daughter."

Shit shit.

"They are concerned, it seems, that perhaps your daughter is not getting enough nutrition in your household."

I just stared at her. *Huh?*

"You must admit, Miss Burke, that Delaney is a tad on the small side, she is awfully thin, bless her heart, and well, we are just concerned that perhaps her health may not be tip-top."

What the actual fuck is this woman talking about? They think I am starving my kid? Just because her classmates are much larger than she is, and some of them are rapidly closing in on obese? Now, somehow, I am doing something to her?

I knew I had better skedaddle right on out of that office before both my temper and California verbal shenanigans got fired up.

"Why thank you, Miss Etchison. I believe I have it handled from here."

With a smile *grimace* I left. I took Delaney out of class early that day and the two of us went for an ice cream. That conversation, and the same one from one of the "concerned" parents two weeks later, did not stop me one iota from taking Delaney to swim practice, signing her up for soccer, or insisting she run around and play outside with Riley.

Cars and Catalina

The other day I was cleaning out my closet and found the pink umbrella. It was smaller than I remembered, faded a pale fuchsia, and surprisingly, still worked. My father gave me that umbrella on my seventh birthday, and for whatever reason I held onto it for decades. That umbrella travelled with me through almost twenty moves across several states, survived multiple husbands, step-children and homes, and is the single remaining remnant of my childhood. I am absurdly proud of the fact that it still works, that I have maintained its functionality for almost forty years. Yet, I also understand that this unreasonably hopeful umbrella does not, in fact, represent anything other than a mentally unstable attachment to something that never existed.

It was during my college years, once I was out and away from my parents' house, barely seventeen, that I realized both people and things had a certain functionality to them. While that may seem fundamental to many, to me, it was not. We grew up in a house where the most basic of things did not work. Take for example, doorknobs.

I had only ever known two homes growing up, the one with the backyard of ice plant and eucalyptus where I lived until middle school, followed by the newly constructed house on the hill of dead avocados. Our first house, moderately furnished, was essentially nondescript, and we lived primarily downstairs, even though an entire second story was filled with junk. My parents called the second floor the attic, and it wasn't until I visited that house many, many years later as an adult that I discovered it had actually been intended as a finished second story, and that my father had declined to have the developer do the work, opting instead to do it himself. Which, of course, he never did.

The house was filled with seventies-era appointments: green shag carpet, rust-orange recliners, and a television with rabbit ears. On his occasional visits, my Gramps would jangle his keys to make the TV change channels, and it never failed to make my brother and me giggle. Those were the years of *Captain Kangaroo* on Saturday mornings, playing with neighborhood kids on the block, and going home when the streetlights came on. Most of the families on the block had small children, and it was not uncommon to hold communal barbeques in the middle of the street while the kids played tag and the adults got drunk. During the week, fathers would leave for work, kids would travel in small herds to school, and our moms would gather during the day for bridge games or grocery shopping.

We played and we played hard. This was long before seat belts and helmets, and my brother and I rode skateboards, scooters and bikes with abandon, jumping plywood ramps, barreling down the slope of our street at breakneck speed, and generally knocking ourselves around with some frequency. On one occasion, we were racing Big Wheels down the middle of the street when my brother decided to yank the handlebar as I roared past. The result was a street littered with broken plastic, a nasty road rash along the side of my face, one broken arm, and the end of that particular game for a while. When my mom called my father to tell him what happened, he came home from work and decided to apply the plaster cast himself. The next morning my mom dropped my brother off at school and immediately took me to the doctor.

At the office, the nurse who accompanied us to the exam room seemed confused.

"You're here to remove a cast?" she asked, her head tilted to the side as she slowly turned my plastered arm.

"Yes," answered my mom. She didn't offer much more.

"And this was applied yesterday?"

"Yes."

"Ummm…did you get X-rays?"

My mom shook her head. I just stared at the nurse.

"I'm sorry, but where did you go to have her arm treated?" the nurse asked as she began to take notes.

"We didn't," said my mom. "That's why we're here."

My mom and the nurse looked at each other for a few very long seconds. Finally, the nurse turned to leave the room.

"I'll get the doctor," she said. "We will need to get this off and take Dorriah's x-rays first. Let's see what the doctor thinks."

All I knew was by the end of that visit I had a really cool cast instead of the lumpy and tight thing my dad had wrapped around my arm, complete with the doctor and several nurses signing it and making jokes about how cool I was having survived a crash of that magnitude. Apparently, I had a pretty good fracture, and Dr. Birch did have to reset the arm. As I read *Highlights for Children* while the plaster dried, he pulled my mom aside and told her how the decision to bring me in had likely saved me from having my arm rebroken and possibly even have surgery somewhere down the line. My mom said nothing. She just listened.

Boy, was my dad pissed at her that night.

Since we were one of the few houses with a swimming pool, a gaggle of kids would show up to swim with us. We would swim until our fingers were pasty and wrinkled, eat soggy potato chips and press our bellies to the warm concrete. Endless hours were spent in the water playing mermaid, Marco Polo, and holding diving contests. "Jaws" was a favorite game, each of us taking turns lying atop the raft with eyes closed, a delicious tingle vibrating through our bodies as we waited for that fatal bump from the water beneath.

With our perpetually wet towels hung across white deck chairs, we would swim until our hair turned green. From early spring until well into the fall we played under the hot California sun, noses peeling and shoulders freckled, squabbling until dark over who could hold their breath the longest. It wasn't until my father had alienated all of the parents on the block that the neighborhood kids stopped showing up.

While we lived in that neighborhood, we were particularly close with my cousins who lived in the next town and were our same age. About once a month we would gather either at our house to swim, at my grandparents' to play in the orchard, or at my cousins' house. Despite the frequent visits, my cousin Rachel and I would write letters to each other during the week, sharing which boy we had a crush on, whether Leif Garrett or Shaun Cassidy was cuter, and our favorite names for our future babies. Her younger brother, Craig, was a year younger than my brother, and the four of us spent a lot of time together. I absolutely adored spending the night at Rachel's house. It was so starkly different from my own that I was practically frantic to visit. Her mom was relaxed and kind, and both her parents had such a calm presence I felt as though I had been drawn a long bath, complete with candles and balm, so that I could soak luxuriously as long as I liked. Dinners consisted mostly of cereal or pizza, we had neither a curfew nor any rules, and I cannot recall a single time that a voice was raised or a fist was curled.

While my aunt was entirely casual, my uncle was both frenetic and a hoot. He bounced from scheme to scheme, always looking for a way to make a buck, and many of his ideas were both entertaining and outlandish. For many years he raised birds: cockatiels and parrots, then exotic roosters, and later peacocks and Guinea fowl. Their backyard was a cacophony of sound, and falling asleep in my cousin's bedroom was not unlike an Amazon safari, the screeches and calls echoing, then slowly fading along with the light.

I even found my very first boyfriend while staying at my cousin's house. His name was Gene, and he lived four houses down from Rachel. I was about eleven at the time and was mortified to find out that Rachel had told Gene I liked him. I was not remotely a confident kid, and the prospect of interacting with a boy was akin to peeling off my own skin. But Rachel held firm, insisting since she had negotiated the fact that Gene and I were "going steady," I was beholden to actually talk to him.

Rachel, unlike me, was a confident kid. She was funny, light-hearted, had a great tan, and the boys loved her. She maneuvered her way around them as easily as a gazelle during rut, clear in her allure, switching her tail to signal whether they could approach. Her parents were river people, boats and jet skis filled the driveway, and they caravanned to the Kern River and the Sacramento Delta throughout most of the summer. Rachel and Craig made friends easily, as their parents were both social and welcoming. Gene, my impending boyfriend, was one of three brothers, and he and his family regularly accompanied my cousins, aunt and uncle on these river excursions. Rachel, of course, was much more interested in the eldest brother, Rick, whom I considered as accessible as a cosmonaut. She was undaunted, and pursued him mercilessly, while I, on the other hand, struggled mightily to put together a single coherent sentence with Gene.

I think Gene and I lasted a sum total of two weeks before he lost interest in the mute girl who wasn't allowed to go to the river anyway. Rachel landed Rick eventually, went on to have many boyfriends, an even better tan, and finally married an entirely different suitor after high school. Many years later, she ended up with five kids and continued to spend summers at the river. My aunt died of cancer when Rachel and I were in our thirties, after a long and protracted battle. By the end of my aunt's illness, we were both hollowed out, and my uncle ended up moving to the Delta to be closer to the place where he and my aunt had spent so many happy years.

When not swimming or visiting with our cousins or grandparents, my brother and I would spend long hours playing in our unfinished attic, despite the blistering heat and open rafters. My mother had a sewing table up there, and we used that table to play endless games of restaurant, NASCAR, and school, alternating as customer and waitress, driver and checkered flag bearer, teacher and student. By then, since most of the other kids didn't come around to play with us any longer, my brother and I became adept at finding ways to amuse ourselves. And while we were fairly isolated socially, together we were not lonely.

When my mother inherited the insurance money from her uncle, my parents developed grandiose dreams of building a large custom house on the top of a hill, surrounded by fertile groves of citrus and avocados, like most of the homes surrounding the ten-acre parcel of land they eventually selected to buy. After the sale of our tract house and my graduation from junior high school, we moved to a tiny mobile home placed on a small scraped piece of dirt at the outer edge of the ten acres while the new house was under construction.

This house was designed by my parents rather than an architect. It had enormous vaulted ceilings, an afterthought of an upstairs balcony, tiny, ill-conceived bathrooms, a front door at the rear of the house, oddly angled step-ups, and was situated so as not to take advantage of the sweeping views. Once the shell had been constructed and the basic amenities like water, sewer, and appliances had been added by the contractor, my father decided that he could save money and took over the installation of the tile, flooring, paint, and hardware. As a result, the house stood for nearly forty years without doorknobs. And that was only the beginning.

Although the house had been designed for John and I to have our own bedrooms, which were disproportionately enormous, as well as our own bathrooms, my father never completed my brother's bathroom. Ever. So we had to share. Which meant my brother had to walk through my bedroom to use the bathroom. Every single day.

It was like that everywhere in the house. Spiral staircases, left incomplete, traveled to nowhere. A wet bar was never finished and served as a storage area for discarded boxes and cases of Jim Beam. An upstairs balcony was left without bannisters and served as a fall zone for early visitors and small pets. The breakfast room floor was covered in dark brown tile, likely purchased at a close-out sale, and our father laid the tile himself. It was ugly, uneven, and looked like it had been installed by a three-year-old. The kitchen cabinets had been installed, but not leveled or finished. It was left to my twelve-year-old brother and me to stain and varnish them.

While it could be explained away when the house was brand new, as the years wore on, it was at first an embarrassment, and later, as visitors became extinct, ignored. In one of my last visits to their house, I barely registered the hole in the kitchen door or how the upstairs carpet had rotted to the point that the plywood underneath was exposed and black with urine and mold. Because now that the refrigerator was no longer functional, my father resorted to using an ice chest sitting on the kitchen floor; because the stove had not operated for years, he now cooked on a hotplate; since the electricity had shorted out due to rats gnawing on interior wiring, he ran an extension cord from the garage into their bedroom. Whether he noticed no longer mattered, as nothing could be said, and nothing would ever be said. This was a 4,000 square-foot house surrounded by multi-million-dollar homes in some of the most expensive real estate in all of California...and it looked no different from a Tobacco Row shanty.

The outside of the house was not much different. I know that over the years neighbors had complained, and from time to time, various city and county inspectors would leave notices on the locked front gate. But because the house was on ten acres and could not be seen easily from the road, it was difficult to make the claim that it was an eyesore. As long as my parents mowed down the weeds in accordance with fire regulations, they were safe from prying eyes.

For the first couple of decades they lived there, they had no driveway or cement patios, no lawn and no landscaping. Whatsoever. When it rained, the dogs ran outside to piss and crap in a swamp of mud and trailed it back into the house where it would dry. California mud is a particular type of sticky, viscous and dense with black clay, so trying to get back and forth from the street to the house was always a chore. John and I simply left our "mud shoes" by the front gate when we left for school in the morning. My father's solution was to lay plywood from the mailbox to the house. Later, my solution was to buy them a driveway when my mom started using a cane.

And the bees. I cannot forget the bees. During the original construction, my father had built a small wooden shed just outside the house to store his relics from World War II. A few years later, some of the local bees took up residence in its eaves. We lived in agricultural California, where small white boxes dotted most of the hillsides, full of hives and queens specifically housed to pollinate the local orchards. It was a fairly common occurrence to see large swarms fly overhead seeking new locations as they split from the master hives. When our swarm took up residence, rather than call the local beekeeper, who provided his services for free so that he could keep local populations intact for the acres and acres of farmland around us, my father ignored and neglected the relocated bees. These bees finally took over the shed entirely, making it impossible for anyone or anything to enter, and then later, set up hives within the walls of the house itself. After four decades, the hive was so enormous that the back of the house and garage area were entirely coated in bees, was impassable, and two-inch thick swaths of workers flew home at dusk to enter the broken duct they had homesteaded in the first place. Even the dogs avoided passing by.

For some people, a lack of access to park your cars in your garage due to a hive of bees might seem nonsensical, but to us it was just another in a string of lunatic choices. For every decision and choice around us was tied in some fantastical way to another series of crazy. Like the bees, like the door-knobs, like the cars. Cars had always been a thing. Ever since we were little. For one reason or another there was always drama around cars.

I think it started when we were still in the other house. My mother had owned a Jaguar at the time. In fact, I think she brought it into the marriage. Apparently, my father, without her permission, took her Jaguar to the dealership and traded it in for the Corvair. While I was too young to really remember, the brazenness of it rings true, so I believe it.

This was back in the day when my mother still stood up for herself, and on this occasion her outrage outpaced itself and she decided to go to Catalina as an escape from the argument they had over the Corvair. At the time, my mom no longer owned her sailboat *The Seabird*, but together with her mother and my uncles she owned a power boat— *The Contessa*. She was a thirty-six-foot Chris-Craft made of white birch, covered in classic teak, and for many years taken out by my extended family on regular excursions to Catalina and the surrounding Anacapa Islands. My grandmother and uncles were proud of this boat, and my earliest memories consist of raucous gulls, sliced tomatoes on the aft deck, one jellyfish sting, and the occasional Coast Guard intervention when the engines died.

When my grandmother fell sick many years later, my Gramps gave the boat to my mom, knowing that she loved the islands the most. Nobody wanted to go on any trips without my grandmother, so the boat lingered in its slip in the Channel Islands Marina for almost a year. It was during this year that my father declared to my mom and everyone around him that since he paid the slip fees, the boat was now his, and no one was to either use it or even go aboard without his permission. I think this may have been the impetus for my mother firing up *The Contessa* and heading to Catalina the evening my father brought home the Corvair.

That evening was one of the only times I ever saw my father actually frightened. He spent most of the night calling the harbor master and the Coast Guard, frantically trying to find her. I distinctly remember sitting with my brother at the kitchen table, frozen, watching as he paced through the kitchen, the phone cord knocking over his drink. While

I do not remember the specifics of what happened on her overnight trip to the island or whether the authorities were involved, she was eventually found and returned to us a day or so later. After that, she never set foot on *The Contessa* or returned to Catalina again.

It was my junior year of high school, when I first started driving, that I tried to go to the marina on my own, to stay on *The Contessa*, to try to fix her, to try to make it like it used to be. It was a short-lived and futile effort on my part. My mother refused to acknowledge my resolution, I didn't know a thing about boats, and I could only wash the decks with a cracked bucket and some Palmolive soap, watching in dismay as the brass oxidized and the canvas rotted. My extended family had long ago abandoned any interest and I did not bother to ask. People offered to buy her, anything to restore this classic, gorgeous boat now left to die in the overhead sun and lapping bilge water, and I would smile and collect their information, knowing my father would throw the names and phone numbers away, and my mother would remain mute. *The Contessa* floated in that slip for over fifteen years before she finally sank to the bottom of the marina with only an angry, brisk call from the harbor master as her eulogy.

Cars and Catalina II

C ars, much like *The Contessa*, suffered a similar fate.
My first memory of a broken-down vehicle languish-
ing in our driveway was the ill-fated Corvair. When I was
about five, I vaguely remember trips to the grocery store,
my brother and I careening wildly across the backseat as
my mom took turns too quickly. But that is about the only
early memory I have of that car actually operating when we
were kids. Eventually, the lack of oil changes and any general maintenance caused the engine to seize, and so it sat for
years, buried under dried pine needles that fell from a towering tree in the driveway.

Like the bricks, the attic and so many other piles of utter
junk, the Corvair was towed to the house on the hill, to
park alongside the blue and white Chevy van that my father
used for work and the Ford Granada my mom drove. Over
time, each of these vehicles joined the Corvair in what John
and I as teenagers coined *The Car Yard*. Now that we lived
on ten acres, my father had plenty of room to simply add as
many vehicles, discarded barbeques, telephone poles, rolls of
fencing, and other odds and ends as he saw fit. To this day,
I have never understood why he took so little care of anything mechanical, instead choosing to buy a new *whatever*

whenever something broke. From the day my father brought any vehicle home, shiny and always brand new, to the day it joined the other hulking rust corpses in *The Car Yard*, he would not wash it, service it or otherwise maintain it in any way. The county would send notice of violation after notice of violation for too many inoperable vehicles—which he ignored by simply moving the cars further onto the property.

Once a new car arrived, piles of dog hair and mud would ruin new upholstery, discarded soda cans and trash would amass on the floorboards, and brake dust would completely coat once shiny tire rims. Sooner or later duct tape would hold side mirrors and baling wire would hold up bumpers. It did not matter how expensive the car, or what year it was bought, they all ended up the same.

It was my sophomore year of high school when the school district decided that the school bus could no longer make the long climb up our hill to pick up so few students. There were maybe three families living along the winding road at the time, with perhaps five kids in all. As a result, John and I were left with the choice of either our parents dropping us off at the bus stop about two miles down the hill—which of course would never happen—or walking, which meant we would have to get up at 5:00 a.m., as well as navigate the excruciating climb back up the hill at drop off.

My father's brilliant solution to the bus problem was to fix the mangled, disintegrating Corvair decomposing in *The Car Yard* just enough so that I could drive it up and down the hill to the bus stop. Ignored was the fact that I was barely fifteen and did not know how to drive, set aside was Ralph Nader's bombshell article "Unsafe at Any Speed," which made the case for the rear-engined Corvair being the most dangerous vehicle on the road, and discounted was the gaping hole in the floorboard next to the brake pedal. Instead, my father commissioned my cousin, a mechanic, to come and fix the engine for a case of beer, while he proceeded to tie up the exhaust pipe with a clothes hangar and throw a Mexican blanket over the exposed springs in the back seat. It was both ludicrous and exceedingly dangerous.

I drove back and forth to the bus stop for several months before, inevitably, one morning I pulled in front of a car and it slammed into us. The police arrived to find John and I sobbing, convinced we were going to jail for a very long time. Luckily, neither of us nor the other driver were hurt, but I ended up having to go to court with my mom, where I was given a warning, the judge looking hard at my mom over his glasses.

For the remainder of high school, and once I had my license, I continued to drive the deathtrap Corvair or otherwise bum rides from my friends with much safer cars. It was around this time that my father began to make it virtually impossible for my mother to get around. When one vehicle would die, he would simply buy another, which he would confiscate for his own use. He owned his own hospital supply company by then, having highjacked customers from his previous sales job. My mother ran the home office, typing invoices and answering phones, while my father ordered supplies, talked to the nurses and doctors at the hospitals and delivered the orders. Like so many things, it was another supremely isolationist approach to life, and my mother was essentially trapped in the house with no means to drive. My father took over all of the grocery shopping, all of the errands, and essentially cut her off from the rest of the world. She never said a word about it.

At seventeen, when I left for college, I was dropped off at the dorms without a car and did not have one until I turned twenty-four and could buy my own. Since I lived primarily on campus, it was not that big of a deal until I needed to get back and forth during school breaks or over the summer. If I could reach my mom by phone before my father answered, she would generally come and pick me up. If I did not, I might have a long wait.

By this time, John had convinced my parents to help him buy a 1968 VW bug to get back and forth to high school in his senior year. The Corvair had long been relegated to *The Car Yard* after a final oily gasp, and since my brother was a stand-out athlete he clearly needed transportation. The VW was old and fairly beat up, but it ran, and since my brother was handy with the engine, he managed to keep it running. My freshman year he visited often, traveling back and forth the several hundred miles every weekend to the University of California, Riverside, crashing on my dorm room floor as often as possible. My newfound college friends found him absolutely delightful, and despite my annoyance with that, I chose to ignore it because I knew he was doing whatever it took to get out of our parents' house.

The summer between my freshman and sophomore year of college I worked as a lifeguard at a local pool, teaching little kids to swim and generally destroying my skin with cocoa butter and baby oil. My mom let me use her car for that job, which of course meant she had no transportation. From time to time, my brother would take me to work or friends would drop me off, but finding a ride was always a huge deal. My father made it exceptionally clear that he expected me to pay my own way at school, which meant I had to work full-time both over the summer and part-time during school, but he thought nothing about the fact that I had no car, hence no means to make money. In fact, every chance he got to yell at me for taking my mom's car, he would. As I would silently absorb his rants, head down, I could only picture circles, big circles, little circles, endless circles, loops and loops of circles, no sense of beginning and no sense of end, no sense at all, just like a snake swallowing its tail.

I loved my job as a lifeguard. Although the water was cold during the morning lessons, I enjoyed watching the kids figure out how to swim. After hours of motorboat bubbles, torpedo arms and dolphin kicks, our red one-piece bathing suits and hair reeking of chlorine, we would lie on our towels on the hot pool deck and sun ourselves like Galapagos iguanas. After lunch, it was time for open swim, and each of us would rotate from lifeguard station to lifeguard station, armed with whistles around our necks and kickboards to swat away the enormous black-and-yellow striped bumblebees that dive-bombed our red suits. Those hours were very happy hours for me. I would volunteer for extra shifts every chance I got, both because of the extra money for school and the fact that I loved the people I worked with. We were a close-knit group of swim instructors, and every graduating class of seals, dolphins and otters brought me a sense of both accomplishment and joy. Many of these kids came to open swim in the afternoon, where together with their moms, they would cluster around us like we were celebrities. I couldn't get enough of it.

As that summer came to a close, I had about a week to register for school, secure housing and get an on-campus job. I needed to use my mom's car to drive down to campus, which of course my father said no to, so my brother offered his VW. He needed to use it the next day for basketball camp, so I had one full day to drive the two-and-a-half hours down, register, find employment and housing, and drive two-and-a-half hours back. It was tight, but I made it, finally heading back to my parents' house at about 11:00 p.m. that night.

About an hour or so into the drive home, the car began to wheeze as I climbed a steep incline. I started to panic. This was La Tuna Canyon, a highway even now entirely bereft of any homes, offramps, or businesses. This was well before cell phones, and the prospect of the car dying on the freeway with no street lights, phone booths, or people, for that matter, terrified me. The VW did not care one bit that I was frightened, seizing entirely about midway up the hill. I barely coasted to the side of the road before even the interior lights flickered and snuffed out.

I sat there for several minutes. I was eighteen, naïve and really scared. I was not sure if I should get out of the car and wave someone down, sleep on the side of the road or start walking. All of my options sounded tantamount to rolling in a bed of scorpions. So I did what any clueless eighteen-year-old would do. I froze.

Just then, a car pulled to the side of the road next to me. A young guy, maybe thirty or so, got out.

"You okay?" he mouthed, motioning his arm for me to roll down the window.

Ah shit.

I rolled down the window and smiled my best please-don't-murder-me smile.

"Yeah, I'm okay, just not sure why the car stopped."

He nodded. "Let's see if maybe it isn't something simple."

He asked me to try to start the engine, and when the car would not even turn over, he nodded his head again.

"I think your alternator is dead," he said. "Do you want me to take you to a phone so you can call someone?"

"That would be great. I would really appreciate that."

The two of us piled into his Chevy truck and drove up and over the canyon to his home about twenty minutes away. When we got there, his wife came to the door, and although surprised to see me, was gracious enough to offer me the bathroom and a drink. Her husband, Gabe, ushered me to the kitchen to show me the phone. By now it was about 1:00 a.m. and I was wildly uncomfortable interrupting them in their home.

I dialed the phone. My father answered on the second ring. "Hello?"

I started babbling, already aware I had lost the 50 percent lottery of my mom answering.

"Dad. It's me. John's car broke down. I'm in La Tuna Canyon at some people's house. They let me use their phone. I don't know what happened. The car just stopped. I know it's really late, but I need a ride."

"Tough shit."

And he hung up.

I was so stunned I almost pretended to continue the conversation, as though I was having a typical father/daughter exchange like the ones I had seen between my roommate and her dad, or even that *Family Ties* episode where Mallory and her dad yuck it up because she forgot to fill the gas tank, a two-second fantasy of my father huffing lightly and laughing at my tomfoolery before shrugging on his windbreaker and coming to get his kid.

Instead, I stood in their kitchen holding the phone, Gabe watching me with an earnest expression. I started to shake, a dumbfounded look on my face, the phone inches from my ear. I could hear the buzz of the empty line on the other end.

"So?" asked Gabe.

"He's not coming."

"He's not coming? Who? Your father?"

"Yes. He said he won't come."

Gabe gave me the most quizzical look. "What do you mean he won't come? I don't understand. How are you supposed to get home?"

"I don't know."

I began to cry, tears of dismay streaming down my cheeks, my face burning with humiliation. Gabe's wife came in the kitchen just then. When she saw my tears and heard Gabe relay what had just occurred, she told Gabe he absolutely must take me home.

I said nothing as Gabe and I drove back to the VW. He had no tow kit nor any means to pull the car other than to tie a rope between his bumper and the VW's front bumper, with me steering from inside the VW cab as he pulled with the truck. At 2:00 a.m. that morning, we began our harrowing journey home along a semi-deserted freeway, the next two hours my hands grasping the steering wheel so tightly they ached, the occasional cars roaring past us, the rope eventually breaking, sending me careening off to the side of the road. I screamed and cried most of that trip. After the third snap of the rope, Gabe tied an orange extension cord as a last resort, with the tacit understanding that if it broke I was likely on my own, until finally we made it up the final hill to my parents' house at 4:00 in the morning. Gabe did not even pretend to want to meet my parents, quickly untying the frayed extension cord and tossing it in the bed of his truck before driving off in a cloud of truck exhaust and disgust.

The next afternoon I told my mom what had happened. She had no idea. He hadn't even woken her up. And John was furious at me for breaking his car.

Over time, and as the various cars piled up in *The Car Yard*, my mother eventually stopped any attempts to leave the house. She spent the majority of her days reading or watching TV, and since John and I were by now out of the house, mostly alone. She had the dogs and cats and birds as company, but as the house fell apart, she no longer hosted dinners or holidays, and her life became more and more centered on my father and his interests.

After several years of this I could no longer stand the utter control he had of her life, even her ability to leave. And the very minute I could afford it, I gave her my Toyota Forerunner and bought another car. She was thrilled.

She used that vehicle to meet me for lunch, go the library, take the dogs to the vet. I could sense she was rejuvenated, taking every chance to drive the minute he left the house for work. She even joined a gym and began to lose weight and get stronger. I joined the same gym and met her every chance I could. I could sense she was feeling better, and her health was improving. We used our meetings at the gym to exchange books, sharing with each other those we thought worth reading, and discussing over post-workout lunch why we liked or disliked those we read. Because we both adored books and reading, it was a natural thing to bond over, and with my father not always present, it gave us an opportunity to have uninterrupted conversation.

Her joy lasted a sum total of about a year before his work van broke down and he confiscated the Forerunner. About two years later, the Forerunner joined the other six or seven vehicles abandoned in *The Car Yard*. My brother told me all it needed was a new battery. It didn't matter. My mother never drove it again.

Southern Comfort

Part of being a grown-up includes the ability to enter relationships in a rational and composed manner. In the language of my daughter, at that I am an "epic fail." Why I continue to choose men who use me or take advantage of me is not something I seem to be able to figure out. At all. I suppose a lifetime of counseling should have illuminated something, but the only light that shines within me seems to be the spotlight on my continued failure. The number of times I have fallen in lust or love is the only thing that is epic. Any possibility of success is quickly sucked into a vortex of betrayal, pain and hopelessness.

He is perfect. This last one. This new one I find while living in Georgia. We have been living in the pool house for a long time, cramped, uncomfortable, but that too, is forgotten. His bright blue eyes and chiseled jawline draw me like a bee to pollen. We met on one of the internet sites that promises eternal love, much like the promise of that final rose. Forgotten is Delaney's father and our divorce. From the moment we begin talking, there is a connection, a spark. We talk and talk and the promises flow. One week, one month, longer and it could be love. He says, *texts* it first, that singular word gorged with intent, that it is down our path, possible.

Not for me. I am not worthy. He speaks of meeting for a reason and the bonding of our equally damaged childhoods, how my story meshes with his, how he *feels* me. I fall in it, I soak in it, luxuriate. Now it will finally be different. The fact that my marriage has failed and I am alone at this age eludes me. This will be different.

We are athletes, he and I, we are coaches, we love to run and to coach young runners, we are readers, we like salty French fries, we are parents, we exercise three to five times per week. We are funny and drawn to each other. Our trauma, our healing, is mutual. We plan and plan and plan. It is brilliant fantasy. We consummate and I am sexually napalmed. To sleep with my nose pressed firmly between his shoulder blades assures me that I will *not* end up alone. He reaches for me in the night, soft murmurs of *why are you so far away baby* and curls his arm around me, the mix of our smell like a forest floor, rich and alive. He calls me "honey" and "baby" and "sweetie" and I know I am special. The sheer release of it is overwhelming. I am raw and open and full of desire to *be*. So I tell him.

I tell him all about the pain and the strangeness. I tell him about my parents, my child. I empty my soul to him. My fear of exposure is buried beneath a tidal wave of snot and tears. We cry together over my un-winnable choices, the guilt of my parental betrayal, my selfishness. He soothes and comforts me, his words like brandy and warm milk, his soft Southern drawl a blanket to draw around me.

He speaks of how he brags on me, my accomplishments, how I am so together. In his eyes I am different from other women, Superwoman, somehow separate and distinct, I have it all. Inside, I shake my head, *no no no, you don't know the absolute despair and brokenness*, but I smile and giggle and allow myself to believe if only for a tiny while that he might be right. He is the first, this one, in a long, long while to capture my attention. I have had a string of lovers over my lifetime, inconsequential urgent meetings of bodies that are designed to leave me empty. I am post-divorce, I am not ready for any form of commitment other than getting my child to school before the tardy bell rings. I have been a motherwarrior, fierce in my determination to free my child from our own insanity. This has been my world for the last year. A world of avoidance and focus. A place where I live only for my daughter and the idea of escape. Love is a concept that seems utterly foreign and impossible, I am an American woman in Baghdad, I have fallen with the Mir Space Station. For a long time, I have been okay with this. Mine is a world of work and chores and dog hair and homework and school events and meaningless threats to make my daughter sleep in her own bed. I take one antidepressant and then another. I use Xanax to breathe and Clonipin to sleep.

I am afraid of my ex and terrified of the future before me. I do not know if my move to this place is correct. I am struggling with the South, its people, its history. I find that once again I do not fit in. I am an outsider, an anomaly. I do not attend church, a staple in our community. I am not married and I travel for my work as a consultant to various clients in various locales, a condition my new Southern female friends find uncomfortable, almost shameful. I have yet to travel back to California, instead calling my mom every few days to hear her say exactly the same words. I have gone from living in my own home to living in a tiny room in the backyard of a college friend.

The fantasy of this life has turned into the reality of cramped quarters and living next to a carefully fabricated family constructed of lies. What began as an escape from my past and California has now taken an unbelievable turn. Over the course of the year, Delaney has become increasingly frantic each time I leave for a work trip. Despite closing on almost ten years old, she starts to revert to childish behavior, tantrums, refusing to sleep alone. I chalk it up to the rotten kids at school, but am shocked to learn that it is not school that is bothering her now, it is my absence. It takes some time, but I eventually coax out of Delaney that Diana is simply not nice to her. I cannot tell if Delaney is exaggerating or if it is entirely true. My heart cannot hold the pain, the betrayal. I have to get away from this house and I am frantic to find a place to live.

I find old bottles of Hydrocodone and feel good for those few days. I steal some from a friend's medicine cabinet and feel no remorse. The *after* of those days blur. I do not drink. I never drink. It makes it easy to justify other addictions. I have kept my head full to avoid falling into the abyss of memories. My past is my Lot's wife. If I look, I will turn into a pillar of salt.

So we talk, this new Huntsville, Alabama man and I, of small things and large, our individual pasts and our maybe could be almost possible future. It is so tempting to believe that in the space of one email I can feel so alive again. That I can look forward to things, that my colors vibrate and my heart can beat outside the lonely rhythm of one. These conversations compel me to seek a greater understanding of who I am, who I have become. Maybe it is his part in it, the fact that he is shattered into so many pieces over the loss of a twenty-year marriage. Two deeply damaged people seeking solace in each other's pain. We met for a reason, he says, and I choose to believe him.

The dreams begin. I wake swathed in sweaty sheets, tangled and angry. I can feel my heartbeat, not just pounding, but swelling outside of my chest like a coral tendril, searching, reaching, my blood the ocean tide. On these days, I retreat. I pull away and become remote, tentacles retracted, difficult to reach. *I am untouchable. Who am I to even assume another's affection? He will hurt hurt hurt me.* I create my own insular tension and hold mental summits, complete with panels of failed relationships.

You're not worth it, says my ex.

Idiot, chime in boyfriends six through nineteen. They high-five each other.

My daughter's father shakes his head and grimaces. *You stayed in it with me for ten years and it still didn't work. You are too selfish to feel. Our child deserves better.*

I sob and agree. This stranger of weeks become years, this Southern lover, texts of driving through tornados to see me and I am whole again. I am lost.

"Michelle?'

"Hey," she mumbles through a haze of time zones. "What time is it?"

"Dunno. I can't seem to remember. It's hard going back and forth between states. Sorry."

I can hear her rustling around in her bed, the funny sound she makes in her throat as she stumbles to wakefulness. She is my best friend of thirty some years and I miss her. She is the one thing from California I desperately miss.

"Yeah, it's okay. Everything good?" The phone scratches and rattles.

"Yup. All good. You?" *Liar, liar, pants on fire…*

"Not really." She yawns. "Looks like Baxtern is closing its doors this year. Moving the headquarters to Pennsylvania. Time for a new job."

Crap.

"That sucks. I'm sorry." *Can we talk about me now?* "How's the man front?"

She laughs. "Well, the janitor likes me."

I can tell this is a good day for her. She battles vicious depression and I tread lightly.

"I'm seeing someone." The minute I say it, I want to take it back. Saying it out loud is like jinxing it.

"Really?" She is animated and awake now. "Boytoy? Potench? Speak."

"He's really nice. Different. He's from here. I'll send you a picture."

There is a pause as she waits for her phone. I inspect my torn cuticle.

"Oh, hey. He's cute. He has kind eyes." I smile. *He does.*

"Yeah. I really like him. Which means I'll probably fuck it up."

Michelle laughs. "No, you won't. You deserve something nice for once."

So we talk and laugh and the conversation wavers between men and sex and relative dick sizes and popcorn and age appropriate behavior and daughters and everything that encompasses a decades-long friendship. When we hang up, I feel good. Connected. I put his name into the universe and it did not implode.

My phone rings as I leave for work. It is my dad. I stare at the screen. Pick up or ignore, it doesn't matter, I feel like shit.

"Hi, it's your dad." *He says the same thing every time. I know it's you.*

"Hi." My stomach rolls. "What's up?"

"Just wanted to let you know your mom isn't doing too well today."

When has she ever? "Okay," I answer. These weekly reports shred me.

"I was thinking," he says, "I will replace the garage doors. Your brother can come down and move them. We can use them to build a barn for a horse. That way Delaney can ride and you don't have to pay board. Maybe I can help with the costs. I'm sure you're tired of Georgia by now."

Oh Jesus, here we go. Because using thirty-year-old warped broken garage doors makes perfect sense to build yet another half-assed project on your property, because I want my daughter to live in squalor, surrounded by splinters and grief, watching her mother go mad. Another promise, another project gone undone, or done only the way you can see it, which is usually off, or maybe I need to be there to do it right, to save mom, to clean, to replace the pictures in my head with a story that is sane, to insert reason in the place of humiliation and shame. Hey, why don't we build it next to the bricks?

"Sounds great."

The dreams are back that night. They never really go away. They only hide in the darkness of my brain, waiting until I have just enough serotonin to mask their existence. The very moment I feel good, they return. My Southern gentleman makes me feel good, this kind and gentle internet man who spends hours with me on the phone. He is my chemical dependency. He fills me with hope. I should always know better.

Tonight is the blue dream. There are about five variations to it, but it usually ends up the same. Even as I fall asleep I can sense it coming. I struggle to stay awake, but it pulls me down. It comes at me like an old film, spliced and patched, skipping across my mind, chopped images. Not black and white, but blue. A series of snapshots, but the voice remains the same.

The candle sits on the blue dresser. Its flame throws a long shadow on the wall and there might be music. It is my childhood room, four-poster bed, and everything is blue blue blue, the walls, the furniture, the air. He sits on the edge of the bed, his hair long and blonde, tall for his age, seventeen. He is talking, but I cannot make out the words at first, only the soft tone of his voice, soothing and calm.

He is there to take care of us, babysit while my mom goes to school at night. He has put my baby brother to bed and the room is blue. The reel breaks and the film jumps, I am three, four, maybe five, and the candle flickers and I am so small. My mind is not formed, but I am aware. These images are the truth of me.

In this version he is explaining.

"You are a good girl," he says. His hands are enormous, they are disproportionate to the scale of him.

I don't speak. I never do in these dreams. I am only *aware*.

"I love you so much. Everything will be okay. I promise."

I am uneasy and I want my mom. He makes me feel icky and I don't like him. And I positively, most definitely want him to turn on the lights, because in the light we can play Candyland or I can spin the Life wheel around and around and around.

"Let's play a game. I'll show you how."

But I cannot speak because he is unzipping his pants again, and that enormous part of him that sticks in my face, and chokes me and hurts me is back, and I cannot breathe and I don't like this game and when is mom home and why does she let him be here, and this game is the mouth game, but there is the ticklefingers game and the bouncy lap game where I go away in my head because it hurts it hurts it hurts, and mom goes to school and he is always there and the room is always blue and I don't understand why he loves me this way.

When I wake up, I stumble to the shower to wash myself with hot water that never scrubs away the revulsion even after forty years. This will be a bad week. I will make others around me pay, I will become stoic and silent and unapproachable. It goes away eventually, but I will be destructive. I will be frustrated and angry. I will not be able to say or feel. I will work and work some more until the dream fades and I can become whole again, or my version of whole, the one that functions and bleeds, the one that carries on, Superwoman. And when my kind man calls, I am difficult. I question and withdraw. I work for days and do not reach for him. Why doesn't he fix it? Make it go away? He must be able to read my mind. If he cared for me, he would just know. When he doesn't and things become tense, I blame him. Our plans become tenuous. I don't just fuck it up as I predicted, I *am* fucked up.

When I receive the message that he is missing, I am confused. We had just spoken yesterday. He is gone and no one can find him. His friend is in a panic. They think he is with me. His last words to his sister and family were that he was planning to be with me. He has not returned any calls for the last twenty-four hours, including my own. I assume he is angry with me for my withdrawal.

The scenarios and desperation grow as the hours go by. I speak with his sister, his friends, no one can find him. He has four children. He does not just disappear. I become unsettled and scared—who am I in this? I know of our words and our tears, our desire and attachment, but I feel outside of this unfolding drama. It is his wife of twenty years who becomes centric, no matter the separation and pending divorce.

His sister calls. He has spoken of her many times, how close they are, how they share and talk and guide each other.

"This is so not like him," she says. "He always answers my calls."

I am numb. "I sent another text," I answer.

"I don't want to panic my mom. We won't tell my dad. We can't. Should I call the police?"

"God, Vicki, I don't know." My hands feel cold. *What is happening?*

His friend beeps in on the other line, panicked.

"I have called his friends, I have left messages, I have begged him to tell me he is okay. He hasn't answered anyone. It's been two days. He just doesn't *do* this."

I don't know this woman from Adam. Never met. But she pulls me in, scares me.

"He speaks so highly of you. He is supposed to be with you." She is crying now. "I have never heard him speak of anyone like he talks about you. He has been so sad, though. The divorce crushed him. God, I don't want his kids to find him."

Find him? What the hell is she talking about? Like, dead? Suicidal? Is this really happening?

And I realize I care. I really do. I start to shake, my body cramping and tearing at me. It had to take something like this to unwind me, make it safe for me to feel him, not question him, not predict our failure.

She is sobbing now. This is about our tenth call, this newfound best friend and I, this woman who thinks the world of me based on what he has told her, and how badly she wants a future for us, knowing his pain, his betrayal, pouring her own desperate hope into our story. I feel blame and guilt wash over me, scraping my skin raw.

"What if he is in a ditch somewhere?" Her voice catches. "He is supposed to pick up his kids today. What if he doesn't?"

I can hear her talking, but not the words. I am sick. I rewind and replay. I question every conversation, every syllable. I re-read our texts and emails, repeat our conversations in my head. *Am I allowed to show up if there is a funeral?*

I think of his children, his pain and isolation, much of it a mirror image of my own. Is this the reason we were brought together, so I can feel yet another loss, a deep and grinding pain that should be distinct from the small amount of time we have spent together, but is not?

There are many more hours of this, no word, no contact, nothing. I walk and think and worry and pray and listen to the birds and fantasize how good we could have been together, how I could have been the salve for his wounds, he, the man to shut down the voices in my head. This cannot be the reason we met. We were a beautiful baby bird, perched on the edge of the nest, new plumage, belly full of worms, ready to fly, now crashed and broken through the branches, crumpled at the base of the tree.

Hours before the news, I waken. The blue dream is back. No more, no less, just the same. This day I cannot scream over that tiny girl that I was or the missing man of my future. I am tired and worn, beaten, sad. The sheer volume of despair is overwhelming.

I still do not speak or cry out in my sleep or within the dream itself. My voice is lost. He comes and comes and comes, never leaving me, never letting me heal, only soothing words of love, promises, words to make it okay and seamless, not the wicked wrongness that it is. I cannot control the impossible decisions I was forced to make, his long blonde hair, nor can I halt the blue blue blue dreams, his voice, the candle, my pain. When I am her, this tiny baby of four or five, I only know that I should not question, should not ask, that it must be safe and fine, that I should trust him. He is my brother after all.

So when the call comes from my sweet missing Southern love, I am wholly unprepared.

"Hey, it's me. Thought I should call."

The relief floods me, he is fine, he is safe, he is not dead. As quickly as the relief forms, dread follows. I cannot think. He sounds so cavalier, so fine with things. Do you not understand that your family and friends, your lover—*yes you called me that*—were panicked over your disappearance for two days straight? We sobbed over you.

"Yeah, I'm sorry I worried you. I just need to be honest. I was with someone else this weekend."

And like that, the truth becomes me again. It cannot be hopeful and bright. It can only be blue.

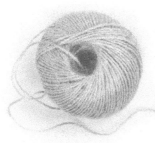

A Glass Shelf

There was a time when I suppose I was happy. I cannot remember when that was, or the circumstances surrounding it, but with the span of so much time it had to have happened. I have a good friend who revels in her childhood: the vacations to Bali, the simple and pleasant rivalry with her sister. I have known her and her family for many years, but they know nothing of me.

My childhood is a vague and third-party affair. I can re-tell it to others much like a circus barker sells the wonders inside the tent. But when I tilt the top hat over my eye and singsong about backyard barbeques and skateboards, the magic lies in the lack of color. Success lies in a subtle shift to their own tales, mine forgotten and bland, small exoskeletons of a life never lived.

My mother and brother look eerily alike. Both have dark curly hair and large, sad eyes. They are overly tall and carry their bodies like loaded backpacks. In a strange and beautiful symmetry, their hands and feet are large, their necks long, and both must buy custom-made clothing. Most people stare at them, not only because they are so unusual, but because they are stunning. Early photos of my mother show an otherworldly goddess, Veronica Lake with brunette hair and pouty lips, eyes a lapiz blue. There is a black and white of her and a girlfriend leaning on a boardwalk fence, stylish bathing suits drawn straight across the thighs, hands clasped together while each cocks her leg ever so slightly to the right. Both women are gazing away from the camera, but there the similarity ends. While the pose and age may be the same, the women are no more alike than Orion and a dwarf star. Her lines, her grace, the groove of her clavicle, are drawn by Pyramus to Thisbe. Hers is a mythic beauty, a photo negative that flashes in memory despite the erosion of age and alcohol.

I, of course, look like my father. Angular and sharp with uneventful brown hair and a sloping, predatory nose. My mind and tongue are razors, and I hone them on those who are kind to me. It is a skill I learned from him when I could not hit back, when hatred and humiliation blended into one rancid mix, soothing me, defining me. Maybe it is the beauty of my brother that drew his wrath, maybe it was my pulse.

I find it odd that people around me can recall so much of their early years. Mine is sketchy and unfinished; an old reel edited together, burn marks skidding across the screen. One therapist suggested *dissociation*, a PTSD reaction. Another, that I am bipolar. I think it is much more simple—I choose it.

John was only three in my earliest memory. It is the four of us and we are sitting outside Baskin-Robbins. I remember it as a treat, pistachio ice cream on a cone for my father and my mother and brother and I with Rocky Road. The wall is short and uneven and requires my mother to draw her knees up under her in an awkward stance. My brother sits to her left and somewhere above us, our father hovers. I can feel the sun of the day, the whoosh of cold air from the store as the door opens for each passing customer. I know I am small and

I know I like the feel of the nuts crunching in my teeth as I bite down on the ice cream. I don't like to lick it from the bottom of the cone like my brother, I prefer to chew it.

There are people around us, there might have been a fountain. I am warm on the outside and cold in my tummy when my brother spills his cone onto the concrete.

"Oops," said my mom, reaching down to pick up the cone.

Before she can even touch it, my father lashed out with his foot and kicked the cone.

"Fuckin' idiot!" he screamed. "What the hell is wrong with you!"

My cone is suddenly ugly and inedible to me and I want to cry. John begins to wail and my father yanks him up by his arm and yells at him to be quiet. Parents around us begin to silently maneuver their children away, frowning and mumbling, one father even pausing for a moment. My mother stares mutely at the melting smear of brown on the ground.

I cannot remember anything much after that, whether there was a beating, whether it smoothed over, or if we lived the next year violence-free.

My mother was gone long before she left. Occasionally, when I gather my daughter in my arms, I wonder what she felt when and if she held me. I have memories of dresses being sewn, lunches made, swim lessons attended, but I simply cannot recall actually touching her. She was never mean, just apart. Radios and electronics never worked around her. She lived within her own frequency, scrambling any attempt to be in tune with her. As a daughter it was confusing. I never got the *here is how you wear makeup, pick clothes, like boys, do homework, plan a wedding, have a birthday, tell each other I love you.* My basic needs were met, but I received no map, no guidance, more like a vague direction that there was someplace I was supposed to go, that it wasn't here, it wasn't defined, there were no instructions, yet I was expected to show up on time.

She tried once in a while to create things she knew were expected. My sixteenth birthday was one of those times. During my junior year in high school, all of the girls around me were atwitter with Sweet Sixteen parties, new cars, and over-the-top gifts. I fluttered at their periphery, smiling at all of the right times, nodding in enthusiasm, desperate to be able to issue my own invitation. I wasn't exactly popular, but there were some who accepted me, most likely due to the fact that we lived so far out from the school that the handful of kids who lived in the area had no other choices. And even though I knew better, I kept waiting for the surprise, the big gift, the announcement of *my* Sweet Sixteen party. It was no more realistic than my joining the homecoming court, but every day I still believed it might just happen, like the purple velour jacket I wore the day of the homecoming nominations *in case my name might be called.*

When my birthday came and went, I finally asked my mom if I was going to get a present.

"Oh God, what is today?" she had asked.

"May ninth."

She looked wildly around the room. "Let's go to the mall. I'll get you something."

"Yeah, okay." It was better than nothing.

She took me straight to JC Penney. I told her on the way that I had wanted a stereo for a long time, the kind with the turntable *and* a separate receiver, the kind that automatically made you cool. She was distracted and probably would have agreed to a wooly mammoth—so I got my stereo.

Back at home I spent the next several hours setting it up just right, laying out the speakers, adjusting the reception, rearranging my room so the stereo was the central focal point, making John as jealous as I could. It was awesome and for those few hours I *was* cool. Even though my birthday had been forgotten, there was no special party, and getting a car was about as probable as singing at a Journey concert, I was happy. My mom had spent a lot of money on the stereo system and I even felt guilty about it.

My dad got home around seven that night. I was in my room listening to KFI AM 640 since I couldn't seem to get an FM station. Air Supply was all out of love and my brother was pouting in his room next to me. I could hear the yelling from downstairs.

When he pounded up the stairs, John immediately snuck into my room. Even at fifteen, he still cowered in my father's presence, and we *always* stayed next to each other when the shitstorms started. We had no idea what this one was about and it really didn't matter, his anger was as regular and consistent as the tides, sucking everyone and everything around him out to sea.

I don't remember what he had been angry about. I don't remember if it was at me or my brother or my mom. It never mattered. His face came into the room before the rest of him, like a serpent rounding a corner, the hiss of him enough to make your bowels loose. He focused on me first, coming at me quick, the words pounding me, the volume so loud, and I knew the fists would be next. As I writhed to get away from him, he saw the stereo. His eyes narrowed and he turned.

"What is *this*?" he spat.

I couldn't answer. I never could. My voice had self-locked deep within me, trapped like a rodent in a burrow. John looked at me, his eyes imploring me to say something, anything, to make this stop.

"If you think your fucking sixteen-year-old fucking attitude is getting away with this—" *please please please tell me what this is if I knew I really could would answer,* "you are wrong."

He turned, and in one movement, grabbed the five-hour-old stereo and smashed it to the ground.

"No!" I screamed. I could see my brother out of the corner of my eye as he crawled on the carpet towards the broken pieces. Snot and tears blurred my vision as I bent to pick up the turntable, now shattered. I didn't even own an album yet.

He was screaming "answer me," but I had no idea what I was supposed to say. Just then he grabbed me by the hair and pulled me back. It hurt so bad I felt like my head was on fire. He chased me into the bathroom, getting more furious the more I tried to get away. In the small space I was completely trapped, and when he finally shoved me into the glass shelf along the wall, we both shattered into tiny pieces.

My mother never even came upstairs.

I am not remotely surprised that I am crazy. I can fall so far within myself that the strongest of serotonin uptake inhibitors cannot touch me. I can also present myself as smart and together, funny and irreverent, only nipping at the Valium to keep the illusion from fading. I can be acerbic and witty, make others laugh, get them to follow my lead. Maybe I got that from her. I do remember my mom's wicked and finely tuned sense of humor, an uproarious and watched-for affair much like Halley's Comet. Mom, John, and I would laugh sometimes until our sides hurt and tears were streaming down our faces, the most often topic my father.

I can still laugh when I remember the sad absurdity. At one visit shortly after my daughter was born, she and I were sitting downstairs in *that* house when we heard a loud crash from the upstairs office. Even then the house was full of filth and cardboard. The office he occupied had one small pathway between towers of old invoices, *National Geographics*, paper grocery sacks, and check registers from 1959 to 1978.

I jumped. "What was that?"

"Probably your father," she answered without looking up.

"It sounded like he fell," I said.

"Yes, it did," she answered.

We sat for a moment, both watching the baby squirm and reach with her hands. I wondered how much dander a baby could inhale before it was dangerous.

"Do you think he's hurt?"

"Probably."

I paused. "Think he's dead?"

She stared me dead in the eye. "One can hope."

We laughed so hard that she had to take off her glasses. It wasn't until my father came down the stairs screaming *couldn't she fucking hear him and that he could have broken something for chrissakes and what was she fucking deaf* and I snuck out the door with him yelling and neither one noticed.

University

My parents were far from stupid. Both had attended college, my mother majored in math and my father in biology, but it was clear they both had flunked social etiquette. While either could complete a crossword puzzle in minutes, neither had a clue that fathers paid for weddings or that TV Guide became obsolete after fifteen years. They played games like other parents paid attention to when their kids took their SATs or needed to send out college applications. They couldn't have told me what grade I was in, but they could have scripted the questions for Jeopardy. Monopoly, Parcheesi, Yahtzee, and Scrabble stood sentry over stale cereal and discarded bread heels lost beside them in the kitchen pantry, only Sir Gin and his side-kick Thimble more noble. While kids on our street raced bikes through the neighborhood, spokes sputtering loudly with clothespins, I was counter-pegging at cribbage. Penny ante poker and booze-logged tumblers boogied almost every night, when my parents would wager and swear until both were stumble-drunk. I could bet the river, play lowball, and out-bluff anyone in Texas Hold 'Em by the time I was nine. But my mother was the always the winner, no matter the game. To this day, her Ziplocs full of pennies lie deflated throughout the house like sun-stroked jellyfish, their copper innards tarnished and bloated.

In an epic repeat of my childhood, my transition to university living began with a wave and a curb drop-off, freshly laundered sheets and 1960s Samsonite in hand. In B2 East, the all-girls hall where I was housed, freshmen roamed with parents and furniture, chattering loudly and instructing fathers on exactly where they wanted their lofts built and eye-rolling while moms put away underwear. I felt so wildly out of place it was breathtaking. I was not wearing the latest clothing—in fact did not know that Dittos had a shelf-life—had no fashionable sausage curls alongside my ears, and my concept of make-up was that other girls wore it. Watching the fluorescent colors, loud noises, and brightly rouged cheeks around me was like standing in front of the parakeet cage at PetCo. All I could do was stare numbly at the slip of paper that held my room number.

My roommate's name was Robin and she was a junior. Her side of the room was neat as a pin, posters tacked in perfect symmetry, Laura Ashley comforter folded neatly back from her two matching standard pillow shams. Her boyfriend and sister were sitting in the room and jumped up when I entered.

"Hi, you must be Dorriah!" said Robin, her smile and hair so perky my eyes almost exploded.

"Yeah."

Her sister came over and took my suitcase. "Wow, this is awesome," she grinned, "want some help?"

Robin smiled enthusiastically and grabbed my sheets. "Let me get these so you can go get the rest of your stuff."

"Uh, I don't have any other stuff," I answered.

"Oh. Well." She paused and looked at her boyfriend, a nondescript boy with dark eyes. Her eyes slid around our room, taking in the sparkling new typewriter, green desk lamp and closet stuffed with clothes. On her side.

"I can just take you to the campus bookstore and we can find some cool things to put on the wall, then."

Her hazmat smile was back. Apparently we had just successfully navigated our first *uncomfortable moment.* As I learned later, Robin and her sister, Sandra, detested uncomfortable moments. Both would avoid loudness and confrontation at any cost and the silence that surrounded my dorm room those first few weeks confused me. I had never experienced anything like it and the dawning revelation that I no longer had to live under the same roof as the rage freak was stunning.

Few memories from that first year stand out quite as well as my first day of classes. With the help of Robin, I had somehow figured out how to get my class schedule, find the cafeteria, and get to the basement laundry for all seven outfits I had brought along. At twenty, Robin was also a Mary Kay saleswoman, and the watery pink plastic compacts covered every surface of the room. My pale, freckled face just begged for her handiwork, and orientation week was spent mixing and matching Ivy Garden with Lavender Fog, frosted lippens and eyebrow polish. By the time classes started, I looked like a freakish version of early Madonna.

But I felt good. For the first time in my life I felt like I *existed.* I was outside the gravitational pull of the horror house and could ignore my biological beginnings with a new ease. Unlike the other parents, mine didn't call. My mother mailed me an avocado once, but that was about it. I was on my own. So when the day came for classes to start, I was ready.

I had borrowed Sandra's sand-colored wraparound skirt and worn it with my flat white boots and Robin's leg warmers. My hair was nuclear with hairspray and I think I might have even had a sweater draped across my shoulders and tied in front. Leaving the dorms that day for campus I felt alive and confident, a girl who belonged, not some mongrel begging for fish entrails along the wharf. I just knew my hair was good, my outfit rocked, and my backpack bulged with books and fresh, white paper just pleading with the pens to scratch across them with incredible new things. I could almost forget that John had called two days before about the pitchfork.

So when people began to say hi and wave at me, I really knew I was right where I was supposed to be. It was a long walk from the Aberdeen and Inverness dorm to get to the Bryant Physics Hall, where my eight a.m. class was being held, and I was enjoying every minute.

"Wow," yelled a boy from across the street. "How are *you?*"

I smiled and waved back. What a great place. Nothing like the intestinal blender I came from. People here were nice. Friendly.

A group of girls from behind me were yelling for me to wait up. They were from my hall and none had really paid much attention to me until now. People all around me were laughing and smiling, pointing and waving. It was like a parade.

The girls finally caught up and gathered next to me.

"You're a freshman, right?" asked Tori Amerson, a sophomore at the apex of the food chain. She and her friends lived at the end of the hall, where second-year residents lived. The smell of popcorn and popularity wafted regularly from their room and freshmen weren't even allowed to pass the midway point.

"Hi, I'm Dorriah," I had answered, cocksure in my painted revelry, not even bothering to adjust the headband that threatened a headache.

"It is *great* to meet you," said Tori, shaking my hand. She smelled like a combination of waffles and Obsession. I was intoxicated.

As she and her girlfriends walked on, a group of guys passed from behind and a few turned and waved at me. *God I loved this place. Nobody knew me—knew them.*

It wasn't until I got about half a block from the physics hall when I realized something was off. It was one of those moments when your head says absolutely *not* and your stomach curls in on itself. I *couldn't* but I *had* to reach around behind my backpack for my skirt. It wasn't there. All I felt was air and underwear.

My skirt had caught in my backpack strap and yanked all the way up until my ass was swinging for all to see. It wasn't remotely funny, it was horrifying, and in less than a split second I once again became *that* girl, that very same girl who could not become something other than who she was.

John and I grew up in a fairly typical suburban neighborhood. Those were the days of coming home when the streetlights came on and mothers yelled from porches that dinner was ready. It was probably just as dangerous as it is now, but we didn't know it and that made all the difference. Behind our house was a stretch of fields about ten acres across

that ran between the homes and the local drive-in. Called
The Bends, the fields were thick with scrub oak and mustard,
discarded skateboard ramps and broken bottles. Along the
west side ran a row of tall eucalyptus, tree after tree of soft
blue leaves, peeling bark and carved initials, always shady and
smelling of winter croup washcloths.

By some kind of little kid radar we knew the areas to
avoid: the ones with mattresses and bronze-colored glass. We
knew where the high school kids went and we knew to avoid
the bend in the creek where the tree fell across. We would fill
our bike baskets with acorns and bird skeletons, my brother
constantly on the lookout for shotgun shells. Most of us were
forbidden to play there as The Bends was known to harbor
hippies. But hippies meant nothing when pollywogs could be
had. The stream we frequented was actually effluent from
a storm pipe, and the pollywogs were more likely mosquito
larvae, but the concept of riding our bikes on forbidden
ground was glorious.

Saturday mornings after *Captain Kangaroo*, my brother
and I would hop on our Schwinns *purple with a banana seat* and
head to the ditch. I called my brother "Johnny Appleseed"
when we played and were getting along, "butthead" when
we weren't. After pollywogging, we would sneak across a
long field full of tumbleweeds to the back of the drive-in
where the grate had rusted through and the bars twisted at
weird angles. We would spend the next several hours looking for dropped change or racing around the speaker poles,
flying up and over the asphalt humps like motocross racers
on crack. At dusk those bars looked like a yawning mouth,
and every time I squirmed back out, my skin would twitch
and crawl past my shoulders as I waited for the teeth to close.

I suppose we spent one month or ten years playing at The Bends. The memory blurs as does time. It was our last visit that is etched as clearly as seabroken jade. We had decided to mix it up a bit and go to the drive-in first. John had seen a particularly appealing squirrel carcass the week before and was hoping it had rotted enough to bring home. So it was late afternoon by the time we got to the pollywog pond. The sun was low and several teenagers were hanging around the storm drain smoking cloves. It wasn't until they scattered that my brother looked up.

It was *him* and he was *pissed*. He didn't say a word as he grabbed us both by the arm, shoving us to our bikes.

"Get those goddamn bikes and get home," he seethed. My stomach felt like I'd swallowed a leaky car battery. My brother just started crying. We must not have been much older than eight or nine because Johnny Appleseed had to have a running start, swing his leg over the balljammer bar and start pedaling madly since his feet couldn't reach the ground. Our dad was so mad he walked faster than we could pedal. By the time we dumped our bikes on the lawn and walked in the front door both of us were so scared we could barely walk.

"I told you two fuckwits *not* to go to The Bends, didn't I?" he screamed the minute we were inside. My brother stood just behind me. I could feel the fear vibrating from him like a tuning fork.

My mom was in the kitchen. We heard her unloading the dishwasher.

"What the fuck is wrong with you? Answer me."

Neither of us could speak. We never could. And it only made him madder.

Suddenly he threw a picture frame at us. It shattered against the wall behind us, barely missing my brother's head. I slunk to the floor whimpering, *this will be baaad.* There was also a part of me that knew other kids were gonna get caught at The Bends and that their parents would be mad. They would be punished or grounded, maybe even spanked. But even in my little kid heart I knew that what we would get would be so much more *unspeakable.*

"Okay, since both of you think you're so fucking smart, I'm gonna let you find out just how smart you are," he said. "Go to your rooms. Now."

I ran into my brother's room with him and we both pulled ourselves under his bed, shaking and crying. We heard him crashing and cursing down the hall, his wolf words and size growing more ferocious as he got closer and closer until we were just little piggies waiting for the walls to fall down. Instead he yanked the bed back and pulled us both out from underneath. In his hand he held the leather dog leash.

"You first," he said to me as he wrapped the leash in half. He pushed the ends together and then back with a loud smack.

"Bend over you little know-it-all. You will listen next time." He shoved me head first over the end of the mattress.

He hit me so hard the first swipe that every cell in my body felt it. I had never felt such a hot rainbow of pain.

"Maybe you'll *think* about it the *next* time you decide to *disobey* me." Every few words were emphasized with an increasingly wicked smack of the leash against my legs and back. I felt the skin across my shoulder blade split open, the warm blood oozing down my back like lava across a volcanic field. He didn't stop.

When my brother saw the blood he screamed and grabbed at the leash. My father laughed.

"Oh, so you're a tough guy," he spat. "Bend over. Your turn."

As the shrieks began, I realized pretty quickly that what I had received was insignificant compared to the *focus* my brother got. From that beating forward, each time I thought I could not handle any more, not one more pummeling, not another fist or hand or kick, I still wished I could somehow take *more*. *More*, so that what Johnny Appleseed got would somehow be less horrifying and not so imbalanced and unfair, so wicked and sideways with hate, *more* so that the leather end of the leash would lash his body like mine and leave welts and marks and not be *turned around for godsakes* so that the metal snap on the end of the leash is used like a club and leaves bruises and cracked ribs and scars and he cries and cries and cries and this is just the beginning of it.

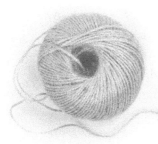

Another Go

The pain is magnificent at times. A whole body, all-encompassing event like laying atop a barbeque. I suck for air. My tears don't fall, they heave, and the idea of her lying there suffering consumes me. Why don't I do something? I try to call, but her responses now are muted, almost unintelligible. This is the mother of my now, a bed-ridden, sodden mess. I can only hope physical therapy is helping, that the doctors are monitoring. This will be the third year in a row she has forgotten my birthday. I am trapped between living and her dying.

My escape from her misery is a second attempt at a post-divorce relationship. I have no business doing this again after the disaster of Alabama man. But I do not want to be alone, I do not want to sit endless evenings thinking about my choices, I want distraction. This time he is Columbian. It is a fascinating dance of language and lust. He speaks several languages and likes to play word games. Once again, he is generated from online algorithms designed to capture exactly what is wrong with me. He is crafty and persuasive, tall with longish black hair that he knows women comment upon. He can eerily imitate an owl and it makes my daughter laugh. He is relentless in his pursuit of me and I thrill at the attention. The small alarm bell jangling at the end of my brain stem at the sixteen-year age difference does little to dissuade me. I am sucked into the whirlpool of emotion and promises so mightily that I breathe through gills.

It is clear that as our rumba begins I have forgotten the string of failed relationships behind me. This one is clearly different. I have finally gone outside my comfort zone. He is not of the chiseled jaw and All-American boyish charm. Instead, he is pot-bellied with irregular teeth. His long hair is unique and almost beautiful, but he himself is awkward in his own skin, cannot even swim. I find this almost funny after he tells me of his coyote journey across South America and Mexico in a desperate attempt to gain asylum in the United States.

The story itself is grim. He tells me of how he, his girl-friend, and a few friends planned and plotted to leave their jobs as dentists and students, engineers and teachers at the chance to have faster internet and minimum wage jobs. I am in awe that this desperation still exists, that there are people in the world who do not have automatic freedom and opportunity. I realize my Anglo-centric outlook is appalling and I am determined to become enlightened. Here is my chance. There is a photo of him in a Nebraska newspaper holding an American flag from seven years prior, his hair still long, almost thirty pounds of McDonalds and Taco Bell ahead of him. He looks young and goofy. He is twenty-four in the photo and the girlfriend beside him is thirty-seven. I cata-logue that he chooses older women. So this age thing is my issue, not his.

He tells me he spoke very little English when he arrived. I find this fascinating as his English is now almost perfect, even subtle and nuanced. Our email exchanges are full of innuendo, switching between English and Spanish, each trying to catch the other at a mistake. I find his mind challenging and his experiences intriguing, but I am not physically attracted. I convince myself that although I do not find him remotely sexually appealing, this is a good thing, progress even, as all of my previous love interests have been a gene here or there from gorgeous, so *that* must have been the problem. No more. I can explain away my failure at relationships by my own shallowness.

We begin our romance both electronically and transatlantically. He is in France and I am in the U.S. He finds me on the very same matchmaking website as my last relationship disaster and "favorites" me so many times that I am forced to laugh. He is so not my type. He is too young, he is too foreign. He is dark and odd-looking and I am simply not interested. After several days of ignoring him, I finally answer on a lark. And it begins. He writes and writes and writes. I relent and give him my phone number and we begin talking. But his accent is so thick that at first I can barely understand him, so we revert mostly to written form. He is so different from anyone I have known that I begin to find him interesting and I look forward to our evening discussions. He finds out that I have a young daughter and he whistles to her from the phone to make her giggle. She asks him why he hoots like an owl and he tells her that his name means owl.

"So what does my name mean?" she asks.

Without pause he answers. "Blinking Star." My daughter and I are smitten.

For weeks he emails me all day and calls me at night and sends my daughter postcards of romantic French chateaus.

He is charming and cultured, well-read and occasionally raucous. We have phone sex before meeting in person. These
are the ways of Internet romance: instant gratification and
another face just around the corner, intimate encounters with
no consequences for bad behavior, a Ponzi scheme with a
Send button.

So I ask myself *am I finally healing? Is it possible I may have
broken the old patterns of destructive relationships?* The possibility
of it glimmers in the distance like an oil slick on a forgotten
highway, only that one lost car broken on the side that leaves
its occasional greasy remains. I pace myself. I don't allow
him to force meeting in person. I make myself somewhat
calm and thoughtful, sure that *this time* I will make this so
very different than anything before. And I realize another
thing—that I have to. If I don't manage this well, the after-
math will be too much. After marriages one and two and
my most recent disaster—he of the lost weekend—I realize
that my healthy participation in this is critical. Vital even to
my internal belief structure that I am a functioning human
being, capable of things that the child in me was not. After
so much terror and destruction, I hold onto the tiny fragment
that believes I am not broken, at least not entirely.

We decide that our first meeting should be in a neutral
location, somewhere without my daughter and away from
outside influences. I want to see him and judge him on my
own. We decide on Florida. I already know that there will
be no automatic chemistry, at least not the kind I am used to,
that immediate sexual spark deep in the belly, a fluttering in
the veins. While I am excited to meet him after so much discussion and intellectual participation, I am also a bit worried.
I know myself well enough to realize that if I don't develop

some of that spark, all of the pacing and trying to build this thing "the right way" will be for nothing.

I make him send my friend Michelle copies of his driver's license and passport in the off-chance he is a serial killer. I leave air and hotel itineraries, a will and instructions for my daughter in triplicate. I also insist that he pay my way, make all of the arrangements, and choose the location. I am *done* with being used.

"Your flight on time?" he emails. "You excited?"

I send a smiley face and answer yes to the flight info. I am due to arrive in Fort Lauderdale in about an hour. I've gone shopping—a new Ann Taylor skirt and a matching summer tank. High heels rather than my usual flip-flops. My hair is freshly cut and colored, my nails are done, and every single callous that might have considered residence on my feet is history.

"What time do you land?" he sends. I know he knows the answer to this but I think he just wants to chat. He is probably nervous, too.

"2pm," I type back. "Are u picking me up in baggage claim?"

"Just outside along the curb."

"K."

My anxiety builds on the short flight from Chattanooga to Fort Lauderdale. Here is a man who may have everything *new* that I am looking for. He is college-educated, he speaks several languages, he lives in both Miami and France, says he owns his own businesses, is articulate and kind, and is patient with my desire to go slowly. My imagination begins to wrap itself around our midnight discussions, his timeline to have children and a family, his focused interest on my daughter, how it must be hard on the two of us without a father to help, his interest in my career and life path, how different I am from the other women he has dated. I barely notice the accent anymore when we talk.

In the email exchanges the week before my arrival he had asked about my breast cancer.

"How long ago were you diagnosed?"

"Six years."

"Are you in remission?"

"Yes." This conversation is hard for me. I don't like it and I don't really want to talk about it. Talking about it adds the jinx element, and the tendrils of all-consuming fear crawl up my back. *I can still remember the feel of that godforsaken lump. The shower water turned cold on my skin despite the heat, and I knew without any doubt what it was before any doctor made any diagnosis. It didn't matter that the statistics were in my favor, I had no genetic history, didn't smoke or drink or do drugs. It didn't matter that the oncologist at my first visit assured me that it was benign because 85 percent are benign. The minute I felt that pebble just beneath the surface of my skin I knew. I knew deep in the coils of my bowels that this was really really bad and whatever happened from this second forward with these drops of water on my body and my husband of the moment staring bleakly at me through the shower glass that I wanted this out of me. Now. But I had to go through the motions, the tests, the health insurance approvals, felt up by more hands than possible, to just get to it. Take it out. So they finally did. Dr. Sperry, the surgical oncologist, smiled and laughed that morning as the nurses prepped me.*

"We're good. This will only take a few hours. We will do a frozen section during surgery to make sure we get all of the margins. Nothing to worry about. I've seen this before and I'm ninety percent sure yours is benign."

Really, Doctor? We are good? Don't know about you, but this whole deal isn't doing much for me.

The next thing I remember is waking up in recovery. My husband, Delaney's father, is sitting next to the bed and his face is grey like the walls. He starts crying the minute I open my eyes.

"It's not good, honey," he says. His nickname of Crumpleface is very fitting. It's as though his cheeks have slagged off the bone, his eyes are deep, sad sockets, and the skin around his mouth looks crooked. It has been ten hours of surgery, not four, and I have lost half a breast, four lymph nodes, and most of my hope.

And so begins the hell of my life for the next several years. My baby is only two and I cannot care for her. I can only puke so loudly that the walls shake. I can only die one cell at a time, each cell agonizing at its own demise, the pain and chemotherapy in a pagan dance of lost fertility. At one point my organs fail and I am rushed to the oncology ICU where I spend four days in a circular room of dying patients and loud nurses. I do remember wishing my parents would come to say either hello or goodbye. They did neither.

I survive radiation and Lupron, forced menopause and more surgery on my ovaries, my uterus, whatever womanparts I have left that insist that I must have hormones, periods, babies. But I come out of it after these lost years with dark and curly hair, a melonballed boob and the determination not to have that again.

"Do you still menstruate?" This email jerks me back to reality.

"What?" I reply. This guy is straightforward, almost insouciant.

"Can you have more children?"

I cannot reply to this. It goes to the core of me. The fact that my childbearing years were stolen from me—that I was forced to be fifty-five at thirty-eight.

I answer. "Don't you think we should meet first?"

Dogs

I called John the other day. It was one of those days when I was feeling particularly mean-spirited, as though I somehow deserved another to suffer in my stead. I was tired of carrying my guilt, tired of the fact that he lived safely away from our mother, and had for years, while I struggled with the last year of my absence on a daily basis. While I would like to believe that I carry a magnanimous love for him, that I am somehow righteous and apart, the reality is that I harbor equal parts resentment and indifference, and it is our history that compels me to stay connected. When I talk to him, I face an internal scrutiny so fundamental that it innerves me, a stark understanding that I cannot escape the core of who I am and that my insatiable desire for some sort of familial normality always, *always,* ends in disappointment. But I call anyway.

This time it was about dogs. He had adopted yet another throwaway, an animal equally as broken as he, found along the road, at a job site, discarded by a drug-addled friend, it didn't matter, they were usually the same dog. It was a far departure from the pedigreed yellow labs that our parents bred and sold for many years and I suppose that was much of the point. From the time we could remember, there was always a pack of Labradors around us and these dogs represented our parents and their odd and tenuous connection to the world around them, even more so than my brother and I.

"Hey, do you remember that weird terrarium thing at the Northam house? Our first house?" he asked.

"The one on the side, below the hill?"

"Yeah, remember how we used to play on that hill, under the eucalyptus trees until dark?" I can hear him inhale his cigarette. "I can still remember the smell of those trees. Sometimes I buy cough drops just for that smell."

I chuckle and my mind wanders as he talks. I remember those enormous trees lined atop the far end of our yard, the house and remaining yard below with its spiderfield of bricks, its oddly out-of-place pool in the midst of weeds and discarded wooden pallets, the sloping hillside covered in succulent stalks of ice plant, their bright purple flowers and hardy root system requiring no care and little water. My brother and I would play long hours on that hill, hide-and-seek, tag, running, hiding, skidding down trampled chutes of burst ice plant, breathing deeply of the late afternoon smells, knees stained lavender.

In the front yard, long before it was fashionable, well before whispers of California drought conditions, and far unlike the weekend-tended, manicured and lush lawns of neighbors around us, ours was a house of minimalism, with little to no landscape, dense Zoysia grass and cement hardscape. As children, we always wondered why our grass was so hard and weird and not at all fun to play on, and it was only when we were older that we realized that the grass had nothing to do with either kid comfort or aesthetics, but was merely our father's way of avoiding spending money and expending effort on anything not directly related to himself.

"….thinks it might be some sort of collie," John says.

My mind dips back to John's deep, almost South Texas voice. Despite his distinctly California upbringing, at one point he reinvented himself as something of a cowboy, complete with a slow, honey-thick drawl and paddock boots. While somewhat diluted now, his adoption of this accent has remained for many years and threads its way through this conversation. He has always been an adept imitator and can bring a room to tears with impressions of rushing trains, staid politicians, and wildly inappropriate sexual dalliances between species. It is this part of him that I love the most, his wicked humor and depth of observation. He has an irreverent and uncanny ability to dissect the deepest, darkest recesses of those around him to a disconcerting point of hilarity and distress. I have seen people doubled over in laughter, women openly grasping at their crotches to stop from peeing, grown men with tears flowing down their cheeks, as he serenaded them with ribald songs or rude jokes at their own expense. His is a towering, lumbering *hilarious* presence, equal parts Dana Carvey and Larry Bird, too large to ignore and too funny to miss. There have been moments when I have literally been unable to breathe at something he has said, a subtle comment he has made. For some reason, to this day I cannot hear the word "nectarine" without bursting into laughter.

But this is also the part of him I mourn the most, this untapped talent shared with only a small coterie of sister and drunken bar acquaintances, this deep, unending well of clear notes and crisp watchfulness. I can easily imagine him a successful singer, comedian, playwright. He could have, might have, and I am certain we both know this.

In this most recent identity iteration he is a biker, his Facebook page chock full of Harleys and bearded road buddies, red bandanas wound tightly around middle-aged wrists and sun-speckled foreheads. Faded tattoos adorn overweight arms and motorcycles gleam from hours of polish. To my untrained, non-gang-affiliated eye, these weekend bangers look no more likely to take down a kill than overweight zoo lions panting diligently for their next bucket of meat. And to me, my brother is no more a biker than he is a cowboy. Or perhaps he is both. It doesn't really matter anymore.

Along the path of self-evolution, he has also adopted the nickname "Falcon" for himself. He even claims it is his middle name. His fantasy of reinvention has the girth of many years and I both envy and pity him for it. It is not at all surprising that he has found a way to be anyone other than who he was, and this is the part I envy the most—his ability to morph like a chameleon, to phase with the colors and emotions around him and become that person that others will most easily accept. I have failed miserably at this talent, instead becoming more and more entrenched in who I am, strident and with little to no regard for the caustic burns I inflict on those around me.

"Swimming with you all day and playing hide-and-seek with Sergeant, those are my earliest memories," he says.

I snap back into the phone call and laugh. "Yeah, he was a great dog. One of the few."

I find that it has become harder lately to stay focused on our conversations. I catch myself moving back and forth in time like some sort of illusory sea anemone, attached only

temporarily to the seabed of the present, my memories swaying with the tide and my ability to pay attention anchored
entirely to chance currents. This is one of those times. My
mind skitters across generations of dogs, seemingly unwilling
to land on a single snout, a clear visual of which dog entered
which phase of our lives. I can recall their names—Patrick,
Argyle, Brigadier, Stewart, Rob Roy, on and on—with the
words flickering like a CNN ticker tape at the bottom of my
eyescreen, but the faces and the shapes and the bodies of all
of these dogs are just one dog. One yellow, indistinct smear.
Above me, I can hear my brother on the surface of the sea,
talking about this new dog, insistent and muffled, as though
he is speaking at me through the depths. All I can hear is the
rush of the water while I reach out lazily for his words.

Instead, my mind goes back to the dogs. So. Many. Dogs.
Like the majority of so many convoluted, ill-conceived and
poorly executed plans of my father, he decided when we
were about twelve and thirteen that because they liked our
first Labrador, that they should become breeders. Sergeant
had recently died and I suppose much of this decision was
based upon the fact that my parents were selling our childhood home—*that of the ice plant*—and now owned ten acres
of land and could hide their lunatic plans from prying eyes
due to our isolation and the fence that surrounded the property. But I doubt it. In all actuality, like so many things my
father decided to do, this, too, was based upon some form of
desire to be the best at something and to be able to talk nonstop about it to anyone within earshot.

So breeders they became, and for the next almost forty
years my parents had anywhere from two to six dogs and any
number of puppies living in the house. Our childhood dog,

Sergeant, is the easiest to recall only because he was the first, but the rest blur together in a haze of fur, shit, and mud. I do know that one adult side effect of growing up in a house full of dogs is that I am now and forever mentally allergic to dog hair. Recently, I have irrationally, insanely been losing my temper when I see balls of animal hair in the corners of the rooms in my home, as though the animals should somehow know better and that my daughter should have cleaned them before they formed.

My parents adored their dogs. So much so that outings, trips, and activities often came to screeching halts because they "had to get home to the dogs." Years were spent with piles of puppies, shit-stained newspaper covering the floor beneath the breakfast table where we ate, fights between the male dogs and generation after generation of increasingly paler versions of the first pair. The first few litters were almost *but not quite* fun. After a while, to my brother and me, it became idiotic and made no sense. As the number of litters grew, so did our resentment. My parents care and affection for the dogs were directly disproportional to us. We hated those dogs.

This obsession and adoration even transcended the danger the dogs posed as my parents grew older. Labs are large and clumsy dogs, with sweeping tails and boisterous personalities, much better suited for young families and kids, not older people with mobility and drinking issues like my mom. The first time they knocked her over, she hit her head on the tile counter. She recovered fairly quickly, suffering a black eye and torn rotator cuff. My father brushed off the accident with noises like *she'll be fine, no need for the doctor.* The second time they knocked her down on the cement patio as they raced for the yard, and she fractured her pelvis, which resulted in her needing a cane to walk. The third time, and a couple years later, they knocked the cane straight out from under her. She fractured her pelvis and her hip, and finally was forced to go to the doctor because she could not walk or get up the stairs to her bedroom. At no time was it discussed that maybe having five one-hundred-plus-pound dogs running around might be a bad idea. At no time was it considered that health might be an issue. This was the beginning of her end.

The day of my daughter's birth was no different. My mother spent a sum total of one hour in the hospital with me, before my father ultimately dragged her out with some excuse about needing to buy dog food. I remember thinking at the time that it was par for the course. How could a newborn granddaughter possibly compete against the dogs?

And at twelve months old, she actually did compete. And lost. My mother wanted to see the baby and asked that I bring her to their house. This was about the time of the second dog knockdown and my mom was having trouble getting around. The only way she could spend any time with Delaney was if I made it happen. This was also about the time when I began leaving brochures about hip replacement surgery so that my mom could get around and help me with babysitting. In my mind, it was a perfect sequence of events: surgery, recovery, babysitting, divorce, live with me. My fantasy of her leaving him was most certainly rekindled with the hope that a granddaughter close by would lure her away.

Since Delaney was not yet fully walking when my mom requested we visit, the idea that she could remain off the filthy floor was justifiable. It was clear from the onset of my arrival that the female breeding dog, Bubbles, was jealous of the attention that my mother gave the baby. She would constantly circle at my mother's feet and try to climb up onto the couch with her while she held her granddaughter. My mom, like always, let the dog clamber up and settle next to her, despite the curled lip and flat ears. All I could see was how close my daughter's face was to her mouth.

When I mentioned that I would be more comfortable with the dog on the floor, my father spoke up from the kitchen saying that his dogs were the friendliest, most loyal creatures in the world and would never hurt anyone. My spidey senses said otherwise. No sooner had my father said those words, did my daughter reach from her grandmother's lap for Bubbles's fur. In a blur of snarling teeth, the bitch snapped at her, my mother only just snatching her away in time. In absolute panic, I grabbed my daughter and yelled at the dog, "No!"

My father came screaming around from the kitchen. At first, I thought he was screaming at the dog, only to realize that he was screaming at me.

"What the fuck is wrong with you? Don't you *dare* yell at my dog. This is *her* house, not yours."

I remember not being able to speak. I was so stunned *although why should I have been* that he was mad at me, that he had zero interest in the safety of my daughter, his granddaughter, or that he would stand up for the civil liberties of his pet over his blood. So I stood there with my squalling baby, my silent mother and a growling dog, surrounded by swirling motes of dog shit and dander, while my father yelled more insults at me, my mind already out the door and driving down the long, winding hill to the safety of my own couch. I never took her back after that. And my mother never asked.

My brother laughs then coughs across his cigarette, "Do you remember how we used to hold his collar and make him pull us around the pool?"

"Or when we would attach his leash and have him pull us up the side of the hill?" I reply.

"I really only liked him, and maybe Brigadier," he says. "Most of the other ones were useless. Except for The Boys."

Ah shit. The Boys. We hadn't talked about them for a long time. They were a different matter altogether.

He takes a deep breath. I imagine he is releasing it through clenched teeth. "So fucked up."

There was a small period of time right after we moved—*brick by fucking brick*—to that hill of dead avocados, when we were dogless. Sergeant had died just a few months after moving, and my parents had not yet begun their breeder-quest. We still had cats, plenty of cats, oh and parrots and chickens and a couple horses. Ten acres could fit quite a few more animals than a tract house, and we had collected them quickly.

It was the summer just before I started my new high school when The Boys first appeared. One morning I went outside to feed the horses and there was this wiggly little white dog falling all over himself to get me to pet him. He had brown spots and a pink nose, rust-colored ear fringes and an ability to move his hind end in the fastest side-to-side wag I'd ever seen. I immediately fell in love and named him Freckles. It didn't take much to get my parents to agree to let me keep him, and I spent that entire summer with him by my side.

It seems that the area we lived in was a haven for abandoned dogs. Perhaps it had to do with the sprawling hillsides, or the ability to hide your treachery in the surrounding orchards, but that very same summer my brother brought home two more dogs. He had been hunting squirrels at the bottom of the hill and the way he told it, these two enormous black dogs just materialized in the trees behind him. He told us he thought they were going to eat him they were so big.

I had never seen dogs like these, and it was my mother who knew immediately that they were Newfoundlands. Brothers it seemed. And only about a year old. They were stunning, with long, rough obsidian coats, noses that shined like apache tears, and the sweetest disposition of any animal I have ever known. When they showed up they were clearly hungry and, surprisingly enough, Freckles had no issue with them vacuuming his food. That very night the three of them snuggled up in a pile of dog and were thereafter known as The Boys.

The Boys spent that entire summer traveling the hills surrounding our property with my brother and me. If I rode my horse down the hill, they followed. If John went out hunting, they trotted behind. My mom absolutely loved them, especially Buck and BJ (as the two black Newfies became known) and spent countless hours brushing their luxurious coats. They were huge and kind and clumsy and fun.

So when the day came that The Boys decided that a rousing game of chase-the-kitten was in order, and one of them either played too rough, or perhaps Freckles may have bit-ten—no one really knows for sure—my father lost his mind. He brought the limp body of the kitten into the house, screaming at the top of his lungs that the dogs had murdered his cat.

We knew immediately to scatter. As our father thun-dered through the house looking for the dogs, shrieking that he would kill them, I grabbed Freckles, and my brother took Buck and BJ. To some families, this might seem a hollow threat, but we knew better. And when he came around the corner, gun in hand, we knew to run.

He saw me first. For the next ten minutes or six hours he chased me around our property waving the gun at me to stop, that he was going to kill that fucking dog. I finally found a hiding spot in the shed and remained there for several hours shivering with an equally frightened dog. My brother had taken off at a lope down the hill with Buck and BJ following. Neither of us returned for many, many hours.

The next day we had to go to school. When we stepped off the bus that afternoon, my mom was waiting for us. She had tears in her eyes and a horrified expression. Our father had taken all three dogs and had them euthanized that morning.

There is a place in Cabo San Lucas called Ventana del Pacifico, just off Medano Beach. This Window of the Pacific is a vertical keyhole crack in the rocks next to the Cabo arch that allows boaters on the Sea of Cortez to see through to the Pacific Ocean. It is a wild and dangerous spot. I took Delaney there one year for vacation, and while bobbing in the taxi boat only feet from the opening, it reminded

me of a dragon's maw, the water heaving and frothing, the sharp scalloped edges of the rocks only too willing to chew us up, the water taxi captain continually backing the boat to stop us from being sucked into the hole.

The only difference between that angry, seething mouth and my father, was the view.

Horses

I t all started with Heather. She was fat, black, and quite sassy. She had an attitude a mile wide and a rear end to match. I met her the spring I turned fourteen, and it was love at first sight. Although our introduction was a bit sketchy, with me trying to brush her stomach, followed by her immediate swift kick to my kneecap, after that day we were inseparable. Over the years, she had the ability to dry my tears no matter how many I shed, and she never, ever once failed me. She was my best friend, my confidante, my escape—my horse.

I did not have much to do with the acquisition of either Heather or Andromeda, the two mares that became members of our family on that hill seemingly out of nowhere. Like so many other things, my father had controlled and orchestrated every single aspect, from the purchase, to the setup of the corrals, to the tack and feed that we were allowed to use. I had always loved horses, but from afar, collecting Breyer horses for Christmas and going on the occasional guided trail rides paid for by my grandmother. The idea of actually owning a horse had never crossed my mind, no more realistic than appearing on the cover of *Tiger Beat* magazine or spontaneously combusting—so I was stunned when I heard the news.

My mom was the most excited of us all. "Ready to go see something special?" she asked.

My brother and I just looked at each other. Special could mean so many different things in our house.

"No, really, you guys," she smiled. "This will be fun. I bet you can't guess what it is?"

"Disneyland?" said John.

"Too easy," she answered. "Try again."

"The beach?" I asked. I didn't want to try very hard, because getting our hopes up was always a dangerous game. Ours was a family that did not go much of anywhere other than those places specifically selected for my father's enjoyment; we did not do vacation, we did not *go see something special.*

"C'mon, you aren't even trying."

With that, my parents loaded us up into the back of the Ford Granada and drove several miles to a small farm just outside the abandoned JungleLand amusement park site. When we got there, my father handed some guy in a checkered shirt a roll of bills and told me I could learn to ride on the shaggy, manure-covered mare with her head down in the pipe corral behind me. I practically wet myself with glee.

Despite my protestations, we drove around the bend to another ranch where we got out to see the most gorgeous creature I had ever seen, grazing serenely in a pasture. A round, rosy-cheeked woman banged out the front door, wiping her hands on an apron. She told us the creature's name was Andromeda, and that we should approach quietly. Andromeda was a tall, copper-chestnut mare with a white snip on her nose and a tail so thick it looked like Dolly Parton had added her trademark hair extensions. It turned out she was an expensive Tennessee Walker mare from a line of champions and one my father claimed he had bought for my mom.

For the next two months, while the trailer was being leveled on the graded strip of dirt, the corrals were being put up, and the water lines added, I spent every weekend I could with Heather at that tiny ranch a few miles away. My mom would simply drop me off at the barn in the morning, where I would spend hours until dusk. Since I knew next to nothing about horses, I asked my mom to take me to the library where I checked out as many books as I could on the subject. Between the books and the checkered-shirt ranch hand, Rance, who was kind enough to help after observing Heather drag me through the dirt from the wash rack after she decided she wanted dinner rather than a bath, I figured out just enough to get around.

Since I was too naïve to be anything other than stupid, one day I decided to ride Heather about two miles down the road to Arby's, where, I reasoned, I would tie her up, grab a roast beef sandwich, then ride her back to enjoy my meal. I was hungry, and the plan made complete sense to me. Heather had a far different agenda. While the ranch was located back towards the base of the Santa Monica Mountains, Arby's was most definitely on a well-traveled city street. In order to get to there, I had to ride Heather on the shoulder of the street, and she let me know how dissatisfied she was with my decision by dancing and spooking at every car. By the time we reached Arby's, she was beside herself, covered in a froth, and held her ears flat in disapproval. Even my two-month-seasoned-horsewoman self knew I had made a serious mistake.

I somehow managed to get the sandwich and fries, re-mount and head back up the street towards the ranch.

About halfway up, Heather had had enough. She grabbed the bit in her mouth, crow-hopped a couple feet to unbalance me, and took off at a dead gallop up the middle of the street. My food went flying, I screamed loudly enough for a passing car to stop, and I was certain I would die. Heather couldn't have given two shits. She galloped the entire way back to the ranch, with me sloped sideways and hanging on for dear life. When we arrived, we were both heaving with exertion, covered in sweat, and flat pissed. We didn't speak for a week.

Andromeda, on the other hand, was a lady. She was elegant and classy, a Princess Diana to my Heather's stocky Irish barmaid. While I toiled at basic horsemanship covered in alfalfa-flavored dust and ticks, Andromeda and my parents spent two months under the tutelage of Victor, a trainer employed by Zsa Zsa Gabor and her husband, Frédéric Prinz von Anhalt at her famous Silver Fox Tennessee Walking Horse ranch in Somis, California. Andromeda had only the best: the best tack, the best food, the best training, and my parents clearly enjoyed the time they spent with her.

On the two times I visited Silver Fox, I was awestruck, both by the beauty of the facility and the quality of the animals. Grooms scuttled everywhere, sweeping and brushing, quietly tending to every horse and rider need. The horses gleamed and pranced, manes glossy and hooves polished. Tennessee Walking horses are three-gaited horses, known for their flat striding walk, a running walk and an easy, flat-backed canter. These were the days when Tennessee Walkers wore "cans" or "stacks" on their feet to achieve what is known as Big Lick style, an exaggerated, over-the-top foot flinging that is utterly awe-inspiring to the uninitiated. As these horses came pounding out of the barn aisle into the riding ring, I thought my heart would quite literally seize. *That* was what I wanted to do—not sit bareback atop a muddy mare who may or may not wish to eject me.

Eventually, both Heather and Andromeda—Andy to me—moved to their new home in the corrals next to our house still under construction. It was left to me to care for them morning, noon and night, which I did with diligence. I did not know it then, but I had to make do with sparse equipment and little money, but because I was so in love with these two animals, it meant little. Over time, I realized that the horses around us were housed in covered barns with pastures and corrals that drained, as opposed to my horses, who had to stand belly-deep in mud during the rainy season, drink out of an abandoned bathtub that froze in the winter and filled with dead potato bugs in the summer, and received little to no veterinary care. Andy, the princess, did not fare well, and to see her standing in the mud in stark contrast to her life of leisure in the pasture was, at times, heartbreaking. But my father would not relent nor spend a single additional penny on their care, and it was left to me to figure out a solution.

Despite the conditions, I was in heaven, and every minute I spent with the horses made me deliriously happy. When it rained, I would dig trenches so the water would not pool. When their water froze, I would hold the hose for them to drink. When it was so windy that the sunshade roof panel shook and peeled from its clamps, I would hold them in their halters on the leeward side of the house. I may not have had a barn or a nice stall, but I did have elbow grease, and I used it liberally.

I spent hours and hours with those mares every chance I got, often lying backwards across Heather's rump facing the valley below, listening to the trains whistle. Every dawn I would bring them their breakfast, light just breaking, mist swirling around their muzzles as they whickered at me. Afternoons, once home from school, were spent mucking and grooming, cleaning tack, or riding up and down the hillsides around us. I never got enough. My horses were my church, my center, the harmony of my soul, and without them I would very likely have ended up either institutional- ized or lost.

That first summer of horse, my mom found out about a local Pony Club that gathered in the arena at the bottom of the hill where we lived, and I think she thought it might be a good way for me to finally learn how to ride properly, rather than continue to fight the good fight with Heather— who clearly perceived her role as my long-suffering advisor as opposed to my trusty steed.

"I met the mom who heads up the local Pony Club," she told me one day. "Do you want to take lessons?"

I was thrilled. I had been riding both horses primarily up and down the easement trails in front of our property. The prospect of riding with other horses and riders was both wondrous and terrifying.

"Sure, yeah, okay."

She smiled at me. "You will learn a lot. And maybe meet some nice girls and make some new friends."

The following weekend I rode Heather down to the bot- tom of the hill to the local arena where six other teenage girls were sitting on their horses, waiting for our instructor to arrive. I was certain I looked like an idiot, that my horse was ugly, and that I would make a fool of myself. I was so nervous I think even Heather felt sorry for me.

When I entered the ring, once of the girls sitting on a stunning bay thoroughbred rode up to me.

"Hi, I'm Christine. I think we live next door to each other."

Next door where we lived meant within a mile since the houses were so scattered and the parcels of land so large.

"Hi. I'm Dorriah. This is Heather."

She grinned and patted her horse's neck. "This is Twister. You'll see why once we start."

I could only stare at her horse. While I had seen some gorgeous horses at Silver Fox, to see someone my age on a specimen like that was breathtaking. Twister had a thick black mane and tail, with black stockings running up the length of his legs where they dissolved into the most gorgeous caramel bay color I had ever seen. His eyes were curious and alert, amber and widely set, and while we talked, he arched his neck in a way that reminded me of a seventeenth-century manor painting I had seen in the encyclopedia. I felt as though I was sitting on a tugboat by comparison.

"Do you want to ride back up the hill together after we're done?" asked Christine. "I know a shortcut."

"Yeah, that would be great."

Thus began some of the best moments of my life. Just about every weekend and every chance we got, Christine and I rode Heather and Twister up and around the hills, back and forth to lessons, and through the orchards and crops growing around us. It did not matter that my horse was nowhere near as well-bred or as exquisite as hers, that my mare was fat, brooding and cranky while her gelding delighted all who observed him, together we were equals and friends, and the world fell away from us as we rode.

We would pack lunches and disappear for hours to forge new trails, cross streams and jump over any fallen object we could find. One Saturday, we even popped over some sagging barbed wire fence to chase a flock of sheep grazing in the field surrounding a nearby avocado orchard. We thought ourselves quite cowboy until a guy in a red Chevy truck came barreling down the dirt path alongside the field, dust spitting from his tires, and chased us out. Christine and I laughed about that for years.

The two of us ended up as members of the Pony Club three-day-eventing team that learned to jump and ride lower level dressage. It was not the hoof-pounding allure of the Tennessee Walkers, but it was an opportunity for me to learn horse health and care, general horsemanship and a place where my instructor didn't buy into Heather's shenanigans. Since Twister would not, under any circumstance, get into a horse trailer, and because my father would not pay for me to trailer to any shows, Christine and I were constrained to local horse shows within riding distance from our homes. Luckily, there were a few each year, and we would leave at dark the morning of the first classes, ride the horses to the facility, enter our classes, and ride home. I could see that the other kids had nice riding apparel and expensive tack, while I rode in plastic tall boots, a saddle with a broken pommel and a hunter green show jacket with a gold lining that my mom sewed for me, but I didn't care. Atop Heather, her coat as shiny and sparkling as I could get it, flying over picnic tables and oxfords on the cross-country course, I felt no fear, shrunk from no words, and I was free.

My mom never did ride Andromeda. I never understood why. My father, who rode the mare perhaps a handful of occasions, harbored grandiose dreams of showing her, but after a few months of riding, stopped. Thereafter, she was my responsibility. Andy was not a hardy trail horse like Heather nor could she jump or do dressage. She was completely ter-rified of water and would hop over the slightest rivulet, even those from the hose. As a gaited horse, she was bred for what she did, and asking her to do otherwise was almost cruel. As a result, she spent quite a bit of time alone in her stall, while I rode Heather. She became fast friends with the pack of Labradors, and it was not unusual for me to turn her out of her corral and let her graze the long grass around the house freely, the dogs and puppies sniffing around her feet. I did my absolute best to ride her and get her out as much as I could, even taking her to a show at the arena at the bottom of the hill. As the other kids trotted around in the Hunter Seat Equitation class, Andromeda performed a stunning fast walk and awed the crowd. The judges told me they couldn't give me a ribbon because, technically, I wasn't doing what was required in the class, but they acknowledged she was a beautiful horse. I was proud of her anyway.

Throughout high school, I rode just about every day and every weekend, aside from those Saturdays we would head to the mountain to ski. It became my routine and a way for me to be out of the house for long hours at a time. One afternoon after school, as it approached dusk, I began the long uphill climb home. Heather and I had been hacking up and down the easement and she was fairly tired. I thought it would be a good idea to cool her out on the walk home. Heather agreed. About a third of the way up, I figured I would try a new way home, cutting across a terraced piece of land that angled a little more steeply but could save me maybe a mile or so. I could tell from Heather's ears that she was displeased with me yet again, but because she was already tired, she acquiesced as only a snotty mare with attitude can.

The landscape changed as I cut across the terrace. Instead of a wide easement with little to no vegetation, the path narrowed and was surrounded by sagebrush and yucca plants. Our passage was a bit more arduous than I had anticipated, and about halfway through, I seriously considered going back and retracing our steps. By this point, Heather was flat-out pissed. What had started as a leisurely stroll home had now turned into an effort-fueled journey, and not one she had signed on for. As we rounded the final bend near the top, I noticed that the sagebrush had thickened. Heather put her head down and pushed through it, and just as she did, the sagebrush erupted in an enormous swarm of angry, displaced bees. I screamed, Heather reared, and we ran, the swarm of bees chasing us—straight out of a Sunday morning cartoon animation.

As we galloped, the bees stung over and over, coating Heather's back and neck, getting caught in my pony-tailed and slicked-back hair, so loud that I could hear their trapped buzzing inside my head, insistent and never ending. As Heather tore for home, I slapped at my face and head, screamed some more, slapped her neck, slapped anywhere I could to sweep away the bees. This only frightened her more, and she alternated between bucking and running full tilt, with me screeching and crying and hanging on for dear life, petrified I would fall and the bees would cover me entirely.

I am not certain how we ever reached home, but when we did, I rode Heather straight to the kitchen door and banged it open, yelling for my mom, who spent the next couple hours pulling stingers out of my head and neck, back and arms. As she did, Heather heaved and puffed next to us, her neck swollen with welts, her sides shaking from the exertion. She eventually recovered but never forgave me, and from that moment on, whenever we reached the fork in the trail that led to the site of the crime, she tried to throw me off, just for good measure.

After high school started, I would occasionally ride Andy, while my new best friend, Melinda, rode Heather. I met Melinda in Algebra I, my very first class in my brand-new high school. She lived at the bottom of the hill near the riding arena, and when we learned we rode the same bus to school, decided we would sit together. Most of the kids in our high school lived in suburban tract homes, and since we lived so far out and in rural country, our bus rides were quite long. Melinda and I quickly became fast friends, sharing classes, crushes, and dreams, studying for exams together, editing the yearbook, and generally bonding for life. We did everything as a single unit. She came with me to the mountain to learn to ski, watched my track meets, and I joined her at her Mormon dances. We held our first job at Marshall's at the same time, drove to school every day, and graduated arm-in-arm. We were inseparable both then and for the last thirty years. I never did share anything about my family life with Melinda back then, instead maneuvering to spend most of our time at her house. To this day, Melinda believes we both had an idyllic childhood. And we did. When we were together.

I know heaven is a place filled with horses. I dream of fields dotted with California poppies and lavender, short-cropped grass warmed by the sun. I see Heather and Andromeda grazing quietly, their muzzles touching from time to time as they swish their tails under the tall oak trees. My mom sits in a chair nearby, her beloved Labrador sleeping at her feet, reading her favorite book.

Skis and a Watch

My parents met while skiing. My father was a ski patrol-man at a local mountain and my mother at that time was an avid athlete. Throughout the early 1960s, she spent her free time either sailing to the Channel Islands or ski-ing at Mammoth Mountain or our local resorts like Mount Baldy and Snow Summit. She was a film editor for Warner Brothers Studios where she worked on movies like *The Story of the Count of Monte Cristo* and *Days of Wine and Roses*. To hear her tell it, it was a challenging and fast-paced job, and she loved it.

My father was divorced, a salesman for Kanematsu, the first Japanese trading company of the postwar era. He spent his work week as a traveling salesman, and on weekends he volunteered on the mountain as a patrolman, tending to lost toddlers and various scrapes and breaks. His work life bled into our family life. *Crane by Water's Edge*, a Japanese wall screen and several Satsuma Flower vases followed us from house to house, and we ate Japanese food on a regular basis. Even at my last visit, amidst the rotting carpet and decrepit furniture, several beautiful pieces of Japanese art remained. But back then, it seemed his primary passion was skiing.

In those days, skiers wore stiff leather boots with eyelet lace-ups strapped firmly to long pieces of wood. Ski bindings were products of the Inquisition, complete with a cable and heel-release, and skiing was akin to affixing yourself to a slab of lumber with a piece of metal, pointing your feet downhill and hoping for the best.

When I asked my mom about how they met she told me it was a snowstorm and a watch that brought them together.

"It was the type of snowstorm where you couldn't see more than a few feet in front of your face," she said, a faraway look in her eyes. "I had lost my gold watch, one my mother had given me, and I really wanted to find it."

"Did you?" I asked.

"Well, no, but as I was searching, and while everyone else was in the lodge waiting out the storm, a ski patrolman came up to me and asked if he could help. It was your dad."

"And then what?" I was probably about ten years old, and this was the first time I had heard the story. In subsequent years, we heard this very same story every chance our father had to tell it.

"We spent the next couple hours skiing and looking. By the end of the day he had convinced me to have dinner with him."

As the story goes, from there they spent the next six weeks dating—skiing, sailing, and walking along the local beaches. My mom was thirty-three at the time, divorced from her bartender—and ragingly drunk—first husband, and desperate to have children. She told me once, privately, that she accepted my father's marriage proposal after three months because she thought he had all the earmarks of a good provider, and that she wanted to stay home and raise her children. He was loving and attentive to her in those first months, wrote her letters and took her places, and although he had three children from a previous marriage, he told her that he did not see them and that she would not be responsible for raising them. In fact, he had woven a tale of an ex-wife who was belligerent and aggressive, who cheated on him and purposefully kept his kids away to spite him. Which my mom believed. It was in my forties, once I got to know my half-brother, that I learned the truth.

My mom became pregnant immediately and I was born within the year. Both parents still skied and would take first me, and later both my brother and me, to the mountain on weekends whenever possible. Even though I was young, I can still remember the lodge where we stayed. Originally painted a dark hunter green, with pale gray river rocks accenting columns and intricately carved gable boards, it now sloped to one side like a stroked grandfather, the green paint chipping in curled strips along the walls, rocks missing and split from the grout. The walkway to the front door was primarily ice and getting inside was treacherous. Inside, the rooms were drafty and smelled like damp animal. A large, shocked-looking moose head watched from above an enormous stone fireplace, bunk beds filled just about every room, and the wooden floors contracted every night and every afternoon, so loudly that the squeaks and snaps sounded like gunshots. The lodge was only for the ski patrol and the ski instructors, so the dads spent their days on the mountain while the moms rotated babysitting and cooking so they could join their spouses for some time on the slopes. The smaller kids simply played until they smelled like wet sheep and wood smoke for days after.

It was white and cold and fun. We would travel to the mountain from early winter through the spring. Several Easters were spent on the mountain, and John and I believed for the longest time that the Easter bunny was actually a snowshoe hare who dug holes in the snow to hide candy. When our father was on the mountain, wearing his rust-colored and very official-looking National Ski Patrol jacket, he was distracted and not nearly as mean. In that element he got to be both the expert, and in charge; two things he reveled in. My brother and I were left alone for the most part with our mom. Once we learned to ski, we got as far away from him on those weekends as we could.

The lodge roof finally caved in after a particularly brutal snowstorm and was never repaired. It was torn down the summer I turned eight.

After the demise of the lodge, our ski weekends became one-day affairs. We would wake up at the ungodly hour of 4:00 a.m., blearily eat and dress, then drive the two hours to the mountain, ski all day, only to drive home in traffic that night for another three hours. My mom became tired of two unruly and exhausted children every Sunday, and so for the next six years we did not go with our father on his Saturday trips.

When we moved to the house on the hill, my brother and I decided we wanted to ski again, and once more made the drive up the side of the mountain on Saturday mornings. We were both teenagers by then, and once we got our lift tickets, would disappear for the day. At 4:30 p.m. on the dot, after the ski patrol had finished "sweep"—the clearing of all skiers from the ski runs—we would join back up with our parents for the ride home.

John and I both became very proficient skiers after spending the majority of our high school years on the slopes of the local mountains. We learned from some of the best, refusing to mimic our father's wooden, toboggan-pulling style, and instead hung out with some of the most elegant and adept skiers I have ever known. John later became a part-time ski instructor himself, and while by far the largest instructor, he enjoyed teaching kids during his Oregon winters.

Our mom sewed most of our outfits, buying patterns and goose down from The Company Store and spending hours in the garage piecing them together, while her dogs milled about her feet. She made me a bright yellow ski parka and pants with orange underarms and a blue diamond shaped lapel on the back. My brother's outfit was rust with brown and black accents. My mother became incredibly creative as she continued to sew, designing her own outfits complete with ermine collars and Aztec embroidery, leather fanny packs and intricate hoods.

Neither of us ever had good equipment, as our father was far too cheap to invest in anything worthwhile. Of course, he purchased new equipment for himself every year. Instead, we skied on used equipment that other skiers had abandoned on the hill, with boots that rarely fit. Luckily for us, however, our ski instructor friends were pretty good at tuning up our equipment, and it was at least usable. I didn't find out that my gear was crap until I attended a university ski trip with a group of students my first year at college. We traveled all the way to Whistler, Canada by bus, alternately sleeping and drinking both on the bus rides and throughout the entire week. I remember the realization clearly.

It was our first morning at the resort. A group of us were standing below the ski lift holding our skis. One of the guys looked over at me. He gazed at my long red skis and entirely outdated Look bindings.

"Where the hell did you get those?" he laughed.

I laughed, too. I wasn't sure what to say.

"Those things are about ten years old," he said. "And they are way too long for you. You should be on one-fifties, not those two hundreds."

I smiled at him. He had shaggy hair, a crooked nose and wore purple-tinted Oakley goggles. I thought he was cute and I wanted to find a way to agree without sounding like a dumbass.

"Yeah," I answered. "I haven't really been able to afford new skis."

"Oh, sure, I get that!" he laughed again. "I would love to get new boots."

I spent the next couple of days skiing with him and I think he was fairly impressed with my ability, despite my stupid skis and ill-fitting boots. On the third day, he convinced me to rent a pair of skis and boots that actually fit. The sensation was mesmerizing. I felt as though I was floating on marshmallows and making turns was no more difficult than tying my shoe. The technology had advanced so much that my edges simply sliced through the powder and bit nicely into the curved side of the moguls. I never had more fun in my life. I knew then I had to find a way to buy new equipment. And it sure didn't hurt that Randy and I ended up dating when we got back to campus.

In addition to skiing, I ran track throughout high school. I was not all that good, but I was definitely determined. My junior year I finally made the varsity squad and was very proud of myself. Track was both difficult and rewarding, I had to work hard for my table scrap times, and after my junior season, I was very much looking forward to my senior year and the possibility of making it to state finals with my relay team.

That was not to be. That winter, just before my final varsity season, I was skiing with some of my ski instructor friends. Since we were young, smarter than everyone else, and utterly invincible, we skied what was considered the backside of the mountain. This area was only accessible by going around the *Caution – Do Not Pass* sign at the top of the lift, skiing down the Devils' Bowl, then hiking out from the bottom. I had done this before and was not remotely intimidated by the prospect.

My friend Peter was with me. He was one of the youngest ski instructors and the son of the best skier on the mountain.

"Conditions look good today. We should make it out by sweep," he said, pulling on his gloves and adjusting his goggles.

"Yeah, we can just hike to the bottom of Chair Four and wait for your dad," I answered.

We took off over the edge of the crest. I followed about twenty feet behind him, and although he was a much faster skier, because there were so many trees, he toned it down. We stopped after a few minutes to take a break and enjoy the solitude. We were the only ones on the run. The ice sparkled on the pine needles, with the occasional soft slumph of melting snow falling to the ground. My lungs felt like balloons filled with ice water and my quads screamed from the exertion. It was fantastic.

We took off again and as soon as I started, I knew something was terribly wrong. This time I went in front, and about five seconds after I pushed off, the snow beneath me simply disappeared. I fell immediately and began to slide on my side down an ice chute as the snow around me roared. I could hear Peter screaming behind me, valiantly trying to keep up as I slid with the avalanche.

The only thing I could think to do to stop myself was to stab my ski pole into the ice beside me. This backfired spectacularly, as the pole snapped off and the jagged edge bounced back and stabbed me just below the eye. I started to panic. The thing about the Devil's Bowl was that you absolutely needed to dogleg right about two-thirds of the way down to avoid a cliff that towered about four hundred feet above the parking lot. I knew, even in my panic, that I was headed directly for it.

My next attempt to stop was to try to drag my skis. I heaved my body sideways. All I accomplished was flipping around so that my head was below me rather than to the side, and as I did so, I could feel my ski twist, the binding refuse to release, and a sickening snap as my knee took the brunt of the momentum. At that point all I could assume was that I was headed straight over the cliff. So I just closed my eyes.

When I finally opened them again it was incredibly quiet. Apparently, I had triggered a small avalanche. It had snowed during the day and that new layer of powder had caused the top snow to slough from the ice. When I pushed off, I set the events in motion and the snow field had pulled me along with it. Luckily, just before the cliff, the slope curved slightly upwards and caused the pile of snow, some rocks and broken branches, and me, to pile up like a large load of dirty clothes at the bottom of a laundry chute. Peter found me about five minutes later. He literally ran out of his bindings and threw his gloves and goggles to the side.

"Oh fuck, oh fuck, oh fuck. Are you okay? Oh Jesus. Oh fuck. This is my fault. Oh my God. Are you okay?"

The whole thing had lasted maybe about three minutes, but it was an incredibly long three minutes. As Peter disentangled me from my gear and dug me out of the snow, all I could think to do was laugh, a long hysterical, pain-fueled laugh. I could feel the warm blood running down the side of my face and my hands and feet were numb. Peter said nothing, simply continued to get my skies off my boots. His face looked like Italian marble, with gray veins pulsing beneath white slab.

Since we had waited until the end of the day, we also had to contend with the fact that a hike that normally took about fifteen minutes with two good legs, was most definitely not going to happen before dark enveloped us.

"My dad is going to be so pissed," he said. "I have to get you out of here. Nobody knows where we are. Can you walk?"

I had no idea how badly I was injured, but I did know I couldn't walk. My knee didn't hurt, but the prospect of putting weight on it made me weak, as though I might vomit with one psi of pressure.

"No. I'm sorry."

"Fuck."

Peter looked around us. We generally knew where we were and how far we had to go. We had veered from the section of the run that led to the hike out by about three hundred yards. That meant we had about a forty-five-minute hobble in front of us and about fifteen minutes to do it.

Peter left our skis and poles behind, hoisted my arm over his shoulder and literally dragged me for the next hour.

By the time we got to Chair 4, it was dark. Peter's father had placed lift operators on standby at every chair, knowing that would be the first place Peter would head. After the operator radioed our location, the entire ski patrol and every single ski instructor showed up. I was placed for the first and only time in a toboggan and skied down to the parking lot. Peter and his father followed behind, insisting that they accompany me to the local hospital.

My father, of course, insisted that he would prefer to drive me all the way home, rather than take me to the hospital. Even in my haze of pain, I could see the consternation of their faces.

"I think she may be hurt pretty bad," said Peter.

My father just laughed and said, "Oh, she'll be fine. Just a couple scratches and bruises."

I said nothing. I sat in the back seat with my leg stretched across my brother's lap while the blood on my face caked into a brown caul. Every time the car stopped or hit a pothole I wanted to puke. By the time we got home several hours later, the pain was excruciating.

My brother carried me to my bedroom upstairs where I spent the next two weeks. I never was taken to a doctor, I never did get an MRI, I never saw a physical therapist, and I missed the entire track season that spring because my knee did not work properly. It was several years later that I finally had it examined. The doctor said I had a torn medial lateral ligament and that I needed surgery. When he asked me how long it had hurt, I told him I wasn't sure.

Gramps

My brother used to bang his head when he slept. Not soft bounces against his pillow, but hard smacks against the wall above his head. Many nights I fell asleep to the sound of thuds from our adjoining wall. My grandfather Alphonse— we called him Gramps—was the only person who could get him to stop. He would place his enormous hands over John's black curls and singsong, alternating between French and English:

> "Frère Jacques, frère Jacques, Dormez-vouz? Dormez-vouz? Sonnez les matines! Sonnez les matines! Ding, dang, dong. Ding, dang, dong."

Having emigrated from WWI France, his accent was thick, and when he switched to English, it sounded very much the same, "Are you sleeping? Are you sleeping? Brother John, Brother John, Morning bells are ringing! Morning bells are ringing! Ding, dang, dong. Ding, dang dong."

Even though I was likely no more than about six, I understood that what my Gramps had to offer was a deep, spring-fed pool of solace and kindness, something my brother and I craved and sought out as urgently as oxygen or water. Luckily, our grandparents sought us out as well, and we were allowed to occasionally join cousins on weekend sleepovers and rare, but treasured, trips to Death Valley and Hearst Castle. These visits allowed John and I to connect to a short-lived sense of normal, and while the stark contrast upon returning home was always both painful and abrupt, we waited for these moments with frantic anticipation. The only price of admission was Sunday School attendance with my grandmother.

My grandparents on my mom's side were an unlikely couple. My grandmother Allesandra was a court clerk, smart and sophisticated, far ahead of her time in an era when women rarely worked. Gramps was her third husband and not my mother's biological father. Allesandra had a son from her first husband, married my grandfather and had my mother and uncles, and in her fifties, she married a much younger Gramps. This, too, was fairly unusual for the era, and she was known with disapproving tsk's and tilted heads as *that Allesandra, she certainly is modern...*

According to my mother, Gramps was the complete opposite of Allesandra's first two husbands, both businessmen, a clumsy busboy to their sommelier, base and uneducated, a guileless street dancer against Baryshnikov. All I knew was that my grandmother clearly did not care what others thought.

While I was too young to really understand either content or motive, my mother would complain to me about Gramps, that she did not like him, and that my grandmother had married beneath herself. Conversations about weekend visits were always awkward and uncomfortable, and I never understood why.

"Did you have fun?" she would ask on Sundays when we returned.

"Sure, Mom," we would answer.

John, always the optimist, would blurt, "Gramps took us to the liquor store, Mom! I got some candy and a piece of beef jerky!"

"Of course he did," she would smile. "He would never think to actually feed you a meal."

For some reason whenever she made these remarks, I always felt the need to defend him in some way. It never worked in my favor, but I did it anyway.

"Gramps let us help in the orchard today, too, Mom. We had so much fun."

My grandparents lived on an acre and a half of land with a lower orchard full of lemon, orange, plum, apricot, peach, and nectarine trees. The house was at the back of the lot, with a large porch veranda overlooking the valley below. Many Fourth of July celebrations were spent on this balcony *oohing* and *aahing* over fireworks launched from city hall in the distance. The fences along the perimeter were covered in blackberry vines and we ate these, along with the plums and apricots, with impunity, despite deep burgundy finger stains and pretty aggressive green poop. The trees were lush and fragrant and during the fall pruning, the yard was flush with the smells of tangy lemonwood and burnt lumber. In the center of the orchard, like a Stonehenge trilithon, stood a vegetable garden with perfectly aligned rows of zucchini, cauliflower, watermelon, and cantaloupe underneath a cascading grape arbor at its entrance. Tomato vines looped over stakes and strawberries dotted small mounds next to the corn. My grandmother hung hundreds of bird feeders and watering stations and the entire house and surrounding property was awash with raucous blue jays, yellow warblers, black-winged Orioles, and tiny Rufous and Anna hummingbirds diving and fighting for their rightful position at my grandmother's favorite porch feeder.

It was nirvana for a gaggle of small kids that liked to scream and run and play. My grandmother knew this and sent us outside for more hours than we were allowed inside, only interrupting every few hours to feed us peanut butter and jelly sandwiches and sliced fruit along with a tall glass of milk. As a family, we would often gather at my grandparents' house for dinner—aunts, uncles, brothers, sisters, cousins—and grandmother would make her famous pork chops and mushroom rice. While we all ran wild outside, the adults would talk politics and argue in the living room. It was a time for John and I to behave like our cousins, and our parents like the rest of our extended family, to pretend to the best of our abilities that we were a normal family, and in that orchard with those trees and our Gramps we could almost believe it was true.

Come summer, my grandmother would make a variety of jams and jellies, and when harvest week came, my brother and I would help Gramps pick the fruit. Canning and preserving is a hectic and hot mess of an effort, since the fruit is only at its peak for a few days after picking. During the harvest, my grandmother slept little, clanging around her tiny kitchen for that entire week, hair swept up in a bandana, sweat beading on her top lip, every pot and pan covered in a film of red or orange, while the rest of us were charged with the outdoor work. There were so many trees and so much yield that neighbors would come by for baskets of fruit and my grandmother would bring trunkloads of jam for her church friends.

"Oh? Let me guess," my mother would reply. "You ate a bunch of green peaches just like last time?"

My mom would shake her head and start muttering to herself about how some people just didn't *think* and how now she would have to clean up the mess. It seemed that no matter what Gramps said or did, he was always in the wrong in her eyes. It didn't matter that he took us everywhere, taught us to work a harvest, to count in French, cuddled with us in the chair, was kind and compassionate, she just did not like him. While she allowed us to spend time with him, and she did not complain either to my grandmother or to anyone else but us, he was her affliction, her diabetes by marriage, the sore on her gums that she could not stop probing with her tongue. And that dynamic only heightened when our grandmother fell ill.

From our perspective, he was simply magnificent. Now that I am grown, I think the dynamic between my Gramps and my mother had less to do with her belief that he was somehow a sorry replacement for her own father and more to do with the fact that my Gramps saw through her alcoholic neglect of the two of us.

Grandmother Allesandra, on the other hand, was crisp and efficient, prone to overly planned family events and speeding tickets, and proudly served as the staunch matriarch of the entire family. She was thin and statuesque, with flawlessly matched skirts and jackets and an unbelievable collection of brooches, earrings and lapel pins, which she sparingly allowed my cousin Rachel and me to play with under her watchful eye. She was a devout Christian Scientist, clear in her belief that prayer alone could resolve and cure any malady from a cold to cancer.

While raising my mother and her brothers on Catalina Island, she had a reputation for believing that ocean salt water was a miracle elixir, that scrapes and cuts did not ever require stitches, and that living on an island without a hospital built a strong constitution. When her husband died of untreated bleeding ulcers, her faith never wavered. As adults, my mother and my uncles did not join my grandmother in her religious beliefs, but were fine with Sunday sleep-ins while their kids joined her at church. Our grandmother was not particularly soft or affectionate, but she was fierce and protective of her family and to a person, each of us knew exactly where we stood.

My Gramps was altogether different—as gentle and tolerant as a basset hound. As a teenager, he had lived in German-occupied France from 1914 until early 1918. His family lived along the north-eastern Belgian border where the entire population was held under military occupation under strict German rule. Food was scarce, and the German soldiers regularly raided farms and households for whatever provisions they required while their inhabitants were forced to supplement the German workforce as unpaid labor in camps and factories.

My Gramps told us about how the soldiers at first came for his family's cooking pots, particularly those made of copper, and then later, forced his family and neighbors to strip the wool stuffing from their mattresses. He told us how near the end of the occupation, even the soldiers were hungry and cold and many of them walked the streets without boots, despite the freezing cold. He described once beautiful cathedrals and hillside manors as bombed-out shells, torn and gutted like blast fish, left to turn to rot. Many people, due to necessity or pride, refused to leave, to give up their homes, and many starved to death in the process, including his parents. Whenever we left food on our plates at dinner, he would gently remind us how hungry people do not have the food to leave on plates.

He was proud to be French, was proud of his country, and spent hours teaching us its language and culture. Sadly, I remember little of it now, but every time I hear Delaney practice her French for school, I am reminded of him, of his accent, his raucous laugh, his love, and his nickname for me: *pest*. He was both tolerant and big-hearted and would do everything he could to take us on whatever adventure he could. He worked for the Southern California Gas Company, and once a year on Gas Company Night, he would take us to Disneyland where along with hordes of other Gas Company families we would hand over our caramel-sticky E tickets with crazed excitement. He was a ray of light in our ink tunnel and my brother and I loved him completely and without exception.

My grandparents' house was fairly close to my parents', so when my Gramps brought home an enormous white German Shepard one afternoon, we were able to go visit and touch this incredible creature within hours of his arrival. He was a stunning one-year-old male, easily weighing ninety pounds, with a coarse, beautiful, polar bear coat. My brother and I fell in love immediately, and spent many weekends sitting with my Gramps in his corner recliner overlooking the balcony stroking the dog's enormous head. We would wrestle for the treasured spot on the left, close to the dog, while my Gramps would laugh *now, now you crazy galoots* and make sure the coveted spot was evenly dispersed. And even though our Gramps made sure the candy bowl next to his chair was full, that we could watch as much TV as we liked, and that we could run and yell as loudly as we wanted to, we loved nothing more than to sit in that chair with him and caress that dog's muzzle.

The dog had been bred by an esteemed breeder who placed white German Shepherds in the movie industry. Apparently, these dogs were hard to get, and my Gramps had waited a few years before a puppy was available. Even then, the breeder made ownership conditional upon a full year of training and when the dogs came to their owners, they were pristine in both manners and ability. Gramps named him Fritz and thereafter that dog was a fixture everywhere my grandfather went. When he bought a tiny red Datsun two-seater, Fritz accompanied him, jammed regally beside him in the passenger seat. And later, when my grandparents bought an enormous silver Pontiac Bonneville that took up their entire carport, Fritz was a regular passenger in the backseat, his head resting on the front seat between my grandparents. He was glorious, equal parts Cerberus and Lassie, and stories of him circulate in our family to this day, like the time he unceremoniously removed the throat of a Boxer that lunged at my grandmother, or that time he ran into the house *barking barking* until my uncle finally came outside to find my cousin Craig unconscious after falling out of the sycamore tree.

Fritz was both mythical and fantastical to my brother and me, both our guardian and friend, and I wondered if my brother remembered him as fondly as I did. Not long ago, I asked.

"Remember Fritz? I can't think of Gramps without thinking of Fritz," I said.

My brother replied, "Yeah, I miss him more than Mom."

When I was about eleven, my grandmother fell ill. She had had a stroke and was left unable to do many of the things she did for herself with pride. Even in her poor health, she refused to take any medication or see a doctor—*prayer will heal*—and it was left to my mom and Gramps to care for her. Her once bustling home now became something of a hospital ward, with an adjustable bed placed in the living room and my mother hand-feeding medication-laced Jello to her daily. As her illness dragged on, the orchard fell into neglect and the fruit fell to the ground where it rotted in the sun. Gophers and deer decimated the garden and ants overran the hummingbird feeders. Finally, as her health deteriorated and care became impossible without medical assistance, Gramps was forced to place her in a hospice, where she died a few months later.

With my grandmother gone, the relationship between my mother and Gramps became so stilted and difficult that he finally sold the house and moved away to Michigan, where he lived out his final years with his one daughter. My brother and I were inconsolable. The family dinners, the weekends with cousins, the sense of connectedness all disappeared with the death of my grandmother, and despite the occasional valiant effort of an aunt or two, was never really resurrected.

My parents made no effort for John or me to either visit or stay connected with Gramps in any way, and it was many years before I was able to see him again. It was my freshman year of college when I received a call from Michigan that he was dying. I borrowed some money from friends and got the next flight out. When I arrived, I learned that he was in the final stages of stomach cancer and that he had only a few weeks left. For a man that who had eaten only red meat followed by a Courvoisier chaser and half a pack of Marlboros his entire life, this was not remotely surprising. What was surprising was that he had lived to be ninety.

He was nonplussed to see me.

"Well, hallo there, *pest*, where have you been?"

"Going to school, Gramps. I'm in college now," I smiled back at him. *Nothing had changed.*

"Ah yes, you were always my little smarty, always knew you would do something with yourself," he answered, laying his head back against the pillow. "How is Brother John?"

"He's good, Gramps," I said. "He is playing basketball and has a scholarship. He's so tall now, you wouldn't believe it."

My Gramps laughed his thick French laugh and shook his head. "Sure do miss the two of you."

Over the course of the next few days I stayed with Gramps, by the side of his bed for hours and hours, talking and laughing and remembering, until finally he was too weak and ill and it was time to go. It was over those few days that I learned a lot of things about my family and more importantly, the full story of Fritz, something my Gramps had never shared with anyone until then.

It seemed that while he lived in occupied France during WWI with his family, the German guards heavily patrolled the Belgian border near his home, as many Europeans tried to flee across the border into unoccupied territory and scatter to the United States or other countries. These German guards patrolled night and day, without fail, accompanied by enormous white German Shepherds specifically trained to catch and kill anyone attempting to cross. After his parents died, and left with nothing and no one, my fifteen-year-old Gramps finally, desperately decided to run, no matter the outcome. When he reached the side of the road, he said, the guard saw him, as did the dog.

And it was then, he told me, that the guard paused, then walked the other way, crisply pulling the dog along. "Come Fritz, there is nothing here for us to see."

Acceptance

I began to realize the truly fundamental weirdness of my upbringing the first couple years of college. I am not quite sure if it was because I was away from that house, that I was older, or the stark contrast to the other students and their families, but the realization was distressing. After the initial shock, I felt neither anger nor hatred, but an embarrassment and dedication to a fabricated self-story so intense that it woke me at night with the fear of exposure. I instinctively knew I would not be believed. So I made it up instead.

All throughout our younger years and high school, John and I simply did not talk about it. About any of it. We never even discussed our home life with our Gramps, the one person who truly would have understood. These were family matters, not to be shared outside of the home, and certainly not with strangers. These were the days before social media and awareness ads and counselors and teachers with an eye out, but rather, the days of abuse with impunity, bruises covered with Jackie-O glasses, and keeping your mouth shut for fear of an outcome far worse than the possible, remote idea of help. You simply kept quiet, covered your head and waited for the bullets to stop. If you got hit, well, that was the price of war, and we knew it. Field triage was a fairly regular occurrence, and one we became accustomed to. I had a vague idea that our upbringing had been abnormal, but since I had nothing to compare it to, it was like trying to compare apples to dinosaurs. And the more I got to know the students around me, the more this gaping chasm became apparent.

My first surreal conversation occurred my freshman year the second week on campus during orientation. I was asked if I wanted to rush a sorority. I had absolutely no idea what a sorority was, why I would rush at anyone, and when I asked the girl covered head to toe in purple, tooth smiling at me from the quad table what she meant, she looked at me oddly.

"Umm, a sorority, like a group of sisters on campus?"

I still didn't understand. "What does it do?" I asked.

"Umm, well, we all live together in a house, and we have parties and we support the fraternities and we take care of each other," she answered.

I could tell from her expression that she thought I was either a) dimwitted or b) messing with her. I was doing neither. Up until that day I had never even heard of such a thing. In fact, I was so woefully unprepared for college and campus life it was frankly a miracle I got in, much less graduated. Those first few months I was like a baby otter that had been raised by cobras, shown the water, yet unable to truly grasp what was expected of me. My parents had not once discussed college with me. They did not pay attention to my grades, they did not ask where I wanted to go, they did not take me on tours or schedule me for SAT prep classes. When the time came for college applications, it was my calculus teacher who asked me where I was applying, and when he found out I had no idea what to do, he arranged for the high school guidance counselor, Mrs. Gutierrez, to help me send in my applications.

That, too, was a fairly awkward conversation.

"So, Dorriah, you have great grades, you scored well on the tests, I think you can apply just about anywhere," said Mrs. Gutierrez the day I showed up in her office.

All of the other kids had already applied, and I was weeks late. "But we do need to get these in quickly, the deadlines for some schools have already passed."

She showed me a list of universities that were possible and handed me a checklist of what I needed to do. To her credit, she never once asked why my parents were not involved. Today, I find it hysterically, and perhaps neurotically, funny that I am preparing for Delaney's college résumé years in advance, clear on her options, what pre-SAT testing looks like, and making notes of subjects she may want to consider for her essay. I mercilessly quiz friends with kids already accepted, determined to make sure I have not missed a single avenue, not overlooked any possible opportunity to help her get where she wants to go.

But back then, in Mrs. Gutierrez's cramped office, college brochures strewn across her desk, I was awestruck by the possibility that there was somewhere else to go, somewhere that could be far away and different from where I was. For those next two weeks, I worked hard on several applications and essays, applying to an Ivy, a prestigious private, the University of California, and a state school "insurance policy" option, all under her watchful eye.

When the acceptance and rejection packages started arriving, all of the kids would report in to Mr. Culberson, our calculus teacher. He kept a running tally on the chalk board, right below the quotes from Einstein, Copernicus, and David Van Halen, showing which student was going to which school. Every morning at 8:52 a.m. he performed this ritual, and we loved it. It was fun and exciting to watch the list grow and became something of a competition between the honor students to see who got into the most prestigious schools.

My best friend, Melinda—who I've already mentioned was devoutly Mormon—her option was BYU and BYU alone. Mr. Culberson had already written her name with BYU beside it before the acceptance packages even arrived, and we all found that quite hilarious. My other friends, Susan and Amy, had been accepted into UCLA and Wellesley, so our friend group was three-quarters giddy. For several weeks, my name remained with a blank next to it due to my late applications. Luckily, there were a few other kids in class who had either applied late or had not yet heard back, so Mr. Culberson made sure not to embarrass any of us. It was agonizing nonetheless.

I will never forget the day the acceptance letter from Stanford arrived. I absolutely could not wait to share the news with everybody, Mrs. Gutierrez, Mr. Culberson, my classmates, the world. I practically bounced to school that morning, hugged Melinda so tightly she coughed, and was over the moon with excitement. I felt so proud watching my name go up on the chalkboard, like I had finally, really, accomplished something of note, that this magical place hours and hours away—*Northern California, where is that anyway?*—was within my grasp. Maybe I could be a normal, college-bound high school senior, not the cowering incompetent I was at home.

Telling my parents seemed like an afterthought. They had little to nothing to do with me getting into Stanford, so when I finally told them a month later, it was almost in passing.

"Want to see my acceptance letter?" I asked them one night at dinner.

My mom was already a few drinks in, so I knew her response was inconsequential.

It was my father who looked up from his plate. "What acceptance letter?"

"I got into Stanford," I said. "I leave in August."

He just looked at me. This was a man who said he had gone to the University of Southern California on a WWII Veteran's Fund, understood the value of a college education, and knew exactly what Stanford meant. While he had never interacted with me on the actual process of my education, it was *understood* that college was mandatory.

"You leave in August," he repeated.

I did not know what to say. *Yeah, you fucking nutwing, I am out of here and you can't do a goddamn thing to stop me.*

Then he started to laugh. Not a funny chortle as in *you great kid, you made it into a top tier school*, but a nasty, *you fucking idiot* snicker. "And I'm going to guess you think I will pay for that?"

At that point I just stared at him, my eyes blinking and my mouth moving open and closed like a broken Levolor blind, my brain slowly pulling on the cord. I had not even considered that. That school cost money, that I was still somehow inexorably connected to them, that it wasn't as simple as sign and pay later and just because I got accepted that I actually got to attend.

Needless to say, there was no further discussion. Nothing about financial aid packages, student loans, taking a second on the house. He would not help, my mother would not contradict him, so I would not go. It was never discussed again. And that was the end of it.

The next day, Mrs. Gutierrez simply gazed at me over the top of her glasses for a long and uncomfortable moment when I asked her what to do.

Finally, she pushed up her glasses and pinched the bridge of her nose, answering, "Well, we figure it out, that's what we do."

As it turned out, I ended up attending one of the University of California campuses, just narrowly escaping a state-school-back-up-plan which would have meant remaining in my parents' home. I convinced my mother to give me the first semester of money and thereafter worked and won some scholarships while I went to school, alternating between lifeguarding and tutoring, whatever I could do to pay my tuition and dorm fees. In retrospect, I am fairly certain Mrs. Gutierrez pulled some serious strings to make that happen, since my acceptance package arrived about one month before I actually left for the university. And despite the fact that Mr. Culberson knew what had happened, he never did change the chalk tally.

Part of what made our upbringing so incongruous was the fact that certain elements were mind-screamingly, hair-pullingly normal—like games. We could experience a day when our father would come home pissed and throw a water cooler across the room and shatter a counter full of wine bottles, to the next evening sitting down to Parcheesi or a game of cribbage. I think it was during these briefly sane moments that my brother and I both sowed a deep and lasting hope within our beings that things could *and would* somehow end up average and calm; if we could just outlast the *other* existence, these minutes would morph into our true reality. Both of us harbored this hope for many, many years, always trying and always failing to create some semblance of family with our parents, trying to connect, trying to be like those other families we watched around us, much like TV sitcoms, the laugh tracks playing loudly and discordant, out of sync with the sounds coming from our home. And no matter how often we tried, and no matter the effort we put into it, the outcome rarely altered, and despite this, despite the fact that we *knew,* despite the fact that we *always knew* what the outcome would be, we were bewildered by it nonetheless. For as much as we tried to imagine our father as a human, he was in fact an animal, a serpent or a crocodile, with big teeth and an equally bigger jaw that could unhinge and swallow you whole, the curved teeth piercing first your face, then your back, and finally your soul, until you were deep in its belly, the acid slowly dissolving your heart.

But the games? The games were fun. We were all good at them, and enjoyed playing against each other. Monopoly was a favorite, as was penny ante poker, and we would spend hours some evenings playing around that ridiculous breakfast table, with dogs and puppies bustling around our legs, cats watching from the fireplace ledge, the lights in the valley below sparkling outside the window. If you turned your face just so, you could unsee the piles of cardboard in the corner and the torn window screen that would never be fixed, and if you rubbed a little Vicks Vaporub under your nose you could handle the stench of puppy shit, and if you looked past the third scotch—*now a double*—next to my mom's elbow, it was fun. So my brother and I became adept at doing just those things: seeing the ordinary in the extraordinarily terrible. We became emotional snipers, able to shoot out the sad or the mean of a past week in order to laugh over losing Park Place, or giggle when someone skunked the cribbage board. We became adept at ignoring and unseeing so many things that they became our normal, because nobody came to the house anymore, and because nobody knew anything at all.

It was the unseeing that left me so muddled when I arrived at college. As the world around me came into focus and I began to realize that so much of my life had been a bizarre cabaret of narcissistic clowns and knife throwers, it was then that I learned that my parents were just *off*. When my roommate received a care package from her parents that first month of dorm living, full of Reese's Cups, microwave popcorn packets, Hershey's Kisses, quarters for the dryer and some graph paper, I asked my mom on the phone for one. It seemed like most of the girls on B2 East were getting regular packages in the mail like this one, and I wanted in. I got one about three months later. It included some outdated National Geographic magazines and a typed recipe for avocado soup signed "Love, Mom."

From time to time, my mother would try. In her own way, I think she meant to connect with me, with us, but like a wobbly foal, never really found her legs. Instead, I found myself spending more and more time with my new set of college friends, girls with whole and complete families. Sure, they had issues, the occasional divorce, parents living in different states, a friend's brother too terrified to come out to his father that he was gay, but those all paled in comparison to the twisted fables I could have shared.

When Thanksgiving came and the dorms emptied, I found myself bereft, hollowed out at the thought of returning. Several of my hall mates invited friends to come home with them, friends who lived on the East Coast or those who could not afford plane tickets back and forth more than once or twice a year. But my friends knew I lived only a few hours away, so no invitation was issued. I felt sick. Finally, on the last day that the dorms remained open, I called my mom and asked her to come get me for the five-day weekend.

"Oh sure, honey, I can do that," she answered. "Your dad is at work, so I can come now, before he knows I've left."

Standing in my dorm room with the phone in my hand, the halls empty of laughter and wafts of buttered popcorn and Pop Tarts, I just leaned my head against the cinderblock wall. This was another one of those *things*—how weird he was about cars. And, of course, like everything else, this had to be a clandestine mission, couldn't just be a *hey mom can you come pick me up like every other fucking normal freshman is asking their parents right now?*

"Yes, please leave now or I won't have anywhere to sleep tonight," I answered.

And because those were some of the years that my parents had more than one car and because those were the years that my father actually allowed her to drive one of them, she came and got me. And like so many other rare moments when I had her alone, I spent the drive trying to convince her to move near me, next to campus, anywhere away from him, to bring my brother, bring the goddamn dogs I didn't care, just leave, but she only laughed and said "oh honey" and we got home in three hours and it was still the same, and more windows were broken, and there were five dogs and my brother was so skinny because my father had padlocked the pantry and the yelling had never stopped.

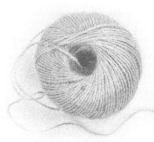

Delaney

S o here's the part that scares me. I have a temper. I have a temper so wicked and wide that it scorches the earth around me, as atomic as Hiroshima and as corrosive as battery acid. It's as though a switch flips in me and I have zero control. Before I know it, I am off and screeching, the back of my neck sweaty and hot with anger, nails digging into my palms, vile and caustic spittle spewing from my mouth. I see, hear, and feel my childhood in these moments, yet am helpless to stop myself. It's as if I am someone else—*him maybe*—a ruthless shadowy visual effect. I can sometimes even stand outside myself watching, mouth agape watching *watching* while the anger sheds from me in white-hot, oily waves. I can almost feel some evolved section of my brain nudging me to stop, while the limbic portion roils on.

One of my college boyfriends even named my anger, called it The Rage, and subtly, and then not so subtly, suggested counseling—*get help, you need it*. At the time, I saw his pleas as weak, as less than, as incapable of dealing with the reality and pressures of life and school and that what I was doing to him was not wrong or spiteful but a natural consequence of being together. He disagreed.

Before college, the only tangible target of my anger was John, and by the age of twelve, once he outgrew me by almost a foot, my efforts were futile. Back then, in reality, it was only a fledgling representation of what it was to become later. Like later, at fourteen, wishing to stab my brother through the eyehole for stealing and destroying my belt; later, as in twenty, punching a guy as hard as I could in the side of the head in an argument; later, as in right now, screaming at my daughter because she made a mess. Not a rational, frustrated huff like I've heard from other parents, but an insane over-the-top rant, screaming and losing my mind and not being able to—*for fucksake stop*—despite watching her eyes well with tears and her shoulders slump from the onslaught.

The idiocy of this is that I love her more than anything I have ever known. From the day I held her, she was mine, and mine alone, a symbol of something that was good and right, a tiny, living, breathing creature that would one day love me. But love and anger are equal parts of who I am and I am helpless to control either. I have tried to be better and I have tried counseling and I have tried medication. For whatever reason I always slide back, back into that hateful horrible hole of a temper, where others suffer mightily, and I loathe myself for days and weeks thereafter.

Of course, and not at all insightfully, the well-meaning and competent therapists *so many along the way* have linked my anger to both nurture and nature, citing the genetic components of my personality to my father, and the lashing out to my inability to control my childhood surroundings. Great. So what? The knowledge of this is no more helpful than trying to stop a car knowing that the brakes have been severed, or watching a documentary about Auschwitz and hoping for a better ending. Intense intellectual and behavior modification exercises are short-lived, because when I go, I *go*, and there is no governor, no mechanism I can physically call upon to short-circuit myself. The only thing that has ever helped is drugs. Not the fun, high inducing, enjoy yourself kind, but the Lexapros, Effexors, and Abilifys of the world, those that file the mental edges to the point of dullness and antipathy. They work in the sense that I am unable to summon the rage within and instead find myself ambivalent about almost everything. Sadly though, I am that patient who cannot function on these drugs, suffers from extreme vertigo, and generally feels like shit. I am a miserable and disconnected mother, and a frankly, incompetent employee. Neither of which is an option in my world.

I have also tried recreational drugs and alcohol, the go-to for the majority of my nuclear family. And in both cases, I have found little joy. While I may revel in the short term, at the end of it all, I find myself sadder and more bereft than when I began, accompanied by a nauseated stomach and a rising fear that I have begun down a path to addiction. I avoided these experiments for many years, all the way through college in fact, serving as the designated driver and dorm parent to every other drunken idiot student. It was such a displaced pride, even when snubbing glasses of wine and two-cube Scotch on the rocks as my parents shoved it in my face at every single family function. For many years I looked down the arched tip of my nose at John, for his early forays into pot and beer, cigarettes and whiskey, all of it lending itself to my vast moral superiority, which of course, was fucking ridiculous. It wasn't until much, much later—maybe even now as I write this—that I realized he was the one that had it figured out, that surgery could be withstood with anesthesia, that to observe your reflection in a circus mirror makes it more possible to bear. I held onto this misunderstanding for almost three decades, and it wasn't until I was in my late twenties that I began to partake. I suppose the timing may have had something to do with the fact that by then I had simply given up that my life would somehow be different or better if I were somehow different or better.

As a result, there were a couple of years in between divorces when I even dabbled heavily in cocaine, surrounding myself with overly friendly neighbors and acquaintances who wanted nothing more than to get high and watch from my couch as I got up for work in the morning. These same neighbors owned restaurants and night clubs and weekends were spent in a bleary haze of late mornings, afternoon barbeques complete with unbelievably tasty grilled garlic shrimp, blue cheese wedge salads, ahi poke, and the inevitable drug-fueled late-night parties. From one day to the next, any number of people from any number of houses throughout the block would be passed out somewhere on someone else's furniture. Fridges were raided, partners were swapped, sex was traded for drugs, and no one seemed to mind nor really care. It was an offbeat, slightly nomadic existence, and one that my neighbors seemed genuinely comfortable with. I joined primarily on weekends due to my day job.

I absolutely adored that drug, and I wasn't just invincible—I was magnetic. I felt like a maharaja with a cult following, my every move perfect, my every thought sublime. On occasion, I would literally hold court, sharing my wisdom and courage with anyone who would listen, convinced that their glazed expressions denoted rapture as opposed to oblivion. Looking back, I don't think the alarm bells about being hooked ever really rang, mostly because I both felt no pain, and because I had done such a *fine* job of not drinking or partying for so many years.

What finally stopped me had nothing to do with an epiphany or an intervention or anything remotely interesting. I was with a friend one night in her VW bug, Red Hot Chili Peppers blasting, on our way to a club. We were both stoned out of our minds and ready for another night of dancing and whatever sexual partners might cross our paths. On the way, she stopped at a gas station. While she was pumping, I started having trouble breathing and I panicked. I knew early in the evening I had snorted perhaps a line too much, but that steady progression had truly escaped me. I could not figure out how to rap on the glass or to open the door. My brain would not fire and my hands would not work. Even my survival instinct was stoned. As I sat in her car choking to death, I remember watching her through the windshield and realizing I was helpless to get her attention or to save myself. I was going to die right then and there, slumping over in her cute little party car, crushing the blue flower in that adorable little dashboard vase and choking on my own spit. She finally saw me staring at her, mouth gasping like a stunned goldfish, and somehow she was able to calm me down enough to breathe. I don't remember much else, just that it was a gross, dirty situation, much like the drug itself.

I stopped that night. And the only thing I got out of that entire coke festival was the loss of a few pounds, a couple good friends, and I suppose, my reputation.

Despite arriving two months early and weighing a mere four pounds, my daughter was a feisty little thing, refusing to return to the NICU with the nurses, preferring to sleep in my arms and attach herself immediately to my breast. The previous months I had had a miserable and difficult pregnancy—none of that glow and mother earth shit for me—complete with pre-eclampsia and regular hospital visits for stress tests. Despite being well into my thirties and for many years having served as an ardent and powerful voice for women who exercised their right not to bear children, when I found out I was pregnant all of that disappeared faster than a peregrine from a skyscraper ledge. I named her Delaney, Gaelic for "offspring of the challenger," a name I found both romantic and fierce. I imagined her dead Irish ancestors swooning around her, gently touching her nose and whispering tales of great things to come. I did not care that my friends referred to her as the "alien tree frog." She was beautiful. And she was mine.

By the time of her birth, her father and I were already on the outskirts of our marriage, his third and my second, his addiction to Soma and Vicodin far more powerful than the draw of his family. That I had married yet another addict came as no surprise to anyone other than me. We had been married only a year when Delaney was born. Why I had not noticed, nor cared to notice, that his odd behaviors and our diminishing bank account were somehow linked, is beyond me still. I suppose I had chosen the safer path of denial and hope, believing that his choices were in no way a reflection of me or my failings. Instead, I became resentful and distant. And he encased himself in a haze of opioid love.

Even the early years of that marriage were suspect. It was his mother that kept the binds tight, rather than any real inclination on our part. She was a devout Christian, a genuinely loving person and steadfast in her determination to have our marriage last. She spent countless hours encouraging family dinners and offering to watch the baby, assembling Easter egg hunts and Christmas dinners. It was her husband and brother who each approached me separately with dire warnings of my husband's sordid past and penchant for shitty decisions. Her husband, Don, Delaney's grandfather, even offered at one point to buy Delaney and me a place if we would just walk away from him. I did not, of course, and on the evening when Don came to our house after my frantic phone call to him that his son would not wake up no matter how loudly I yelled or how much water I threw in his face, he left after simply taking one look. As he was leaving, he told me to brace myself, this was what people like my husband did, and if I was content that he had a pulse and nothing else, then I had made my own bed.

Finally, when Delaney was about seven, I threw in the towel, exhausted by counseling, failed rehab centers, and an ever-increasing realization that yet another marriage was doomed. The fact that I had a child was little recompense, and I took the divorce hard. I knew deep down in my belly that he would disappear, both financially and emotionally from her life, and in this, he did not disappoint.

After raising our daughter on my own for many years, I would like to point my righteously convinced finger entirely at him for the collapse of our family. But even that is untrue. It was my loathing, my disgust at his ambivalence, and my utter lack of compassion for his struggles that ultimately contributed—*can I say equally?*—to our demise. While I realize that I could not, nor will not, ever fix him, what I did do is leave Delaney without a father. In any capacity. Because in my rigidity and my conviction that his life choices made him emotionally bereft, which may or may not be true and does not matter, she ultimately does not have a father to conspire with, to love, to rely on, and this is completely and wholly my fault.

I continue to do a good job of surrounding myself with people who support how I have isolated her from him and his inane self, but underneath it all, I mourn the fact that while her broken relationship with her father is entirely unlike mine was, it is in fact, the same. I wonder how much of her separation from him is a generational carbon copy of my own dysfunction, and how much of it is based on the reality of her father's actual imperfections. In the end, I know that Delaney and I are doomed to cry watching daughters escorted down wedding aisles, will never attend a daddy/daughter event, resent our friends whose families are whole and balanced, and ultimately filled with a sorrow and longing so immense that we ache with it. And it is in that truth that we share a legacy.

So why is it that, even armed with the years of knowledge and understanding about what intrinsically drives my temper, am I unable to stop it, unable to withdraw it, sheath it like a sword in a scabbard, when faced with the crumpled face of my daughter? I know that it makes me feel like a vile, base creature unworthy of her love. I know that it makes her sad and frightened and pushes her further and further away. Yet, I continue. I don't diminish with time, nor do I control it despite my never-ending love for her.

I've wondered at times if it may be that I actually resent her, her life, her relative peace in our household, the fact that she has so many opportunities and so much support and feedback and lessons and basic information, things that I never had. The fact that I guide her and suggest possibilities and alternatives, and do not leave her with a gaping void where life lessons should reside. The fact that her pets are safe and she will never hide from a gun. She will have a car, her choice of colleges, and somewhere—always—to come home to. She will be safe, she will be loved, and I will always answer the phone in her time of need. But perhaps none of it is enough, and perhaps I am slowly, inexorably eroding her capacity for love and any ability to bond.

It is these musings that drive me for answers within my own family and the family of my father. I reach out to half-brothers and cousins, aunts and uncles who knew both of my parents far before my memories. I find that I need to know what it was that drove my father to torture and maim his own, and it is years before I find the truth.

Hidden far in the depths of a desolate family history is the story of my father's father, my grandfather. He died long before I was born, and I had heard little to nothing about him other than he lived to be close to one hundred. As it turns out, he was far worse than even my father, his rage and anguish an ugly boiling red that scorched everything around him. He beat my grandmother and my father almost to death on multiple occasions. He did the same to his second wife and my father's half-brother in subsequent years. At the age of about forty-five, he became so unruly and dangerous that he was forced to endure a frontal lobotomy, the preferred method of treatment for patients in those days. The details of the procedure and whether he consented are murky, but what is known is he spent the next fifty or so years swaying on his wife's porch swing, unable to speak. As the story goes, she was most unkind to him during those ensuing years.

I am stunned by this, as though a cattle prod has pierced the thin veil of my self-constructed gospel, a slowly dawning horror that I am directly related to this man and the versions of men he sired after him, a litany of men that bred diseased progeny, angry daughters, and sons that molested sisters. And I cannot shake the inevitability of it all. That no matter my resolve, no matter my effort, no matter the fierceness of my love for my child, that my genetics are catastrophic, and my broken neural pathways doom me to a Clockwork Orange existence.

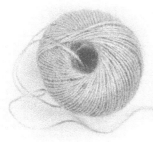

How High Can
You Get

The first few years of Delaney's life I worked hard at my marriage. It was my second, and I was determined to make something of it. Ours was a courtship fueled by highs and lows, followed by a marriage equally as intense, and I was certain I knew how to fix it. The problem was the "it" of it, something as elusive as a snow leopard, difficult to pinpoint, requiring tremendous effort to study, and ultimately doomed.

I tried anyway.

Delaney's father was the ultimate All-American boy: tall, blonde, an exceptional athlete, funny and kind. We met on one of those horrible dating sites, and although we were well into our thirties by the time we met, I was struck by his charm and sense of humor, his disdain for the status quo, and his seemingly successful business. We met for coffee, began a whirlwind romance, and were married three months later. I was convinced this was the guy who should father my children.

There were so many red flags along the way. I ignored each and every one of them, opting instead for those moments of hilarity and family that I hoarded, ingeniously wrapped in a cloak of *wished it was so* draped to self-soothe. He was not a bad guy, just a broken guy, one in a series of shattered pieces I tended to collect. And because love and sadness are such close cousins in your gut, push the same buttons, elicit the same tears, we lasted for almost a decade.

I loved him, and deeply. I gave the relationship the heart I knew existed somewhere within me, and when I found out I was pregnant, I was ecstatic. I was nudging at forty, and knew my uterus was about two years away from becoming a dried-up husk. My doctor kept me under close watch, and despite rising blood pressure and a not-so-fun amniocentesis, I powered through. And when she was born, premature, underweight, but healthy, I knew I had just scooted in under the chromosomal radar.

Those early years, when Delaney was a toddler, and I was completely oblivious to her father's severe drug addiction—*was I? was I really?*—were filled with the excitement of a new marriage topped with the delirium of a brand-new baby. We laughed. A lot. We hiked, we swam, we went to the snow, we had fun. Those were the years I convinced myself that I was capable of holding together a nuclear family, and my upbringing had in no way infected my current life. And it worked. At least for a while. Thinking back, if I were to color those years like a mural or collage, they would swirl with oranges and yellows, bright spots of seafoam green, solidly framed, with a warm gold patina overlay. Only the frame was black.

Every night, before the sun set, we would push Delaney in her green stroller around the neighborhood, naming the thimbleberry, Indian blanket, and black-eyed Susans that dotted the hillsides along our path. She was a curious and talkative baby, pointing and garbling loudly at just about everything we encountered. The walks were cathartic, and we used them as a balm for our ever-increasing disconnect.

One evening we were taking a route that ended in a cul-de-sac in an area that had not yet been built up with homes. In the center of the cul-de-sac was a very large tarantula.

"Are you serious?" said Delaney's dad. "Is that alive?"

"I think so."

Since I had grown up on a ranch of sorts, took care of horses, and generally had survived multiple swarms of bees, I did not consider a palm-sized black spider to be problematic.

"Jesus, don't go near that thing."

I couldn't help myself. I am not sure whether I was trying to prove my bravado to my husband, impress my infant daughter with my etymological prowess, or was genuinely interested, but I decided to go straight up to that spider, kneel down directly in front of it, and peer into its tiny devil eyes.

Just as my husband uttered, "You're friggin' crazy," that nasty-ass creature rocked back on its barbed legs and jumped straight at my face. I could see its warped dome eyes glittering and its hooked fangs headed straight for my eyeball. Everything stalled to a horrifying slow motion. I screamed and fell, scrabbling backwards across the pavement as fast as I could, looking like a character out of *The Ring*, or maybe a deranged crab.

As the tarantula scuttled away, and I picked the asphalt pebbles out of my palms, Delaney and her father howled with laughter. My husband was doubled over, clutching his sides laughing so hard he could barely talk.

"Oh my God, baby girl, did you see that?" He could barely get the words out. "Your mom is a lunatic. She was almost eaten by a spider."

As he laughed, Delaney's eyes lit up and she pointed at me, giggling.

It took us a while to get home that night, as the two of them felt it necessary to stop every few blocks and laugh.

I was not remotely amused.

I suppose I should have paid more attention to the slow erosion of our marriage than I did. Or maybe I chose to ignore it, choosing desire over inevitability. But the allure of the kids around the Christmas tree and the concept of family dinners in a clean house was my version of emotional meth. Over time I saw my reflection changing, my skin becoming a pale, dull gray, my teeth rotting, as my husband fell in and out of rehab centers, yet I continued to inhale, desperate for the high of those fleeting moments.

His addiction was gruesome to watch—the slipping of the flesh from the bones of his youth and promise, the dullness in his eyes as he watched his daughters play, the delayed laugh as he struggled to follow the thread of a conversation. It was both brutal and heartbreaking to live through. Although I had not been intimately familiar with drug addiction, I had snuggled closely with alcoholism, and the side effects were not all that different. Much like my parents, he chose the pills over me, his children, his career, and just about everything else. What he did choose were friends that shared his love of the high. At first, I was under the impression that these friends were lifelong pals that he enjoyed getting together with. He was a guitarist, and from time to time, he and his friends would play at our house, drink some beer and hang out. What I didn't know was this was their platform to deal drugs and get loaded.

When the "band" would come to play, I at first would sit in and listen, enthralled by both the comradery and the music. Hours were spent sitting in the living room at decibels far above healthy. I found his musical ability sexually appealing, and constructed ways to justify his ever-eroding interest in work hours by his musical talent. Unfortunately, none of this talent ever translated to bills being paid or kids being tended.

It was not much of a problem in the beginning. He had inherited some money from his father, and for the first year-and-a-half of Delaney's life I stayed at home, something I had never done in my entire life, having worked since I was fourteen. Her father meandered from part-time job to part-time job, played his music and somehow convinced me that this minimal effort was enough to keep us going. When both his inheritance and his job search ended, it was up to me to return to the workplace. I did this gladly, realizing fairly early on that being a stay-at-home mom was not something I was cut out for in the long run. I found myself practically frantic at times to be intellectually productive and do something other than care for my child. This made me feel both profoundly guilty and a desperate failure at motherhood.

When I did finally reenter the workplace, I am fairly certain I appeared bipolar—at times crying in hotel rooms over my tiny girl wailing for me at home, and simultaneously manically thrilled upon inclusion in an important meeting.

After about a year of watching Delaney run to the living room window and pull back the drapes to watch me drive away, her face crumpled and tears welling, I told my husband that I couldn't be away from her this much anymore and that he needed to return to work once she started preschool the following year. I wanted to work part-time, and I figured with him working part-time or full time we could make ends meet.

That plan never materialized. Instead, he spent the next several years in and out of rehab centers and bouncing from counselor to counselor, never really being able to get it together. While many of these places blur in one green-gray septic smear, one experience was particularly traumatizing.

He had been arrested for snorting cocaine with his buddy outside of his mother's apartment while his three kids slept inside. Why the two of them thought doing drugs inside a car with a lit interior was a good idea is beside the matter, but the cop cruising by clearly saw them for the dumbasses they were. We spent the next half year dealing with lawyers and court dates, only to have him assigned to some court-appointed rehabilitation program designed to keep addicts out of jail. At the time, I was ecstatic that the father of my child was not going to be placed behind bars, and that this could all be left behind us with a short stint in a county facility. Stupid girl.

This was the first time that my drug addiction ignorance came into stark focus. When I dropped him off at Carpinteria By the Sea, we were met by a very friendly front desk nurse who greeted us with a smile.

"So glad you made it," she chirped. "Just sit here while I complete your paperwork."

My husband and I held hands sitting side-by-side on the bright blue couch, muted pastel seascapes adorning the walls around us, glancing hopefully at each other the entire ten minutes it took to have him admitted.

"Alright then, I have you all checked in. Why don't you go ahead and leave your watch, phone and shoes with your wife, and we will get you the rest of what you need."

I remember shaking my head slightly, as in *huh? This isn't prison.*

My husband, on the other hand, was clearly familiar with this routine and handed over his belongings. The nurse placed them in a white plastic bag and handed them to me.

"So, we will see you in two weeks," she said, as she led him to the locked doorway, *Authorized Personnel Only* clearly stenciled on the window.

"Two weeks?" I really did not understand what was happening.

"Yes, we allow family visits after two weeks of detox and rehab. Then we start counseling on the third week."

She then punched a code into the security panel, the door whisked open and they were gone. I stood there staring after them for a solid few minutes. I felt as though I had watched something as conceivable as a rogue wave take my spouse out to sea. I could not comprehend that there was a world where family members simply disappeared behind closed doors to live with a group of people you had never met and that you would not be in contact with them until some vague indeterminate milestone had been met.

I had little choice but to return home, find a babysitter, and go back to work. The lights needed to stay on, my daughter needed to be fed, and since all of this was court-ordered, I had little say in the matter. Like so many situations in my life, I put my head down and plowed through, waiting to see if some small treasure could be discovered at the end of this untenable trail, a jewel-encrusted saber perhaps, or maybe even a sparkling new sober husband, as shiny and delightful as a new Audi.

When the two weeks were up, I traveled to Carpinteria By the Sea that Saturday afternoon. I had no idea what to expect, but was giddy at the prospect of seeing him again and putting all of this in the rear-view mirror. When I arrived, chirpy nurse was there and greeted me warmly.

"Hi! So glad you could make it. Just sign in here and we will take you back."

I signed into the visitor's log and was escorted behind the *Authorized Personnel Only* door, past several rooms, to a cafeteria. The nurse sat me at a table in the cafeteria and asked me to wait while she had my husband sent in. The room was full of high school style cafeteria tables and benches, long counters with sliding rails for plastic trays, tall stacks of plastic utensil holders, cascading napkin dispensers, and the oddest assortment of people I had ever seen.

As I waited, I watched androgynous men and women meander in and out of the room, dressed in sweats or pajamas, wearing blue socks, hair unkempt and eyes cast downward. There was little to no chatter between them, minimal eye contact and the room was eerily silent except for the soft shuffling of socks across the linoleum floor. I felt as though I was in a casting call for *Dawn of the Dead* and it made me entirely uneasy.

A man that reminded me of my husband started towards me and it wasn't until he got right in front of me that I realized it was him. His transformation was utterly appalling. He had entered this place a coherent, healthy, human being. What stood before me now was at least ten pounds lighter, with his sweat pants falling off his hips, hands palsied, and unable to meet my eyes. His pupils were pinpoints and he did not speak. I could only stare. He was so clearly drugged out of his mind, it was highly unlikely he even knew who I was. He finally looked over at me and uttered something about ice cream before he got up and shuffled to the soft serve dispenser nearby.

"Are you okay?" I asked as he shambled back. "What is happening to you?"

"I don't know," was all he could answer. As I watched, he slurped at the chocolate ice cream like a suckling pig rooting at its mother's teat, unaware of the brown drips falling on his lap, the sounds he was making, or my utter horror.

I had nothing to say. I looked around wildly for some sort of doctor or nurse or janitor to explain to me what was happening and why he was behaving like this. There was no one. I stood abruptly and left the room, determined to find someone who could explain how this was remotely helpful or part of any recovery. He didn't even notice my departure.

I never was able to get any acceptable answers out of anyone that day. I left befuddled and sad. Sad for my marriage, sad for my daughter, and sad for the man who had once coached sports with me, watched stars from the jacuzzi with his arm around my shoulder, played Twister with the kids, swam with the dog and was an excellent water skier. That man was a ghost and I was sincerely afraid that he was never coming back.

Upon his release, I discovered that protocol for that place had been to detox patients from addictive substances to medication that continued to drug them but did not have the addictive side effects. My husband, like so many patients, had manipulated the system to stay loaded his entire visit. He cared no more about his recovery than an arsonist cares where the extinguisher resides. This was just another step along his journey to the next escape. That, and the subsequent five other visits to rehab over the next several years only served to light a flicker of hope in my soul, to be snuffed out immediately after. The end result was a series of events: passing out face first in his chicken salad, informing me he now liked speed in Marie Callender's, missing sums of money from bank accounts, another arrest for prescription forgery, dropped pills that my three-year-old picked up. A progression so increasingly bad that my heart gave out.

It did not matter how much I wanted it to work or the fact that I desperately wanted some form of family for Delaney, I simply could not keep up with the frenetic pace of his betrayals. It did not matter that I still loved him, or that I held onto his potential to be better like a fistful of sand, so that the harder I squeezed the more it slipped through my grip. It did not matter that he had children who relied on him, or a mother that was desperate for him to find ballast, he was lost in the fog of his abdication.

He never did return to work. For seven more years I fiercely defended the stronghold of my family until finally, embattled, fatigued, scarred, I gave up, choosing instead to go it alone. I knew then, as I know now, that Delaney would see little of him from that point further and that knowledge alone thrust a rusted dagger into my already tetanused heart.

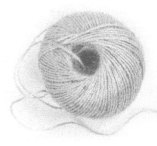

Monkeycheeks

I first introduced my baby girl to horses when she was five. In that moment, and without knowing it, I had forever woven our souls together. Even at five, she immediately fell in love, much like my instant fourteen-year-old adoration with Heather and Andromeda. I could see it in her eyes as she leaned into the horses' muzzle, fearless, breathing deeply of the scent, hands softly stroking the face and jaw. The horse immediately went limp, intuiting both her smallness and kindness, as only horses can do.

There were several occasions throughout my life when I turned to horses for solace of some kind, whether it was a broken spirit or a broken heart, it did not matter: they were my Sedona vortex, my Peruvian Sacred Valley, a place for me to recharge and gather myself up. At twenty-five, I bought my first horse within a few years of securing my first job and shortly after losing the love of my life. We had been dating for several years, and the loss felt fatal. He was six years older, smart, incredibly handsome, and the first person I think I ever truly loved. We had spent many happy hours together, hiking, camping, four-wheeling, traveling to Hawaii—doing all sorts of grown-up things that I never thought myself capable of. When it became obvious, to me anyway, that he needed to commit, things fell apart. Rather than give him the space to make his own decision, I was relentless, foregoing any aplomb or nuance. Instead, I plowed through us like a mule with a harrow, eventually chasing him away altogether. As he grew more distant, I tried and failed, multiple times, to win back his trust and affection, but the damage was done. And he disappeared. It was the first time I understood that I was not equipped to successfully navigate a serious relationship, that I had neither been modeled, nor taught, the correct coping mechanisms, responses or words, that my actions were disproportionate and my desperation unappealing. In hindsight, I suppose showing up at his house and crawling through a window to find him when he would not answer my calls was a tad over the top. I also believe that quite possibly the one or two times he was around my family with my mom passed out drunk, while my father yelled some insult or another, was enough to convince him I might not be the best candidate for a family with children. And finally, I would guess that my inability to step away from him was inextricably tied to my frantic belief that I could never again find someone to love me, that in truth he was an anomaly, an outlier in my otherwise predestined crap life.

Since I had dedicated so many hours and years to our relationship, I now found myself alone, and with no one to turn to, the isolation was unbearable. I spent hours sobbing, watching the phone, unable to function in any real way. My work began to suffer. Hoping to replace him in any form I could find, I moved several times to various friends' houses, therapeutically talking it out until they could no longer stand my presence. Ultimately, as I unwound, falling in on myself like a collapsed star, the only solution I could think to stay hinged was to find myself a horse.

His name was Thunderbird. He was a magnificent Canadian thoroughbred gelding standing seventeen hands with a beautiful dapple-grey coat. I had zero business owning him. He was an extremely talented and fiery upper-level hunter jumper capable of clearing huge fences, while I had not ridden in years. That mattered little to my emotionally-addled self and I rode him with abandon, my mind free of loves lost and futures bleak. Over time, as my job became more intense and once I met my first husband—*he of the obvious rebound*—I lost the hours needed to take adequate care of Thunderbird and eventually sold him to my trainer. I knew even then that horse had single-handedly saved me from some very stupid decisions and some very black places. At the time though, soaring over enormous jumps was just the medicine I needed, the mix of adrenaline and focus better than any Lexapro or Chardonnay. That gelding enabled me to bypass therapy, potential alcoholism and the deep, dark hidey-hole of maybe-I-don't-want-to-be-alive. The day I handed him over was tough. He had been my only companion, my friend, my confidante for over two years. As the trailer pulled away, I had to sit in my car for about twenty minutes. I just couldn't see to drive through my bittersweet tears.

My first marriage was short in both duration and intensity. I realized early on I had made a mistake, that I had simply believed I needed a marriage, not that I actually wanted to live one. My husband at the time was oblivious to my indifference, happily enjoying my professional success with golf club memberships and fat cigars. Much of our time was spent playing golf, a sport I detested, and hanging out with people twenty years our senior. I had little to nothing in common with the other wives, most of whom had never worked, and I could not take off from work every Friday for luncheons. As a result, it was my husband who made friends and was invited to all the gatherings. I lingered just outside the margins, wishing I fit in, but secure in the knowledge that I did not. As expected, most of those friends remained with him once I moved out of the house.

Although a kind and loving man, at thirty-five he was already sixty-five, and I felt doomed less than a year in. I distinctly remember the conversation that preceded the demise of our brief marriage. We were in the bathroom one evening getting ready for a local fundraiser. As I looked in the mirror, I remember being satisfied with my healthy thirty-year-old reflection—one of the few times—thinking to myself that my hair and dress looked good and it was kind of cool that we were going to be the youngest couple at a party chock full of successful people.

As I primped, my husband came up behind me in the mirror, wrapped his arms around my waist and kissed my neck. I smiled back.

"Ready?" I asked.

He nodded and smiled back, taking a step to the side. As we gazed into the mirror at each other's reflections, I remember thinking how nice we both looked, how this was the beginning of our lives, that the world was ours.

As I smiled at him he shook his head and commented, "Wow, we sure are getting old."

I had no response. What could I say? In that moment I realized we were two very disparate people, one who had already settled in, much like an old goat loathe to leave the warm shed, someone who saw his life as set and solid, a future filled with custom golf carts and amber liqueurs. I, on the other hand, viewed myself as more of a racehorse, agitated, pawing to get out, never satisfied with what was, only that it needed to get better. And while the thoroughbred and the goat can share the same barn and happily coexist, once the door is left open, the horse will eventually run away. We divorced six months later.

The second time I leaned on the love of a horse was the year I realized Delaney's father and I would not survive our marriage. The realization was harsh, as was gathering the courage to leave him without either an emotional or financial safety net. I struggled internally, not only with my second strike at marriage, but more so with the fact that I had failed Delaney. I knew my sadness ran wide and I needed something to keep my undertow from pulling Delaney out to sea. While she was only five, she wasn't stupid. She began to insist that she sleep with me despite having her own room, and when she could only fall asleep with her head atop my heart—*she called it chesty chest*—I knew I needed to do something. I figured a horse would keep me occupied and could be something Delaney and I could enjoy together, something that would get me out and away from my crumbling marriage; give me a place to be where I did not have to watch her father flail at sobriety or return to a house with little joy. I needed an emotional alibi.

Little did I know her love for horses would outpace my own.

I still knew people in the horse world, so I joined them to find both a horse and a place to ride. Like so many other resolutions in my life, I jumped in feet first, buying the first mare that came my way. She was a kind, older mare named Ribbons, and she was the sweetest animal I had ever encountered. She had been ridden by a little girl for many years and was both big enough and safe enough for me to ride and for Delaney to learn. It would have been the perfect fit even if it wasn't.

I chose to make Ribbons a Christmas surprise for Delaney. Her father was not at all pleased with any of it and fought the purchase the entire way. He argued it would take hours and hours of time away from him and his two other daughters, the soccer games, our weekend family activities. *My point exactly.* I went forward with it anyway. I decided that since I was the one working and I was the one making the money, I could spend my money any way I saw fit, and if that way included buying a horse for my five-year-old daughter, then so be it. By then, Delaney's father and I fought most of the time anyway, and I am sure the kids could sense the anger and tension that permeated the house. I wanted him to leave, but he would not, so spending hours with Ribbons seemed an excellent way to avoid both his career apathy and my anger.

On Christmas Eve—I couldn't wait another day—I took Delaney to the barn where Ribbons was waiting. She was already excited, thinking a trip to the ranch and surrounding pastures was the treat. Little did she know. My friends held her hand while I led Ribbons out the barn door, a huge red bow on her halter. Delaney's eyes grew huge.

"Momma?"

"Yes, Monkeycheeks. She's yours."

Her hands flew to her mouth and her eyes filled with tears.

"Momma, no!"

I started to cry, too. "Yeah, baby. She's for you. She is your very own Christmas present."

As Delaney sobbed, I led Ribbons over to her and the mare immediately dropped her head to her new two-foot-tall best friend. Delaney kissed that horse right on the mouth and began to whisper the first secrets the two of them would share over the next few years. From that moment on, they were inseparable. My daughter learned to clean a stall with a pitchfork taller than she was by a head, feed a horse that outweighed her by twelve-hundred pounds, and ride an animal that could easily throw her at any time. None of that mattered. To either of them. Ribbons adored my girl and went out of her way to protect her like her own. And Delaney spent every spare moment of her pint-sized life asking if we could go to the barn.

After only a few months, Delaney had gotten pretty good at riding that old mare. The other boarders at the ranch called her "The Tick" for her enviable ability to stay on the horse no matter what happened. It was a close-knit community and I felt safe with other boarders watching while Delaney rode. Most of the owners got quite a kick out of my forty-pound kid muscling her fifteen-hand horse, and the one time she fell when Ribbons spooked I think the other women were more upset than I was.

I took lessons while Delaney learned primarily by trial-and-error. The two of them were hilarious to watch. Delaney, with her always-crooked helmet sitting atop that fat mare and cantering around the arena, her legs barely to the horses' ribs. Ribbons, stopping whenever she felt like it with little consideration for Delaney's boots thumping her sides, looking completely put out at the suggestion of exertion.

They rode for hours those two, and after about six months, I felt safe letting Delaney ride her outside of the arena.

By then, Ribbon's filly, Lila, had joined the stable for training with our trainer. Lila was about four, and quite possibly the singularly most unattractive horse I had ever seen. Her front legs stuck out in front of her at an odd angle, her head was shaped like a donkey's, and she was clumsy. There was little, if anything, to like about the horse, her breeding or quite frankly, her owner—a woman who fancied herself quite the horsewoman, despite her broad midsection, big mouth, and lack of any ability. She was stubborn, ugly, and had a bad attitude—just like Lila. Nobody at the ranch liked her and Delaney and I avoided both of them as much as possible.

There came a day that summer when our trainer decided Delaney was ready for a trail ride. This was a big honor and a huge milestone for a six-year-old equestrian. Delaney was beside herself with excitement, the week leading up to the ride filled with *when's* and *what's*. The only problem was, I needed to accompany her, which meant I needed a horse, and the only horse available was Lila. Much to my chagrin, I agreed, saddling up Lily alongside Ribbons for the ride, her fat owner blowholing advice the entire time.

Delaney, Ribbons, Lila and I set off down a valley and into a winding canyon, the sun shining overhead, and our backpack full of lunch goodies. Delaney sang most of the way, and after about an hour we reached our final destination; a sandy river bottom surrounded by bamboo and wild raspberries. We dismounted the horses and sat in the sand to eat, sharing a bottle of water while the horses stood tied to a tree. I may have napped. Two red-tailed hawks *scree*'d overhead as we gathered up our leftovers and got ready to head back.

As we approached the bottom of the last slight hill before the road to the barn, Delaney and Ribbons started to trot, then canter. As they did, Lila lost her mind. Apparently, she thought her mother cantering was an excuse to be an asshole, so she took complete advantage and began bucking and crow-hopping, ears flat, her stiff back jamming into my spine at every bounce. I yelled at Delaney to stop.

Delaney slowed only slightly to turn and look at me while Lila caught up, all the while grabbing the bit in her mouth and prancing insanely up to Ribbons. I had to tell Delaney three times to stop trotting forward just so I could stay on. When we got even with them, Delaney took off at a dead gallop, whooping and hollering like a cowgirl, her six-year-old arm lashing the air like an invisible lasso, while I hung on to Lila for dear life. That ugly ass horse ran at a heaving gallop, bucking and twisting every two strides, and it was all I could do to stay in the saddle, while Delaney laughed and yelled, "Whahoo!" the entire way. I have no idea how I stayed on that fool animal and cannot fathom how Ribbons ran so fast. Delaney laughed so hard smears of dirt ran down her face. I wanted to kill her.

God, I love that kid.

Something or Other

I look inward on occasion and do not always like what I see. As an example, it is fairly obvious that the reason I am so over-the-top with my work ethic is directly related to the fact that my father informed me at fourteen I needed to get a job. While other kids in the area were shopping at the mall, going to parties or hanging out, I walked the local dogs, babysat, took care of horses in the area, whatever I could to make a few extra dollars. I was given no explanation why I could not ask for, nor receive, any money. It did not appear we were struggling financially. It did not seem as though our lifestyle had changed to any degree. If anything, my mother inheriting the insurance money lifted some of the burden from my father and allowed my parents the opportunity to build the new house. It just seemed to happen overnight, as though some arbitrary switch had been flipped, some post-adolescent fuse had been tripped.

My mother did what she could do to slip money to me, but my father held the purse strings and that meant very little came my way. When I finally left home for college, I tended to behave miserly with my money, not winning many friends when it came time to contribute to pizza or midnight Del Taco runs. My friends always found it odd that I declined to eat out so often, or to join them on road trips, but I simply could not afford it. I did not have a credit card or a bank account that my parents regularly deposited into, I did not have a savings account I could draw from, I had only the money I made from my summer job that went directly towards tuition and the monthly paychecks from my university jobs. And I was far too humiliated to let anyone know how broke I really was.

I had my first full-time job the summer after completing my freshman year as a lifeguard. It was better than minimum wage and a good way to earn the first and second quarter's tuition. I did not want to return home, but I had no choice. I could not earn the amount I needed to save *and* pay rent. The math just didn't work. I became increasingly depressed as the school year ended.

The prospect of returning to that house was especially difficult after having been away for most of the year. I had learned so many new things about social norms and behaviors, how other families behaved, that I now had a litmus test to compare to, and I knew my family was acidic. Come June, a friend who lived in San Francisco dropped me off on her way home and, laundry bag in tow, I returned. The first few nights were okay, as I think my mom had missed me. She made an effort to cook some nice dinners and even went out of her way to slow down on the drinking. She knew I didn't like it, and I could tell she was trying.

Eventually, and as expected, the same shitstorm returned. My mother resumed her post-five o'clock slur and my father renewed his reptilian wrath. I had little choice but to power through that summer, spending as many hours at the pool as I could manage and returning home as late as possible. By then, John had graduated high school and was gone most of the time. He had figured out the very minute he had a vehicle that he could sleep on friends' couches and be fed from unlocked pantries. His absence, like a gas flame turned down, at least brought the physical violence to a simmer.

As that summer came to a close, I remember thinking how we had made it through without any major issues—yelling screaming threats, sure, but no actual bloodshed. I had about two more weeks of summer left when things started to swerve. John had come home one weekend because he needed to work on his car. His VW broke down regularly and seeing him under the hood was not an uncommon sight. My father had an entire garage full of tools—that he rarely used—and when I got home from the pool that afternoon, my brother was outside the garage, his engine torn apart, tools everywhere.

I hadn't seen much of him that summer, and not at all for the last several weeks, so I decided to hassle him while he worked. We had discovered that we now fought much less, and our conversations were becoming more interesting and less fueled by sibling rivalry. Since I was now out of the house, we no longer had to compete for the sparse attention our mother paid us, and I actually found him hilarious and quite clever. If anything, we now sought each other out, innately understanding that our bond was not unlike war veterans, we had each other's back and we knew when the enemy was approaching.

I leaned in under the hood.

"Hey."

He didn't look up. His arms were covered in grease and his veins bulged as he torqued a wrench on some part of the engine.

"Hey."

It was my same old brother. He of the seafoam-green eyes, the lop of dark curly hair hanging in his face, taller and taller by the day. But in the last three months, he had filled out quite a bit—still lean, but very muscular, clearly owning an athlete's body and much more male than I remembered from the start of summer. He wore loose yellow basketball shorts and no shirt, flip flops jammed on his enormous feet. As he worked, I remember feeling almost outside myself, as though I were looking at a picture of him, not him, some other version of him. It was surreal, and for the first time, I felt as though I did not know him that day as much as I used to. He seemed older, hardened, aged like young bourbon not yet refined.

"What ya doin'?"

He pulled hard at the wrench. Then reached for another.

"The fuck you think I'm doing?"

He placed the wrench on the edge of the engine and grabbed an oily blue towel. He wiped his hands for a solid ten seconds before he smiled.

"Idiot," I laughed.

And like that we were three and six again. My little brother, now enormous, taller than me by a head, who could fix an engine and win a state basketball championship was still just my little Johnny Appleseed, my tiny little other.

We spent the next half hour talking about his preparations to go to Colorado State where he had received a basketball scholarship, and how he could not wait to get there, how these next few weeks were interminable. As he worked, I handed him tools, belly laughing over stories of his escapades with his buddies, his multiple girlfriends, his love of cannabis and beer.

Just then our father pulled into the driveway behind us. We both instinctually stopped laughing. Stopped talking altogether. We were antelopes downwind of the lion and we knew it.

"Jesus fucking Christ, not this again," he roared as he came around the side of the car. "The last time you worked on this fucking car you left a goddamn mess of my tools, and I couldn't find my crescent wrench for a week."

He kicked at the tools around him on the ground. He then set his gaze on John.

"I told you you couldn't use my tools, didn't I?"

My brother said nothing. He just stared, arms at his side, all six-foot-six of him mute.

Stupidly, and with no sense whatsoever, I decided to answer.

"He was just trying to fix his car."

Why *the fuck* I chose to open my maw eludes me to this day. The prey does *not* talk back to the predator, it simply runs and hides. The minute the words came out of my recently college-educated-but-wildly-misinformed-in-the-ways-of-the-world mouth I wanted to scream them back into my piehole, will them into nonexistence, shut them in a dark closet forever.

He swung his gaze over to me. He smiled a small, tight smile, his eyes narrowing in that way he had, the way that reminded me of a dinosaur or a crocodile, unthinking and unblinking in its desire to consume. He slowly and methodically set his car keys on the roof of the VW as my brother began to back away.

"Oh, so you have an opinion, do you?"

By now *and far too late* I knew better than to speak any words, to make any noise at all. With absolute deliberation and thought, our father considered the weapons at his disposal. As we stared, he glanced at the tools on the ground before ultimately selecting the digging bar—about five feet tall, weighing about forty pounds with a sharpened metal tip at the end used to break apart impacted soil—leaning against the garage wall.

My brother started to whimper. I couldn't seem to get a breath. This was going to be bad.

While I do not remember the fury-filled words or the logic or even the exact sequence of events, what I do remember is our father chasing us around the back of the house brandishing the long bar like a spear. It should have been impossible for him to carry a forty-pound tool over his shoulder while he ran, but he did. It should never have been a scene in any backyard, yet it was. He ultimately threw the spike at my brother's head, but it missed. As the bar hit the ground, first with a heavy thump of the honed tip, and then a twang as it bounced off the clay, my brother took off down the hill, flip flops slapping the pavement, headed most likely for his buddy's house miles away. He left his car abandoned in the driveway while I ran and hid behind the horse trough.

Once my father went inside, I snuck around the side of the house to find my mother reading in the library. I lightly tapped on the glass door to get her attention. She looked up from her book, oblivious. I slowly opened the door and went in, my mom watching me over her reading glasses. Whispering, I convinced her to take me back to school. Right then. Not in two weeks, not at the close of summer, but right fucking *then*. It was one of the rare moments when she actually did not try to deny it away or to pretend like this, too, would blow over. She watched while I snuck up the back stairs and into my room to pack, then drove me the almost three hours to campus. We did not talk. We did not discuss the impeding repercussions coming her way for getting me out of the house. We did not discuss anything. I simply asked her to drop me off outside the dorms.

While I may have saved myself from a beating, I had severely miscalculated what might happen once dropped off at school. In my haste to exit, I didn't realize the dorms were not yet open. Although the Resident Advisors had moved in, the student rooms were not available. My RA, Jennifer, was kind enough to let me drop my belongings in my assigned room, but she could not let me stay. It was against the rules.

"If I let you do it, everyone will want to come early," she said. "It would be one big party."

I nodded and used the phone in the hall to call my roommate, Joyce. When I told her I was already on campus, she laughed and said she wasn't headed down for about six more days but to feel free to wait for her.

I spent the next hour or so calling everyone I knew to see if I could find a place to stay until the dorms opened. The only possible option was a friend of a friend who was moving into her apartment in two days. At least that way I would have a place for the remainder of the week. The only issue was what to do for the next two days. As I stood in the hallway of the dorms, I realized I might be in trouble, that for the next forty-eight hours I had nowhere to sleep.

That afternoon and evening, and for the next few days during daylight hours, I sat in the campus library, reading, napping, leaving for lunch only to return an hour later and stay until the library closed at nine p.m. As the doors closed behind me, I had no idea where to go so I headed to Denny's, open twenty-four hours, and right around the corner from campus. That first night I sat in the far back corner booth, backpack on the seat beside me, and ordered a Grand Slam. I tried to become as invisible as possible, but after about two hours the waitress came over to my table.

"Can I get you anything else?"

"No, thank you."

An hour later she stopped by the table again.

"Coffee?"

"Sure."

She set the cup down on the table and paused.

"Are you okay?"

Her question startled me. "Umm, yes."

"Because you don't seem like the type of person to hang out at Denny's all night," she said. "Yeah, we get lots of students who stay here to study, but school hasn't started yet. So why are you here?"

She set her dark brown eyes directly on me.

Ah shit. I'm going to get kicked out because I can't order more food.

I could tell she wasn't going to let me wriggle out from an answer, so I decided to shoot straight.

"I don't have anywhere to go and I can't afford a hotel. I need the money for my room and board this quarter. It's only for two nights until my friend gets here Wednesday, but I didn't know what else to do."

She nodded.

"Well, honey, why don't you make sure to stay right here in my station. I have the late shift tomorrow night, too, so you can just make sure to find me. I'm Georgina by the way."

She reached across the table and shook my hand.

And like that, I had a friend. Georgina took good care of me those two nights, never once charging me for the food I ate, stopping to sit and chat with me when the restaurant was empty, every so often setting ketchup and sugar bottles on the table for me to fill. She never once asked me why my family did not help me or why I never even considered asking. She was a quiet and kind companion, one without questions, and someone who seemed to accept that this was my eighteen-year-old normal.

When I did finally leave after the second night, she hugged me hard and asked that I come back. I promised her I would. As I was leaving, she stuffed some money into my hand.

"I want you to have this. I don't know why, I just do. And don't argue."

"Georgina, I can't take this."

"Of course you can, and you will. I don't know why, but I think good things will come for you. But later, not right now. And for whatever you've been through, remember there are good people in the world."

She smiled and walked me out the double doors of the restaurant. All I could do was cry as I walked back to campus, the sun just rising over the hill beyond.

Money was always such an ordeal. And for so long. I never had any and I always needed some. I was so embarrassed about it that I made fun of myself every chance I got—responding with *"alms for the poor"* or *"please, sir, have you any more?"* in a ridiculous sing-song Cockney accent whenever I felt especially humiliated. When I finally did get a job after college, one with a real paycheck, I wasn't quite sure what to do.

I had taken the first job I was offered, moving directly into an apartment upon graduation. I landed a great job in downtown Pasadena with an engineering company and simply could not believe what they were willing to pay me. The contrast from my senior year in college where I worked as a tutor, lifeguard, and for a short-time, as a waitress with Georgina was so stark that I found myself working extra hours, not because my boss demanded it, but because I felt so *guilty* over how much money I was making. I remained friends with Georgina all throughout my years at Riverside, and for many years after. We lost touch at some point along the way which caused me great heartache when I realized I had no idea where she was. These were the days without Internet and I never was successful in relocating her. My heart still stings when I think of her.

Once in the workforce, I think my boss was impressed with my dedication because I moved up quickly, earning a coveted spot on a project team. After about a year, I had saved quite a bit of money, at least by my standards. When I went home for a visit to see my mom that spring, I decided to do something nice for her. By then, the house on the hill was no longer new, it had been around for about nine years, and in that time had already started its downhill slide into neglect.

My mother still did not have doorknobs on her bedroom door, finished flooring on the stairs, or any landscaping. The stovetop did not work, and dog hair balled in every corner. The yard was covered in junk: discarded cardboard boxes, broken hibachi grills, PVC pipe, railroad ties, rusted cans, hundreds of empty plastic bottles, wood pallets, an endless array of utter crap. The one olive tree they had planted near the house during construction was now so overgrown that the branches blocked the entire side of the house, including the windows and doors. We no longer had any family events at the house, and I think my mom had utterly and completely stopped trying to keep up appearances.

I decided to go home one weekend not just to visit my mom, but because my parents were off to some ski patrol reunion for my father and needed someone to care for the animals. As Mother's Day was that same weekend, I planned to pay a crew to clean the yard as a gift. It was going to cost a couple thousand dollars, a vast sum of money in my mind, but I really felt like she would be pleased. She would at least have a clean line of vision to the house and could use the light to read by from the unblocked library windows.

The crew showed up early Saturday morning with a huge dumpster and about six guys. They spent the next two full days hauling junk to the dumpster, cutting back overgrown trees and generally cleaning up. By the time they left Sunday afternoon, it looked about as good as it ever would.

I knew my parents would be home before dark, and I was excited to see my mom's reaction. I never got to. When they drove into the driveway, my father jumped out of the car, leaving my mom behind.

"What. The. Fuck. Did. You. Do?"

He had that horrible grimace on his face that made my bowels weak. I was both confused and terrified.

"I-I had the yard cleaned. For m-mom," I stuttered.

"You had no right. No right at all," he snarled, advancing on me, his fists clenched.

"I just wanted to surprise her...I wanted..."

"You just, you wanted, you had no fucking right!"

With that he came for me, fists swinging at my head. I ran. I slammed through the kitchen door and into the dining room where I stood behind the table. The dogs barked and scrambled around us. He came running after me still screeching with words like "I am going to kill you" and "you will regret this" spewing out of his mouth. He kicked one dog so hard it fell on its side, yelping. By then I did not focus on the words, only knew to keep the table between us as he screamed threats at me.

As I kept running in circles around the table, I think he realized he wasn't going to catch me. When he left the room *for the gun box,* I called 911. I told them my father was going to kill me. And hung up the minute they had the address. Since my father had parked behind my car and I could not get out, I ran about fifty yards down the hill and waited for the police. When the patrol car finally arrived, I waved them down and explained what had happened.

The officer had to ask me three times what was going on.

"Your father wants to kill you because you *cleaned the yard*?" he asked.

"Yes."

"That does not make sense. Are you sure something else didn't happen?"

"No, that is what happened. He threatened to kill me. And he has a gun. This isn't the first time."

"Because you cleaned the yard?"

"Yes. And now I can't get my car. So I can leave."

Th officer shook his head.

"Okay, wait here. Let me go talk to him."

While the first cop went to talk to my father, the second cop stayed with me. As we stood there, he asked me to go through the sequence of events with him one more time. As I did, he took notes. After about fifteen minutes the other cop came back. He motioned for the second cop to come over. The two of them stood conferring for several minutes. By then I was cold. And wanted to go home. My apartment never sounded so good.

The first cop walked over to me. He had a really odd expression on his face.

"So, technically your father has every right to kick you off his property. It is his property. So I recommend you get your car and leave."

"Okay."

"We will escort you, so you can get your car."

"Okay."

The cops walked into the yard with me and told me to wait by my car while they collected my purse and keys.

When the first cop handed me my keys, he looked at me.

"And Miss? I really don't understand how anyone can get so mad about what you did. I think you tried to do a nice thing. But he is mean-crazy, and you need to stay away. He's dangerous."

I just nodded and got in my car. I shivered most of the drive home and took a long hot bath. For the next several years I stayed away. My mom never did acknowledge her gift.

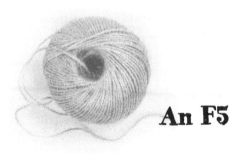

An F5

Delaney loves her swim lessons at the local YMCA. It seems a lifetime ago she took lessons with her father. Swim lessons in the south are indoors, so vastly different from the huge outdoor pools of California, where she and her father would splash and freckle in the sun. These indoor pools reek of chlorine and mold, and I find it so odd that we exit the water when lightning strikes, even though we are inside. And lightning strikes a lot around here. The swim instructor suggests that Delaney join our local swim team, the Hammerheads, so I sign her up the following week.

I use the team swim practice as an opportunity to get to know my neighbors, their kids, some of the locals. It does not go well. Once again, I can tell they distrust me, and the swim meets are agony, hours spent in the blistering southern sun, trying to get Delaney to her backstroke and freestyle lanes on time. None of the mothers help me like they help the other kids. When Delaney forgot her swim cap at one meet, not a single family had an extra, and it was the coach who finally mustered an old cap from his bag. By then, I was becoming accustomed to the snubs. This was going to be a long haul.

There was only one other family treated worse than we were: the Jamisons. Brett Jamison was a tall, successful CFO who worked for a law firm in downtown Chattanooga. His wife, Amy, an accountant, was lovely, fit, intelligent, and obviously adored her kid. Their son Matthew was a good swimmer, younger than Delaney by a year, and a very sweet kid. The only problem with the Jamisons was that they were black. And the only black family on the swim team. In rural Georgia, being black was apparently still a thing to be noticed and avoided even in the twenty-first century, for the Jamison's sat by themselves every single practice and every single meet. I found it abhorrent. So, of course, I had to meet them.

I sat down with them one practice while Delaney and Matthew swam intervals. I think they were surprised when I did. I found out after talking with both for a while that they had understood coming into this they were likely to be ostracized, despite their education and success, they had chosen to live here for the duration of Brett's transfer. They felt this was a good professional move for them. We ended up staying friends throughout that swim season, sharing a canopy during swim meets and pot-lucking our food for the day. Amy was an incredible cook.

I finally learned over time the town was still segregated, that an entire three block radius to the east of downtown was literally called "Blacktown." It was incredible to me—this was 2011 after all—but not to the Jamisons. They took it all in stride, laughing at my liberal outrage. When a F5 tornado hit that spring and wiped out much of the downtown, the Jamison's left. I was on an airplane when news of the tornado scrolled across my phone, and I had never been so frightened in my life. Delaney was at home with Diana and her kids, so I immediately called the house. About two seconds after Diana answered the phone, it went dead. My flight was diverted to Nashville and for two hours I was frantic. Diana, Delaney, and Diana's kids were fine, but the tornado had wiped out many of our neighbor's homes. I will never forget the smell of burnt lumber and the sight of flattened houses when I arrived at dawn, escorted by the fire department. It was surreal. I was most definitely not in California anymore.

Diana's husband was cheating on her. I knew this because he had let it slip. He did not know I knew, and Diana certainly did not know I knew. Unbelievably, and against all sanity, he had been cheating on Diana with the same wife he had when he and Diana started cheating. He and Diana had been married seventeen years, and I learned that this had been going on for years. I found out not because he let it slip in a "I want to be caught" way, but because he was stupid, and thoughtless.

I had taken a trip to Seattle. Diana's husband offered to drop me off at the airport and take my car back to my house. I had always thought he was incredibly thoughtful and mannered, generous with his time and his efforts. I could not have been more wrong. When I returned from Seattle I noticed that my car had been keyed. A long, deep scratch all the way along the driver's side. My car was not all that old, and the scratch really upset me. When I asked him what had happened, he said he had no idea, that he had dropped the car off at my house and hadn't seen it since.

Only three days later I happened to be at their house for a party. I still had a few odds and ends in the pool house and wanted to get them loaded into my car. He was inside the pool house on his phone.

"But why, Sherry? You knew it wasn't my car."

I could tell he was angry, upset. I also knew Sherry was the name of his ex-wife, because Diana had regaled me with stories of how she had "stolen" him from her. After seventeen years, she still talked about this woman. I stood just outside the window and listened.

"I *told* you I had to be there. I had to be with her and the kids. There was nothing I could do!"

By now I had a pretty good idea of what was going on.

"But still, you didn't have to key her car. C'mon, you really think she won't figure that out? She's her friend for christsake. They talk. Jesus, Sherry. It wasn't enough that you wanted to fuck in her bed?"

I took a sharp intake of breath. He was using my house? Where my daughter lived? Where I lived? What?

And with that, I knew. I knew that their family was a charade of epic proportion. That this man who pretended to love and cherish Diana's kids from her first marriage, who had a daughter with Diana now, who had spent the last seventeen years posing as a father, was a charlatan. His cloak fell from his shoulders and I knew him for exactly who he was.

I left the party immediately and took Delany home, feigning a stomachache. That evening I lay in my bed staring at the ceiling. My mind raced and I could not fathom what I had done to get here. What I thought was a solid, stable, healthy environment had turned out to be as toxic as Chernobyl, the two-headed snakes beginning to emerge. I didn't know why I thought this place would be different, that these people would be different. Their stories were no more noble than my own, their facades equally as carefully constructed as mine. I was so out of my element here it was stunning, breathtaking even. It did not matter that the mist from the lake soothed me in the morning as I drank my coffee, it did not matter that Delaney screamed with joy when she found a goose egg hidden in the reeds, I had once again surrounded myself with the fractured.

A Beautiful Mother

My brother and I entered portions of our childhood deeply interconnected, knowing in some innate way to blend together like blue-belly lizards on summer slate. Our games had two volumes—silent if our father was around, and as raucous as nightshrill mockingbirds when he was not. On occasion my mother would join in, and in those moments allowances could be made.

My mother loved to read, both alone and aloud to us. Many days we would come home from school to find her sitting in her paisley blue chair in the living room, hair up in a bouffant do, cigarette smoke swirling around her, deep in her book, dinner and homework forgotten. She loved all things science fiction, and our house was filled with Asimov, Bradbury, and Vonnegut. She was an avid fan of *Star Trek* long before it was cool, and followed every episode closely. While we were too young to truly understand either the plotline or the characters, we did understand that she enjoyed her time in their alien worlds.

At night she would read to us from classic Grimm and Aesop's Fables, literary classics or simply make something up. My brother and I lived for these gray minutes, knowing we had her full attention and that within the cool cadence of her voice lay a certainty that those moments were our own.

The Owl and the Pussycat by Edward Lear was a timeworn favorite, and she would often recite it to us in a butchered German accent. No matter how many times she did it, my brother and I reacted the same, howling with laughter and begging for more.

"Zee owl and zee pussycat, zey vent to sea..."

"Ahahahahahahahahahahahahaha..."

"On zee beevutiful peagreen boad..."

We were not allowed to sleep in each other's rooms, so my mother would alternate sitting on the edge of our beds. One of us would listen from the hallway just outside, shivering both from the draft and our glee, while the other took full advantage of the warm nearness of her body.

"Puzzy said to zee Owl, oh you elegant fowl, how charmingzy sveet you zing! Oh let us be married, too long vee haf tarried, but vat shall vee do for a ring?" With this, she would pull back the covers, ostensibly searching for that ring.

"Zee ring? Vere is zee ring?"

Amongst bong trees and piggywigs we sailed, imaginations soaring, hearts suffuse, and for the moment sane. We would suck deep of the smell of her, lush earth, Ponds face cream and a slight spritz of Benson & Hedges. She was a goddess, a medicine woman, curator of small intellects and ringmaster of wistful lion cubs facing biting whips. She was our toehold to reality and the cliff-edge to which we held. We loved her then with every fiber of our being, so strongly that we vibrated with it.

She was an avid seamstress, and her skill and artisanship was at times mind-bending. She could make anything: belts, purses, jackets, prom dresses, kilts. As I got older, I understood this for the lost art that it was, and I mourned for my inability to replicate any of her ingenuity. My senior year, while girls around me fluttered at mall shops, my mother and I went to Hancock's Fabric Shop and selected an elegant Butterick dress pattern more appropriate for a New York art gala than a high school dance. She spent weeks making that dress, complete with an embroidered bodice and intricate sleeve. It was beautiful.

She bounced between crafts at will, from stained glass to playing the bag pipe; if she was interested, she would try it. Both desultory and beautiful, art pieces languished about our house as unlikely in context as ballerinas in a rainforest— an embroidered Van Gogh's "Starry Night," an oil on canvas still life with lemon, hammered pewter chanteuse atop a swan. It never once occurred to my brother or me that her abilities were vast and enviable, it was just who she was: gifted, original, and as rare as bismuth crystal.

There were many instances when we were very young that his fury became too much, and she would retreat, goslings in tow. Her chosen favorite spot was a Holiday Inn on the California coastline about thirty miles from our home, a place reminiscent of old Hollywood and sordid affairs, just far enough from spouses and LA jobs and just near enough to return at a moment's notice. The faded rooms smelled of cigarettes and stale mussels, but the beach was long and glorious, with tendrils of shore-tossed kelp looped across driftwood, and killdeer and avocets scuttling from the tides. This shoreline was a place for mothers and children and at no point did anyone ever ask where our father was. John and I were practically lunatic during these trips, running up and down the boardwalk like sun-crisped banshees, our faces smeared with melted ice cream, oblivious to our mother just below us staring out to sea.

I suppose her penchant for the beach had much to do with her upbringing. Like so much of her, her birthplace was in itself unique. She was born on Catalina Island, where she and her brothers were raised among sealions and ferries. Her father owned a restaurant on the island, a much-loved getaway for 1930s era ingénues and movie stars like Stan Laurel, Johnny Weissmuller, and Betty Grable. Grainy black and white photos fill family albums, their scalloped edges and careful descriptions reminiscent of bawdy laughter, Gin Rickeys and sunburns.

There are pictures of gallant young men with arms slung lazily over bronzed shoulders, high-waisted bathing suits and Avalon in its infancy. Yachts and dinghies bob languidly in the background, anchored haphazardly, scoffing at the carefully monitored mooring protocol of today. In the corner, one carefully applied snapshot of my mother and her siblings standing on green, slippery rocks and shouting at arriving ferries for tourists to throw coins from the deck, delighting in their admiration and showing off like so many lichen-covered gymnasts. Page after page of these photos resonate with images of Clark Gable's mutiny and Dorothy Lamour's hurricane, their black-filigreed pages crumbling, the gold-corded binding slowly relinquishing both its hold and its complexion.

My mother was a graceful swimmer, having learned on this island. I remember her smile when I mentioned it was time to teach my daughter.

"My dad took us out in a rowboat and dumped us in the harbor," she explained, "then we had to swim to shore or get to the buoy."

I stared at her in horror. "Are you kidding me? That has to be a joke."

"No, I'm not kidding. It's how we learned." She was grinning as she told me, stealing glances at my daughter as we talked. "Maybe you should give it a try."

"So thrashing, flailing kids in the water didn't worry your dad?" I asked. "What about sharks? Or drowning?"

She laughed aloud. "No, we didn't worry about those things then. It wasn't until *Jaws* came out that people started worrying. Yes, there were probably sharks and jellyfish and all sorts of biting creatures, but that just wasn't the way we thought back then."

Needless to say, and as I've already mentioned, my daughter took lessons at the YMCA.

This profound connection to Catalina remained throughout my mother's twenties. In an era when women were expected to be marrying and settling down with children, she set about sailing her sixty-foot schooner, *The Seabird*, between Long Beach and Isthmus Cove every weekend.

In one worn photo, she stands at the bow with her fingers wound around the forestay, an elegant mix of defiance and fortitude. Her hair is tousled and tomboyish, and she is looking to the horizon, an inscrutable expression on her face.

I suppose it was during these years that she cemented her appetite for both turmoil and alcohol, living a racetrack life of harbor bars, studio parties, and hangovers. She was someone I would love to have had as a friend, a person so vibrant you could not help but feel awake, both wildly aware of the speed at which she traveled and painfully cognizant of the danger it posed. It was this woman who ensnared everyone around her, each awestruck by her mastery of crossword puzzles, her partiality for Afghan dogs, and her strained relationship with all things electric. Reader, philosopher, lover of geometry, she was a creature to be guarded, missing only her Anubis.

My brother and I saw only the barest glimpses of this person, but we inherently understood that she was composed of the most intricate fabric, one of iridescent colors, byzantine weaves and a texture almost painful to the touch. While we knew her as our mother, we did not really know her, instead gravitating just outside the pull of her dying star, our galaxy small in comparison. We understood, too, that even as her children, we were also somehow separate and apart, and despite our yearning for a profound connection, it never materialized, leaving both of us inexplicably stunned.

I will never, ever forget the Sunday after one of our infamous Holiday Inn excursions when she perched us down on the couch in our living room, my father sitting in the chair across. She sat erect, her voice clear and her blue eyes almost onyx.

"How do you feel about your father and I getting a divorce?"

John and I looked at each other in abject shock. All we could do was cry. I was seven and my brother, six. The chosen interpretation of those tears was that of resistance, as opposed to its reality of relief. And in that one moment, the dissonance of our future was secured.

But we never heard the word divorce again.

Mothers and Daughters

My grandmother Allesandra did not approve of my mother. But that was not always the case. From birth through her teenage years, my mother enjoyed a close-knit family and the adoration of both parents. Living on a small island off the coast of California, the family did not leave often, instead relying on daily ferries for supplies and attending the local schools. My grandfather, Samuel, owned a restaurant named *The White Cap*—a popular destination for tourists and locals alike, and with his Hollywood good looks he was well-liked both by his customers and his children. This grandfather I never met was a hands-on dad before that was even a thing, spending hours in the water teaching his kids to fish and swim, playing catch with his sons, and doting on my mom.

She was a beautiful baby, with curly hair and enormous blue eyes. Everyone on the island knew the family, and my grandmother was especially proud of her daughter, dressing her in Shirley Temple bows and frilly pink dresses, impeccable each Sunday service. But it was Samuel my mother adored. From the time she was born, the two of them were inseparable. She followed at his heels everywhere he went, and most days he could be found somewhere on the island, running errands back and forth to his restaurant, baby daughter atop his shoulders. Other days he could be spotted fishing in the Isthmus, baby Anne sitting quietly in the front of the dinghy. They were cut from the same swath of fabric, a shimmery ocean blue festooned with threads of silver, lightweight, diaphanous, fluttering in the offshore breeze. As she grew, it was her father my mother went to with skinned knees and tattered crushes, and it was his daughter that my grandfather chose as his favorite companion. From him she learned to sail and navigate the ocean, spearfish just outside the harbor, cook and test recipes in *The White Cap* kitchen, and it was because of him that she decided she wanted to live on that island forever.

Their home in Avalon was a two-story green-and-white colonial on the corner of Beacon and Lower Terrace, just below the Wrigley house perched high on the cliffs above. As children, my mother and her brothers ran up and down the streets of the town with abandon, playing on the steps of the Casino and visiting the Catalina Bird Park whenever company would come to the island to visit. Later, the mother that I knew always loved the screech of peacocks, at one point even entertaining the idea of owning a pair. On the island, she had a particular favorite white peacock at the Bird Park, pulling at her father the minute they neared its cage. My mother may have adored that bird simply for the fact that her father told her its piercing blue eyes matched her own. Or perhaps she adored it because it was unique and rare, much like herself. In later years, the family restaurant became famous for its cocktail *The White Peacock*, and it was said that John Wayne ordered it on every visit.

Allesandra and Samuel ran the restaurant together, spending interminable hours cooking, cleaning, serving, and keeping the books. My grandmother ran the front of the house, while my grandfather the back. It was a difficult business, eating up many hours and causing them significant stress, but the kids barely noticed, spending most days on the beach just in front when not in school. As they got a little older, my mother and her two older brothers helped out, bussing tables, running linens to the laundromat and serving as host or hostess at the entrance. Come summer, when the island was packed, ferries full of tourists landing every few hours, passengers starving and ready to enjoy the island with all it had to offer, the entire family staffed the restaurant, falling in an exhausted heap at the end of the weekend.

As a young teen, my mother and her friends would join ferryloads of their friends from the mainland; sunning on the beach, posing for pictures at every possible opportunity, roasting hotdogs with the harbor master, hiking the island to the Wrigley Tomb and cactus garden just outside, rowing to the Isthmus, lunching at St. Catherine's hotel, swimming, kayaking and diving. My mother favored the modern—and much less modest—two-piece bathing suit of the era with velvet panels and metal zippers, a skort-styled bottom and banded top. Approaching almost six-foot by the time she was fourteen, she looked like a model, her long legs and wavy dark hair the admiration of all the boys and the envy of all the girls. Her teenage photo album is full of these pictures—Inkie, Betty, Flip, Dickie—their bodies brown from the California sun, laughing, goofing off, faces covered in Noxzema cream by the end of the day. Her photo captions tell a tale of a happy girl, self-effacing, funny, surrounded by friends, social and outgoing, alive and vibrating.

As I study her album, I cannot help but think of Delaney, for the physical and attitudinal resemblance is uncanny. I see Delaney in the smirk on her face as she glances up from the beach blanket, the upturned smile, the full and sensuous lips. I hear Delaney in the bubbly world view, self-criticism and empathy for others. And I promise myself that I will not end up missing my adult child as horribly as I miss my mother of those years.

My grandparents tried to protect their children from their troubles, but when my mom turned fifteen, Samuel fell seriously ill. For most of her childhood, he had suffered from a "sensitive constitution," his stomach often upset and accompanied by a tight pain in his chest. Despite running a restaurant, he could eat only mild foods, and over time, began to lose weight. The stress of the job, over a decade in the kitchen, together with raising and providing for four kids became too much, and he began to steadily decline. Although medical help was available on the island, he and his wife chose to pray for relief rather than seek help. Allesandra worried constantly about him, and as he got sicker, the restaurant began to suffer as well, until finally, the family was forced to close its doors. Without an income they were forced to move to the mainland, to June Street in Los Angeles with my grandmother's parents, where Allesandra took a job with the county clerk's office. As it turns out, "sensitive constitution" was merely forties-speak for ulcers, and my grandfather died within the year.

His death came as a shock to my sixteen-year-old mother. She had just started her sophomore year at Hollywood High and was already struggling with the loss of her island home. She knew her father was ill, but her parents had woven a tale of "taking a break" rather than telling their children the truth about the severity of his illness. He died at home, and when my mother arrived after school to find her mother sobbing in the kitchen, she told me later that she could think of nothing to say, nothing to think, nothing to do. She said she simply froze. She could not fathom that the man she adored above all else, the father to whom she shared every detail of her life and dreams, the man she considered invincible, was gone.

The months following his death were a blur, with arrangements and changes and an array of relatives in and out of the house, offering condolences, advice, but little in the way of money or help. As a result, my grandmother was forced to work two jobs, leaving her children in the care of her own elderly parents while she worked. She missed most of my mother's descent into severe depression, focusing instead on keeping food on the table and spending her few remaining hours becoming an even more devout Christian Scientist.

My mother's response to her father's death was to stop caring. About anything. Her grades began to drop, and at one point, she stopped attending classes altogether. She began to drink and smoke cigarettes with friends on the weekends, eventually hanging out with some of the faster Hollywood crowd. In her own fog of pain, Allesandra was both unaware and unable to help. Lost was the ebullient girl of the Catalina years, full of life and promise, now replaced by her new self, the woman captured in almost every photo album of her adult life: Anne with a drink in her hand, face puffy, eyes lidded. Always.

By the time she was eighteen, she and her mother barely spoke. Allesandra was both angry with, and disappointed in, her daughter. She saw that she was making poor choices, understood that she hung out with the wrong crowd, but was unable to do much about it. My mother, in turn, viewed her mother as weak and ineffectual, her reliance on the church supplanting her love for her children. At first they argued, and later, ignored each other. The combination of my mother's distress, her teenage angst and hormonal rages, coupled with my grandmother's stress and fear, turned lethal. Theirs had become a relationship with a half-life, poisonous like uranium but destined to stick around for billions of years.

My mother barely graduated high school. Allesandra informed her upon graduation that she either needed to attend college or move out, that she was not going to be party to my mother's poor judgment. My mother's GPA may have been abysmal, but she tested spectacularly. She was admitted to UCLA as a math major. She spent the next year-and-a-half continuing to party and did little to improve her education. At twenty, she dropped out.

In the meantime, Allesandra had met a new man. His name was Alphonse and he was to become the grandfather, Gramps, of my childhood. My mother detested him, finding him a sad, sloppy replacement of her own father. She made her feelings quite clear until it became obvious to my grandmother that the two of them could not live under the same roof. My mother's response to her mother's ultimatum to get along with Alphonse was to promptly marry the bartender at the bar where she hung out.

Harry was a drunk. A happy-go-lucky drunk, but a drunk nonetheless. He was well known as a bartender, popular and well-liked, but offered little in the way of financial or emotional support. They stayed married for a number of years, with my mom finding work as a film editor, and propping up the majority of their marriage. These were some of the years of her fast life, racing cars and sailboats, seeking her happiness through adrenaline and alcohol. Interestingly, my mom never lived far from her own mother, always within a few miles, and always in constant touch despite their differences. They may have disapproved of each other, but they certainly remained wound tightly together. I suppose my relationship with my mother mirrors their own, and I find myself distraught by how the generational threads from both my father and my mother entangle me in a preordained future.

My grandmother did not approve of Harry, the lifestyle or the drinking. She continued to remain involved in the church, sinking deeper and deeper into church-related activities and people. In the early seventies, she moved from Los Angeles to Ventura County upon her retirement as a court clerk. Gramps had also retired from the Gas Company by then and the two of them lived a quiet life with their orchard and bird feeders. By then, my mother's marriage to Harry had run its course.

She met and married my father only a couple years later and immediately moved within a few miles of her mother. I was born shortly thereafter, and my birth brought my mom and grandmother close once again. Albums are filled with photos of the two of them dressing me, playing with me, teaching me to swim, hiking with me in the mountains. During my infancy, my parents reached a short-lived accord, the drinking and violence had ebbed, and it seems my mom was happy for a while. My brother was born eleven months later.

Allesandra knew that my mother would disappear on occasion. She saw the bruises and witnessed firsthand my father's temper. I do not think she was aware of his rage directed in our direction, or at least I would like to think so. Maybe she knew how bad it was, and maybe she didn't. But those were the days of silence and looking the other way, when men operated with impunity within their own domains, far before anyone thought to stick their noses in other people's business and *certainly not report* anything at all. Yet the two of them never discussed it. Never once did they discuss the possibility of my mother leaving my father. My mother continued to present to the world and her immediate family that all was fine, that never mind, don't look here, not too closely anyway, we are fine and dandy, thank you, and my grandmother chose to believe it. I think she had to.

My mother loved her mother, that much is clear. When my grandmother fell ill at the end of her life, it was my mom who came to her side, visiting in the hospital every day, taking care of her at home when she returned. My grandmother refused medical assistance and medication despite her illness due to her Christian Science beliefs, but it was my mom who ultimately snuck her medication in lime Jell-O, innately understanding that without it she would die much sooner.

When Allesandra did die, my mother was bereft. She retreated even further into the bottle and no longer stood up to our father in any way. I was twelve at the time, and I remember watching my mother relinquish what little zest in life she had left. It was about that time that she stopped worrying about her weight and her appearance. She no longer wore makeup, stopped having her hair and nails done, and stopped participating to any real extent in my brother's and my lives. She became numb to us, to our father, to the world. I missed her then and I miss her now. I miss them both. My middle name, Allesandra, is a constant reminder of just how much.

Johnny Appleseed

As an adult I really struggled with John and who he had become. I did not understand his life, his choices, or his constant lying. It had become somewhat of a joke by then, a wink and a nod, there goes John again, off on his flights of fancy, nope, he didn't have that job, no he didn't ski in Patagonia, sorry, no, that never happened. Throughout the years, he would fade in and out of my life, showing up every so often with a new wife or a new baby, only to have that set disappear in the mist and be replaced by another. He would call every so often to brag about a new job, only to find out later he had been fired. He hopped from job to job, girlfriend to girlfriend, wife to wife, never really setting hooks into any sort of identity. It was difficult for me to follow, so I stopped trying. And when he no longer had contact with his children, I simply stayed away. I found his path to be circuitous and steep, traveled at extremely high altitudes, and I could not get enough oxygen into my lungs to follow.

I wanted a relationship with him. I truly did. I wanted to know him and be proud of him, but he was so deeply troubled that I alternated between bouts of sadness and pity, followed by annoyance and disgust. As the years wore on, I felt that he had become a professional victim, reveling in his inability to accomplish anything because everyone around him was determined that he would fail. His lack of ownership in anything remotely concerning his own poor decisions drove me batshit crazy, and I was exhausted from trying to help. He was also a raging alcoholic, not unlike our mother in his constant commitment to alcohol and the warm buzz it brought him. He told me countless times he was sober, although I knew better, and he fooled no one. For decades, I circled around him in an ever-increasing wide circumference, only intersecting as life brought us together. Harshly, given a lack of familial tie, I doubt I would have sought him out as a friend.

Despite all of my misgivings and irritation, I still looked forward to seeing him on the infrequent occasions we got together. He was so like my parents in that way—his ability to both immediately kindle hope and shortly thereafter extinguish it entirely. I remember one winter when Delaney was about six traveling to a local mountain where he was a ski instructor. He had yet another girlfriend by this time, and the two of them lived on the mountain where they raised her three kids from three previous boyfriends. While I did not necessarily understand or approve of their lifestyle, I did want Delaney to learn to ski from him. He was an excellent skier, Delaney adored *Unca John*, and I hadn't seen him in quite a while. Much like with our parents, I always held out hope that something would be different this time.

When we got to the mountain, he had lift tickets arranged for us and lessons set up for Delaney. He spent much of the day with her and by the end, she was plowing down the beginner slopes like nobody's business, switching between pizza and French fry formations with her tiny skis, an earsplitting grin on her windburned face. When the chairlifts stopped operating, his girlfriend met us in the lodge for après ski, and the four of us sat around the table eating cheeseburgers and sharing stories of the day.

As we sat there, another ski instructor came to our table and asked my brother to come with him to the ski school. When my brother returned, his face was thunderous. He had been fired. For drinking on the job. I was mortified. On the one day in over four years since I had seen him, after he had moved to this tiny ski community not more than a month or two earlier, he was now jobless. Again. As he began to sputter and spew mutinous, red-faced invectives, I left with Delaney. We didn't say goodbye and I had no good explanation for Delaney on the ride down the mountain as to what had just happened.

What saddened me more than the actual firing was his spin of it later. Over time, what I had witnessed firsthand morphed into a concocted fable of how he had been set up, screwed over, fired for no apparent reason by people who had it out for him, yet another in a long string of jobs he had lost due to other people and never *not ever* himself. My take on this latent yarn was one of disdain, rather than any empathy or understanding, simply because I had grown up in that very same fucked-up house and I seemed to be able to keep a job and pay my bills. So why couldn't he? Why was his life so much more impossible and fraught with problems than my own? It all sounded like a load of bullshit, and it made me angry.

It wasn't until just before our mother's death that I finally asked him what it had been like for him growing up in that house, rather than just assuming I knew what impact it had

had on his life, his self, his soul. What he told me froze the marrow in my bones. It changed my perspective entirely. And I kicked myself for not asking sooner.

Growing up, I called my brother Johnny Appleseed simply because I had seen the Disney short film in grammar school, and well, because his name was John. But the weird thing was, I never called him that name out loud, either to him or anyone else. Ever. I only used it in my head. And only when I liked him. Or felt spine-wrenching pity for him, which sadly was often, especially growing up.

John received the bulk of our father's wrath. He was horrid to me, but he was murderous towards my brother. It seemed as though he absolutely hated him and had no qualms about showing it. Even very young, I instinctively understood this dynamic and did what I could to protect him, which wasn't much at home. I overcompensated by guarding him at all times in grammar school. He was not any bigger than the other kids until he turned about ten, and up until then he was picked on regularly. I think the kids in school intuited that he was the runt of our litter and bullied him as often as possible. He was one grade below me in school, so throughout kindergarten and grammar school I had him under my watch.

Back then, he was a quiet and soft-spoken boy, sensitive and caring, reminding me of a tiger cub, eyes barely open and wobbling on its new legs, adorable just before it grows into the killing machine it will become. He cried often and was the boy who would try to nurse a baby bird to health after falling from a tree, stuffing a shoe box full of cotton and feeding it from a dropper for days. I knew he looked up to me, many times sitting at my feet as I would read to him from *Aesop's Fables* or *Grimm's Fairy Tales* on the family room floor. The brother of my youngest years liked goldfish and trains, olive and cream cheese sandwiches, our dog Sergeant, and was deathly afraid of the dark.

We attended grammar school about three-quarters of a mile away from our house. John and I would walk back and forth together to school, across an intersection and through a weed-filled field every morning and every afternoon for six years, brown lunch bags swinging at our sides. When John entered third grade, it did not take long for the other boys in his class to figure out he was a target. One afternoon a pack of them followed him from school to the field just outside school where he and I met for the walk home, and like hyenas, circled around him waiting to pull out his entrails.

As I walked from my fourth-grade classroom to the field, I noticed a clump of boys pushing another kid around. It was about six-to-one, and even before I knew it was my brother, I didn't like it. As I got closer, I saw it was John, and before I could even form a coherent thought in my head, I dropped my backpack and rushed them. All six of them. I think I may have gone a little bit crazy, because I beat the living crap out of two of those boys.

This was back in the day when parents and teachers did not get involved in schoolyard politics, and when the other boys saw it was a girl and a *crazy* girl at that, they backed off. The two I had beaten remained on the ground, noses snotty with dirt, backpacks tangled. John stood away from the fight, eyes wide, tears forming. I think the shock rather than my fists were what kept those boys down.

As the first boy got up, I noticed he had a pocket watch in his hand. My eyes narrowed.

"Where did you get that?"

He said nothing. The other boy answered.

"He took it from your brother."

"That's my Gramps' watch. He gave it to him. You had *better* give it back."

As the kid walked slowly over to my brother and handed him the watch, I gave him his final warning.

"If *any* of you touch my brother again, I'll kill you."

I think they believed me, or maybe heard something of my father in my voice, because my brother never had any more trouble. At least not from those boys, and certainly not while I was in the same school.

During those same years, my brother and I played mostly by ourselves and occasionally with the kids who lived on our block. When we weren't outside playing tag or hide-and-seek until the streetlights came on, we played one of our favorite games we called "Cougar." The object of Cougar was simple—we were both cougars in the wild, desperately eking out our survival in a tumultuous world full of dangerous skunks or rabies-riddled foxes with little in the way of food. We would prowl around our rooms, alternately stalking prey or attacking each other in rowdy, claw-filled battles complete with guttural growls and tumbles from our boulder-covered beds. We loved that game and played it every chance we got, primarily in John's room since he had a bench where he built model airplanes that we could hide underneath.

Our other favorite game was "Bucking Bronco." This too, was a simple game, but one we didn't play as often because we could get in trouble for being too loud on weekend mornings while my parents slept off hangovers. One of us would be the "bronco" while the other was the cowboy. The bronco would lean over John's bed, hooves on the ground, with a bandana in its mouth as the bridle. The cowboy's job was to stay in the saddle all throughout the wild bucking. It was a tough rodeo, but we muscled through, horses sweaty and cowboys invariably in the dirt. Most times we would collapse in fits of laughter, other times one or the other of us would bang our head on the wall after getting launched by the bronco. It was through these games that we first learned how hilarity could make us cry in joy, erase hours past and a mother damaged, how we could feel something other than fear. It was a compensation we would use for the rest of our lives. These were the years that bound us inexorably together, finding ways to laugh amidst the sadness—blood siblings both by the open wounds on our bodies and in our hearts.

I began to see a change in my brother when he was around nine years old. It had become obvious he was utterly terrified of our father and desperate for our mother's attention. It made me jealous how much more attention he received from her, but thinking back now, I believe that had more to do with his efforts towards her, rather than hers towards him. I first noticed this when we played with the other kids on the block. After some game or another, one of the neighborhood kids would always end up getting hurt—a fall, a punch, a bloody ankle from a thrown rock. Invariably it was my brother who was blamed, and invariably, it was my brother who did it.

His fear, an oily, insidious disease within him, was growing and all he could do to temper it was to lash out. Sadly, for him and the kids around him, he lost many friends and ended up isolated, the parents on our block no longer allowing their kids to play with him. Over time, I became his only companion.

At thirteen, John switched to a new school district when we moved to the house on the hill. By then, I was a teenager and wanted nothing to do with him. That summer, after stealing my silver belt and making it into a hat band, he got a gun for his birthday. It was nothing special, but my brother took that gun everywhere. He spent hours and hours walking through the hills and orchards, killing anything he could find: squirrels, rabbits, birds, coyotes, deer, anything he could find with a beating heart. He told me he cried after killing each one of them but could not stop. Instead, he ceremoniously buried each and every single one and marked it with a tiny headstone made of stones and twigs. When he got home in the evenings, our father found more ways to beat him senseless, often breaking his nose, his arm, his collarbone, then setting the breaks himself. The cycle of deranged had begun in earnest by then, and my brother, frankly, had no chance.

It was about that time, my brother later told me, that together with his adolescent hormones, his fear and rage coalesced into a toxic blend of adrenaline-fueled idiocy and alcoholism. He started drinking daily, stealing booze from our parents' stash, and taking money from our mom's wallet. By then he was as tall as our father, and it was then that our father decided to teach my brother to box, not only using the lessons as a way to teach my brother to fight, but also as an excuse to beat him bloody. It was horrifying to watch.

His grades suffered and the only things that kept him out of jail were basketball and track. Even so, he added smoking pot to the mix and moved up from beer to whiskey and bourbon. It was a miracle he graduated, much less got a scholarship to play at Colorado. Once he finally got out of the house, he said, he was able to clear his head a little during his first year at school. Just as I had social revelations my first year away, he discovered many of the same. He found friends not as interested in numbing themselves and cautiously began to enjoy college life. The few times I talked to him on the phone that year I could hear the relief in his voice, even a spark of optimism. His grades were passing, he was going to start as a freshman on the Colorado team, and he had a beautiful new girlfriend studying pre-med. I held my breath for him. Not surprisingly, during Christmas break he decided not to come home, instead opting to stay in the athletes' dorms and play pickup games to stay sharp. I'm sure the girlfriend factored into his decision. It was during one of these pickup games that he fell and suffered a spiral compound fracture of his leg. It ended his basketball career, his scholarship, and any chance he had at escape.

Since he had no money and nowhere to go, he was forced back to our parents' house before his school year ended. It was several months later when I came home one weekend to arrange for my summer job. My brother said little during my visit, spending most of the hours in his room listening to music and smoking pot while staring out the window. The cast had come off by then and he had a slight limp. I had no idea what to say to him. I felt sickened that I had the chance to leave our house on Sunday while he did not, but whenever I tried to talk to him he just asked me to leave and close the door. The second night I was home things didn't go so well. Our mom was already two scotches in and our dad was in one of his moods. Each year that had passed since I had left for college had resulted in my tolerance straining at the seams, and I am sure my father could read it. That night I had earphones in my ears and was sitting at the kitchen counter rather than at the dinner table where my parents sat.

I guess my father had asked me a question, and I didn't hear it, so he yelled at me. When I heard him yelling, I pulled the earphones out of my ears and said "What!" which clearly was the wrong answer. He flew out of his chair and came straight for me. I was sitting in a high-backed stool at the counter, so I was trapped. As he screamed at me, he punched me in the back and head over and over, his ring slicing into my shoulder blade. I could feel the warm trickle of blood down my back. All I could do was cover my head and wait for it to end. All of a sudden, he was no longer hitting me.

My brother had come up behind him and thrown him to the floor. Now topping a cool six-foot-eight inches, he towered over our father, and despite his leg injury he was much stronger. He beat our father to a pulp that night, breaking two ribs and giving him a black eye and bloody nose, while my mother and I watched aghast in the corner.

As my father lay groaning on the floor, my brother told him he had better not touch either me or my mom ever again. Or he would kill him.

Not one of us picked him up from the floor. My mother went upstairs to her bedroom and I packed to leave. All I could hear was my brother sobbing in the bedroom next to me.

At nineteen, my brother decided that a career in drug-dealing was his next best option. He also decided to take the lying thing to a whole new level—who he was, what he had done, who he was going to be, and making sure nobody knew who he really was. The sad thing was, everyone knew he was lying and he ended up hanging out with other people equally as full of shit as he was. The drug experiment eventually led him to cocaine, where he became both addicted and a dealer. With his size and his anger, he made the perfect enforcer, beating the crap out of anyone who owed him money, hanging out with thieves, dealers, pimps, gang members, and a slew of other unsavory characters. He found himself in and out of jail numerous times, and I refused to bail him out.

For the remainder of his adult life, my brother continued to shed identities like snakeskin, moving from one relationship to another, joining motorcycle gangs, nurturing his alcoholism to the point of drinking a fifth of hard booze a day, and marrying whatever bartender or female that showed interest along the way, shrugging off each family as easily as the seasons required. I watched like a NASCAR spectator through all of it, his car flipping along the siderails every other race, his body flung on fire to the gravel. Again, I could not help. I could only watch as he became another, different version of our father; violent, full of hate and rage, storyteller of tall tales, ringmaster of broken spirits, purveyor of damaged goods.

But for all the similarities, he was different in some way. A *forgivable* way—at least in my eyes. For when it came to him, underneath it all, I felt sadness and pity and maybe even some understanding—even through my distaste. He was my Johnny Appleseed after all, my cowboy, my cougar in the wilds, the boy I had protected and loved all my life, who never really had any chance at all to become the soft-eyed man he should have been. He could have, should have been an accomplished—maybe even professional—athlete, he could have graduated from college and gone on to a fine career, he could have raised two happy healthy children with a loving wife. We could have shared one or two beers at a family barbeque, tipping our cans to our grand lives, our parents slowly fading into a quiet retirement, smiling at us from their shady spot beneath the tree.

He had deserved better and received worse. The world had truly taken a grand dump on him, and who was I to say he should be someone other than who he had become?

My Shell

There is one human interaction I am good at. Only one. And those are my friends. I accept that I suck at male intimacy, and I accept that I am not good at acquaintances, casual chitchat, or thousands of Facebook friends. I don't understand the allure of "likes" and "followers" and I don't even try. I don't attend parties where I know few people, and I avoid social interactions with people I find uninteresting. I find platitudinal memes ridiculous, emojis dull, texting impersonal, and all of it a poor substitute for picking up the phone or meeting for lunch. I suppose this labels me somewhat of a social media moron, a recluse, or a snob, but I don't really care. What I *am* good at are solid, interconnected, lifelong friends—the kind where you pick up like you never left off, even if years have passed with the friendship unattended. While I may have failed miserably at my marriages and just about every relationship with a man, I have a handful of girlfriends that I have known for most of my life. None of them know *all* of my secrets. That would be too much, too embarrassing, too humiliating. But they know a lot. And I wish I could tell them more.

Melinda was my touchstone during my high school years. We met at fourteen, just after we moved to the ten acres on the hill, and she remains one of my closest friends today. I didn't share with her what was happening behind closed doors back then because I didn't have the words to put to it, I didn't have the confidence or the knowledge, and mostly, I was afraid. Her family seemed so put together, so normal, that telling her what was happening at my house seemed an affront, an insult to their carefully crafted family, and I simply couldn't. I also could not imagine what would happen to me if I did say something. In my head at the time the concept of the unknown seemed far more frightening than the evil of the known. Would my mother disown me? Would I never see my brother again? Where would I be sent? These questions were unknowable, so I kept quiet.

Melinda's parents were Dutch immigrants with heavy accents and foreign hairdos. Her mother was beautiful, with pale skin and equally pale hair and eyes, lips permanently stained with coral lipstick. She always wore her hair up in a sweeping bouffant, tiny tendrils falling around her face as she cooked over the stove or pulled bread from the oven. She was a kind and attentive woman, deeply interested in her children, their whereabouts, their activities. She accepted my presence in her house charitably, perhaps innately understanding my need to be around and never questioning our friendship despite her deep Mormon faith and my resistance to it.

Melinda's father was tall and balding with heavy brows, handsome in a European way. He wore outdated clothes and shoes but was always impeccable, with his hair slicked back and his vests neatly buttoned. He came across as stern, but his kids had his number, not really buying into the act and teasing him regularly. He and his wife were humble, gracious people, and I found their company soothing, an emotional aloe vera for my burned family skin. Oftentimes, I would pretend they were my own parents, explaining away my dark hair and green eyes as a genetic outlier from the sea of blonde hair surrounding me at the dinner table, squabbling equally as loudly with Melinda and her siblings.

I wonder at times if I had gone to them with my truth what their response would have been.

Melinda and her family lived a few miles from us on their own parcel of land where they raised goats for milk and made most of their food from scratch. The goats were hilarious, finding ways to wreak havoc at every opportunity, the babies each spring melt-your-heart adorable. Melinda had two brothers and a sister, and their version of discord was a little bickering over who had to do the dishes and who got to use the car. It just wasn't palatable to mention a gun to my head in contrast.

I used every opportunity I had to spend time with Melinda and her family: weekends, evenings, Saturday night Mormon dances, Sunday morning church, even seminary in the pre-dawn hours before school. Although I desperately wanted to join the church to be a part of something, anything other than my own family, I could not bring myself to believe in the church teachings. I certainly adhered to their sense of family, harmony, and community, but could not wrap my head around my subservient role as a woman. I knew in my heart of hearts that if I joined I would be lying to myself, and I would be destined for spiritual disappointment.

None of that deterred me from developing a bond with Melinda that was indestructible. She never stopped trying to convert me, and I never stopped loving her for it. Between my horses and Melinda, I was able to survive high school and take gulps of air at the surface of my tormented ocean, my father's hurricane-swept waves washing over us, again and again. There were many occasions when I would simply show up at her house on horseback, excusing myself for just stopping by, when in reality I was fleeing yet another storm. I don't think she ever suspected anything, not for my ability to conceal anything, but more likely because the concept of that type of life was beyond her comprehension. Hers was a life of muted voices and clear expectations. Nothing remotely like my own.

We were editors of our senior yearbook together, played church basketball together, went to prom together, even wore matching outfits every chance we got. Neither of us was particularly popular, but everyone knew us, and mostly because we were always together. Even when I ruined my knee skiing and my father refused to let me see a doctor, I don't think she suspected anything out of the ordinary. She just knew I wasn't in school for a couple of weeks, and we carried on as though all was normal as soon as I returned. I think she just accepted the knee brace I wore as having been prescribed by a doctor and not something my father had ordered from his hospital catalog.

Our graduation was bittersweet, the excitement of leaving home followed by a profound sorrow that we would be apart. We cried many tears that summer with promises to write and made detailed plans for the next summer when we would be home. It was difficult for me to let go, and I was sincerely afraid that I would be unable to make another friend like her. She left for BYU two weeks before my departure south, and the day I watched her drive away I thought my chest would collapse.

As expected, we drifted apart my freshman year of college. She had another life and so did I. We did see each other that summer when we returned home but not nearly as often as we had in high school—primarily because we both had to work. I was busy as a lifeguard and she had found a job as a math tutor. Our schedules did not allow for much time together, and it was a difficult adjustment. Melinda was also planning to go on a mission to Ecuador that next year, and I knew I would not be able to talk to her during those two years. As a result, I didn't try as hard as I could have to connect. It made me sad. And lonely.

When she called me a few months into our sophomore year at college, I was surprised. I hadn't spoken to her at length in many months. I was still living in the dorms, and I answered after my roommate yelled down the hall that I had a call.

"Dorriah?"

"Mel? Is that you?" *I'd know that voice anywhere.*

"Yeah, it's me. Dorriah, I need you." She started to cry. Hard.

"Mel, what's wrong? Talk to me."

She was sobbing so hard I could barely make out the words. When I finally got her to calm down enough so that I could understand her, she told me her father had died of a heart attack, suddenly, at home. Her brother had tried to revive him but could not and the entire family was in shock. He was only forty-two years old.

"I'm coming," I told her. "I'll be there tomorrow."

I spent that entire evening looking for a car to borrow from someone, anyone. A guy I was dating finally agreed to loan me his car and I drove the next morning directly to her home where I spent the next two days helping out with funeral arrangements and holding her up. Melinda was the one who seemed the most torn up over the loss. She said little during my stay, simply holding my hand throughout the various services and sleeping up tight next to me at bedtime. She told me she had no idea how to go on, that her dad had been her anchor, the weight that held her to her beliefs and her faith. She shared stories of how he had taught her to milk the goats, squirting her in the face, laughing uproariously at her reaction, how he had taught her to waltz by first drawing a chalk pattern on their back patio, then having her stand on his feet to feel the rhythm, how he called her every week at school to check on her to see if she needed anything, and when she came home for the holidays always finding a way to slip her a few dollars. She said she was convinced she was the favorite and that she no longer wanted to get married because he would not be there to see it. We cried. A lot. I was drained by the time I got back to school.

And even though my parents lived five minutes away, I never did visit.

Over the years, Melinda and I reconnected through various marriages and children, moves and jobs. There were periods of time when we did not speak for years, but as soon as we did the time and distance fell away. Once our kids got a little older, we began to spend Thanksgivings together, making it a tradition, her family traveling from Utah to California each November, where Melinda and I would catch up poolside while our kids laughed and splashed around us.

I met Michelle my junior year of college. I had made a few friends in the dorms, but none of them really stuck as friends. Melinda was far away at BYU and basically inaccessible, so my best-friend status was pending. I met Michelle through her mom, Bobbie Jean Fernecki, who ran the tutoring center at the University. Bobbie Jean recognized me for the starving mutt that I was, and after knowing me for only a few months, began to invite me to her home every other Friday for dinner. Together with her husband, she lived in a gorgeous home at the base of the mountains just outside the college. Her house was filled with delightful bric-à-brac placed just so, perfectly matched upholstery, briskly swept floors, and thousands of photos of Michelle. I felt as though I had stepped into Disneyland's Candy Kitchen when I first saw it.

Bobbie Jean decided I needed to meet her daughter because, she said, "You two are like peas in a pod."

Michelle was a few years older than I and did not attend the university. To hear her tell it, the last thing she wanted to do was meet one of her mom's geeky tutor strays with "lettuce in their teeth." Bobbie Jean insisted. At the time I was semi-friends with a girl named Suzanne—who at eighteen decided to marry a navy guy. *Dumb.* Suzanne had very few friends and I felt sorry for her, so I decided to throw her a bachelorette party at a friend's apartment. Since she knew so few people, I invited my own friends, including Bobbie Jean, who, of course, forced Michelle to join.

I had never thrown a bachelorette party before, in fact had never been to one, but I certainly knew that raunchy things were supposed to happen. All I could think to do was to go to an adult store nearby and buy the most embarrassing things I could find. My goal was to create games that would embarrass everyone to the point of horror. These games included dick in a bottle, ass masters, and a round of "where is the weirdest place you've ever had sex?"

Keep in mind the audience was a handful of eighteen- and nineteen-year-old girls, Bobbie Jean, and Michelle, none of whom had ever met each other before this party. I didn't care. Decorum was thrown out the window, Fritos and bean dip were set out on tables, and magazines entitled *German Urine Olympics* and *Pepita: Sorceress of the Anus* were distributed. We laughed so hard someone may have peed a little, and I think Suzanne definitely got more than she had bargained for. *Oh, and of course my "weirdest place" was on a horse...*

As she tried to insert the hot dog hanging from a string around her waist into the coke bottle, Michelle looked up at me and smiled. "I knew I'd like you." We've been as close as sisters ever since.

Michelle is the only person I have ever shared some— *not all*—of my childhood with. Over time, over decades, I have rationed it out in pieces, slowly, carefully, not wanting her to abandon me because it was all too much, or because I was just a little too damaged. She always rallied, finding ways to support me when no one else seemed able, showing up when I was most alone. Ours is an entirely irreverent relationship with little in the way of boundaries or etiquette. And that is what makes it work. We have been each other's bridesmaids, thrown each other baby showers, slept in hospital rooms, cleaned up sick messes, and cared for each other's kids through our twenties, thirties, and forties, and intend to remain together until death do us part.

We aren't perfect to each other, or for each other, but we try. We understand that each of us is like an old Mercedes or BMW; we need lots of maintenance, we break down on the side of the road fairly often, our liquids leak, but our tough leather seats will last forever with some TLC. Much like those old imports, we will stick around in each other's driveways for years to come.

Our friendship is based on the ludicrous, the impossible, the insane, and we understand that in its entirety. One of our favorite games, a game we have played for so long we cannot remember how or when it started, is Poopoo Haiku. This is a game we made up and found so stupid that it was hilarious, so, of course, we continue to play. The purpose of the game is simple: string together three to four words in a sequence that will make the other person cringe. Of note are time-worn favorites like "pus crusted nipple donut" and "boiled anus pie." We have played this game for decades and the combinations are endless. We've tried to recruit others, but generally people think we are weird. We are absolutely okay with that. We find ourselves utterly amusing and have found that the game becomes even funnier when either of us is faced with traumatic life circumstances.

Michelle and I tell each other straight up when the other is behaving shittily, and we never ever lie to one another. We have had good years and bad years, but in the end, we're there. She has been one of the good things in my life, a safe harbor, a calm port, and I love her with all my heart. I have survived life's calamities with her by my side. We are not lesbian, yet we call each other Domestic Partners. We are not related, but we agree we are sisters *with Bobbie Jean as our mother.* When I was diagnosed with breast cancer, she was the one who slept by my side in the hospital recliner, she was the one who made sure I had food and around-the-clock care, and she was the one who made sure I stayed alive. Along with Delaney, she is my sole remaining family.

As an adult, I have added a cadre of other close friends: Jennifer, Kylee, Brandy, all of whom have been steadfast in their friendship and support of me. Jennifer is my tie to Catalina, and she and I travel there frequently to honor her sister and my mother. She is a funny, fiery redhead with a wicked laugh and incredible smarts. Kylee is my connection to horses, and while she is much younger than the rest of us, she is an old soul at heart, her dark eyes scrutinizing everything around her at all times. She and I have ridden horses together for many years, and she is the one who taught Delaney how to ride Ribbons. Despite our age difference, I consider her a sister and would trust her with my life. Brandy has a dry wit and a keen eye for detail. She has two young sons she raises with a fierce love, and she travels back and forth from her home in Austria to visit all of us twice a year. As a group, all of us get together as often as we can, sharing mojitos and snack trays, cackling like hyenas until Michelle inevitably snorts some of her drink, and Jennifer can't talk because she's laughing so hard. We are simultaneously ridiculous and sincere. They may not be blood, but these women are my family.

I have shared little in the way of my past with them, mostly because they come from families primarily whole and are able to stay married, have children and prosper in ways I cannot. Rather, I have built a tiny family around myself and Delaney, and all these women form our nucleus. I have come to a deep understanding within myself that I am not likely to marry again, may never have another serious relationship. My daughter will not have a father and I will not *ever* experience the possibilities inherent in a healthy, loving relationship. I do not have parents and my daughter has no grandparents. Ours is not anything in the way of traditional, but I suppose that is how our life imitates life. My childhood has doomed me to repeat the patterns of my parents and my adult failures have sealed my solitude. Interestingly, I have grown beyond my self-diagnosed crazy to a simple awareness that I am broken. It is who I was always destined to be.

Figuring Father

L ike a chained dog, I spent most of my life seeking my father's approval, alternately wagging jubilantly with over-the-top gestures or slinking away with my tail between my legs. I worked hard at school trying to bring home the perfect report card, joined track because that was the sport he loved, came home after college to join him at his business because I thought it might somehow forge a bond. It never happened. Instead, as time wore on, I became increasingly fatigued by his fury and endless assaults, the relentless weight of the links around my neck, and his singular disinterest in anything that did not center directly on him.

He was so vastly different from my friend's fathers, the Walton fathers I watched on TV, those men of fuzzy sweaters and hearty laughs—frankly any representation of fatherhood I had ever encountered—that assigning him a description was no more possible than trying to affix a label to a sweaty wine bottle. I realize now he was profoundly mentally ill, but even that understanding does little to erase the jagged agony of the past, and even more sadly, that realization came so late in life as not to matter. Of course, as children we had no way to know he was abnormal, or really what was even to be considered normal, because with our mother's complicity, we were doomed to endlessly cycle through his lunacy.

The irony of most of our childhood existence was those who came in contact with him always spoke of him with words like "larger than life," "incredible," and "extraordinary." Whether these monikers were tongue-in-cheek were lost on my adolescent self, but more than once I would retreat in shock that those around us simply could not see him for who he truly was. I suppose much of that could be explained by his storytelling, his ability to be the coach, the salesman, the doctor, the expert on demand, and the fact that no one really knew whether his tales were true.

My father was born a twin on a peach farm in Yuba City, California. He was the only surviving baby and his mother liked to joke that like a shark, he ate his brother in the womb. I remember my grandmother, his mother, only vaguely. By the time I was old enough to know her, she was riddled with rheumatoid arthritis and used a wheelchair, but she was known for her irreverent humor and wicked intelligence. In her heyday she was one of a handful of female lawyers in the State of California, and legend has it that she was even allowed to sit in the courtroom, a rare occurrence for women in those days. When my father was a toddler, he was cared for by his grandmother, while his mother went to law school in Sacramento and his father farmed the orchards. It was an unconventional upbringing to be sure, but one he spoke of with pride.

Yuba City, snugged up against the Sutter Buttes, was a tiny rural town known mostly for its fruit orchards and canning warehouses. As a landowner, my grandfather was considered upper-class in town, despite the fact that he toiled in the orchards from sunrise to dark every day. My father grew up amidst peach trees and orange dust, surrounded by seasonal labor and rat terrier hunting dogs. His father raised and bred these dogs to keep the squirrel population at bay, as they could easily decimate the annual fruit yields left unchecked. Blue jays and mockingbirds were also considered scourge, and my father was taught at a very young age to shoot them directly out of the sky on sight. I remember one grainy black and white photo from my grandmother's album, my father about five or six, barefoot, wearing shorts with suspenders, proudly holding aloft a string of about twenty bird carcasses, his father's hand placed firmly on his shoulder. He looks quite a bit like my brother John in that particular photo. It hurts my heart to look at it, both because John never knew a father who would teach him anything—nor ever place a guiding hand on his shoulder—and because I deeply mourn that little boy of the beaming smile, the man he would never become, the father he would never be.

My father's father, John Russell Burke—Rusty to the townies—was a stern and exact man. He was well-known around town both for his height and his anger. At almost six-four, for the era, he was considered a giant. He had enormous hands and a temper to match. Most in town steered clear of him, and I am certain he beat my father and grandmother regularly. Whether this was due to his concept of discipline, or simply his inability to control himself, I do not know. What I do know is his fists were the first tendril of a common generational thread.

My father's grandmother was known for her Johnson Peach Pie, a recipe that the family guarded religiously in order for my great grandmother to defend her Sacramento

State Fair pie title every year. That pie recipe was passed through multiple generations until my mother finally took possession. I am not sure if it was the home-grown peaches or my great-grandmother's touch, but while my mom was a fantastic cook, a baker she was not, and that poor pie recipe died a harsh and undignified death after multiple blackened crusts and soggy innards.

Once my grandmother Lillian began practicing law, my father, his parents, and his grandmother all moved together to a home in Los Angeles. My father was about eight at the time, and the transition from farm life to suburban life was not easy for him. He had trouble adjusting in school, fought quite a bit with other kids, and generally caused some ruckus. His father could not stand what he considered "city life" and returned to Yuba City after less than a year, where he later married a heavy-set neighbor and together they raised my father's half-brother.

As a teenager my father attended Dorsey High School in Los Angeles, where he was a nondescript student. His senior year yearbook shows a dark-haired, grinning young man, and despite his lifelong claim of athletic superiority, there is no mention of him on any team or club rosters, no photos of him with a football or leaping over a hurdle. Instead, he stands, a gawky boy, at the back of the science club photo and the scribbled notes along the yearbook margins refer to him as the "Darkroom Cowboy" and "Shutterbug." The gleaming varsity athlete he always claimed to be is nowhere in sight. It is only the awkward photography buff with a definitive interest in getting signatures from those same varsity athletes in evidence.

One of the earliest stories I heard growing up was his desire to join the armed services at seventeen. The adult father I knew rarely, if ever, spoke of the war, but apparently his mother Lillian did, and mostly to my mother. She told her that at the time of his decision, my father was living at home with his mother and grandmother. His father had already started another family so was not a factor in any family decisions. That December 7, 1941 the Japanese bombed Pearl Harbor, and along with hundreds of thousands of other young men, he was eager to join. The U.S. government had committed itself to victory over both the Italians and Germans in Europe and Imperial Japan in the Pacific. My father enlisted in the U.S. Navy immediately upon graduation. He was sent to boot camp in San Diego, where they discovered his penchant for science coupled with his high test scores. Upon this discovery, he was sent to San Diego Naval Hospital where he attended hospital corpsman school and from there was sent to advanced training at an epidemiology laboratory school in Virginia. Concurrently, and from the vantage point of the admirals, warfare in the Pacific was not going particularly well with regard to the health of the fleet. Both marines and sailors were coming down with malaria and other tropical diseases in droves, and there was a dire need for vector control and tropical disease management. My father was one of the first groups of naval corpsmen deployed to the Pacific Islands of Palau and Guadalcanal, in a concerted effort to thwart the spread of disease among U.S. troops.

Once he completed corpsman training in Virginia he was sent to Camp Elliott for training with the U.S. Marine Corps, since naval corpsman were deployed to medically support the marines, and from there deployed to Noumea in New Caledonia on a Dutch frigate. For several months he seesawed back and forth with the 7th fleet while the 5th regiment rested. He finally was assigned to combat on Guadalcanal where he served as a triage corpsman for the next two years.

At the unimaginable age of seventeen and eighteen, he was responsible for treating injured and dying marines up and down the coastline. I believe most of this to be true, as several boxes tucked in his attic contain photos of dead Japanese soldiers and my father as a very young man, bare chested and dog-tagged on a beach, his arm slung around his buddy, Corky, who died on that same island.

Decades later, when *Saving Private Ryan* came out, a WWII acquaintance contacted him to say the first twenty minutes or so of the movie had accurately captured exactly what it was like on the beaches of Guadalcanal, despite portraying the Normandy landings. These were the nineties, a time when WWII veterans were receiving quite a bit of attention and being honored in a number of movies. My father emphatically refused to go see the movie. It was the one time I ever saw him visibly upset about the war.

He was, however, enamored with the television series *Victory at Sea*, broadcast by NBC in the fifties. The original broadcast aired twenty-six segments, many of which were replayed on the History Channel at regular intervals. Episode six, "Guadalcanal" aired some actual footage of my father and his friend Corky on the island, the two of them covered in mud, helmets askew, squinting at the cameras. When the documentary was finally released on video, he bought the entire series and would watch all twenty-six episodes every so often, two glasses of whiskey neat sitting on the table beside him—one for him and one for Corky.

I can only imagine the horrors of that war and what he experienced. I can only think perhaps somewhere in those fly infested trenches, covered in the blood of his friends, dogged in his desire to live, grasping to normalize the images around him, that quite possibly he snapped. It is a reasonable and plausible explanation for the man he later became. It also explains his belief that he was capable of field triaging our broken bones and various ailments throughout our lives. This knowledge does little to poultice the wounds he inflicted on our family, but for me at least it provides some explanation for the atrocities he later exacted upon us.

According to my grandmother Lillian, when my father first returned from the war, he was different. She told my mother he was angry, sullen, distant, and that his temper had taken on a new dimension—one of hatred. At first she gently, and then later not so gently, suggested he enter college and move out of the house. Post WWII, universities were accepting war veterans with open arms and scholarships, so at the age of twenty my father was admitted to the University of Southern California.

For our entire lives, and to anyone within earshot, my father would describe his years at USC and how he played football and ran track. He would describe in detail his feats on the field, how his efforts on the track team led him to become an alternate in the decathlon for the U.S. Olympic team. He would watch USC football games religiously on TV, and cheer loudly every Rose Bowl. No matter how well my brother John did at basketball or track—and he was very good—no matter if I scored a goal on my college soccer team, the conversation would always come back around to him and what a magnificent football and track athlete he had been in his day. New boyfriends were always regaled with these stories, family members at holiday gatherings were forced to hear them over and over. We, of course, became immune with time.

One Christmas not long ago, I asked my second cousin to bring his son to my house Christmas morning. Liam was only three at the time, an adorable baby with curly blonde hair, an inquisitive mind, and a personality as wide as his smile. I was very much looking forward to his visit, joined by my first and second cousins, and Delaney was thrilled to have extended family around the tree.

When they first arrived, Liam went straight to Delaney, grabbed her hand and asked her to sit with him.

"Dany, please come with me."

Delaney smiled her impish smile at him and together the two of them sat cross-legged under the tree. It was distinctly obvious they were related, with their almond green eyes and dirty blonde hair, heads bent, conspiring. Watching them made my chest warm. Liam, of course, wanted to get straight to the gifts.

"Dany, is that for me?"

Delaney looked up at me. "Mom, can he open it? It's the one from me."

My father had not yet arrived, and for some reason, I felt compelled to wait, always stoking that irrational hope that maybe he would want to be part of something bigger than himself, a Christmas with a sweet baby first comprehending the magnitude of all that wrapping paper, his granddaughter and his nephews.

"Hang on a minute, honey, let's give it a few minutes."

She looked at me, her head tilted to the side. "Why?"

"Because your grandfather will be here in a few minutes."

Delaney was only ten at the time, but her answer rocked me back. "So?"

And like that, I knew she knew. All of my attempts to build a sane nuclear family around her had been futile. She was no more likely to be connected to my father or my mother than I was, and she knew it, her tiny, still-forming self knew it and felt no compulsion to explain it away, to hang any hopes or expectations on it, but to simply move it aside.

Just then, the doorbell rang, and they arrived. My cousin went to help him unload gifts, while I went to put on some coffee. The kids sat impatiently by the tree. Once we got settled again around the tree, Delaney played Santa, handing out gifts. She handed the first gift to Liam.

His eyes were like bush babies.

"Did I ever tell you about my coach at USC, Button Baker?" boomed my dad to my second cousin beside him.

Startled, my cousin smiled politely. He clearly wanted to watch his son open presents.

And for the next hour, my father talked nonstop, all about playing under Coach Baker, his exploits as a running back, his glory days. Never once did he ask a question. Never once did he stop to watch the kids open gifts, never once did he stop talking.

I remember being so angry I could barely speak. The kids had tuned him out, my cousins were simply being kind, yet all I could think about was throwing him down the side of the hill. The thing about it though, despite my anger, despite the obvious fact that he was a boor, none of us ever interrupted him or asked him to stop. It was as though his presence was an underlying current, a riptide, once caught in it if you struggled and fought, you would drown—the best you could hope for was to swim sideways, your eyes on the beach, knowing you would be exhausted and depleted, but ultimately survive.

That very same thing happened when my father's only grandson came to visit a couple of years later. Like so many of his grandchildren, he had fostered no relationship with him, and the nineteen-year-old kid sitting on the couch just watched his grandfather from hooded eyes. This was the kid who would carry on the legacy of the Burke name, the youngest male heir to my father's side of the family. He was a strong, beautiful boy, capable with his hands, talented on a motorcycle. Delaney was entranced by him, and the two of them fought like siblings. Yet, my father did not ask him a single question about who he was, what he was about, what interested him, what he wanted to do with his life. He had not seen this boy in ten years. Instead, he spent the entire two-hour visit talking about his days on the ski patrol, how many wondrous and awesome feats he had accomplished, how magnificent his days on the slopes were. My nephew said absolutely nothing to him the entire visit.

When he finally left, I put my arm around my nephew.

"I'm sorry."

"For what?" he asked. "Him? That's not on you. That's on him."

"I was hoping for better."

"He means nothing to me, don't worry about it." He squeezed my arm and left to swim with Delaney.

His father, my half-brother Ken, handed me a Dr. Pepper. We just shook our heads.

"It never changes," he said.

"No. It doesn't."

Ken was the middle child of three sons born to my father and his first wife, Ginny. All the way through high school, the only thing I knew of my half-brothers was they were what my father referred to as "his bad result." I had no idea what that meant, but once Ken and I got to know each other as adults, we grew close.

Theirs was not a happy marriage. According to Ken, whom I met in my twenties, they both drank heavily and fought often. Ginny left him after she had a gun shoved in her mouth while her five and seven-year-old watched. I guess Ginny had a taste for a certain flavor of violence, because she married my father's half-brother only a few months later and proceeded to birth a few more children. To hear Ken tell it, the violence and rage ran deep in that bloodline, for both of those men beat the women and children in their lives almost to death.

Ken told me he had only one distinct memory of our father since he was so young when he left. At fourteen, grown weary of the constant beatings by his stepfather and uncle, Ken rode his dirt bike for miles through suburban side streets to get to our father's house. Stressed and near tears he knocked on the door, not knowing what to expect. At the time, he said, he simply wanted somewhere safe to sleep. My mom answered and invited him in. She fed him a sandwich and together they waited for my father.

What Ken didn't know, and couldn't have known, is that his timing was impossibly wrong. Just one year earlier, his older brother Richard had been living at the house with our family. Despite not having raised him, my father convinced my mother to take Richard in, let him live in the attic until he got his act together. He had shown up one afternoon and knocked on the door, much like Ken a year later. Richard, seventeen at the time, and unbeknownst to anyone, was a sexual predator. He had been kicked out of his house for molesting his younger sister.

For the first few months he was well-behaved, helping around the house and not causing any trouble. Since she had some help, my mom decided to take geology classes at the local community college. Richard eagerly offered to watch my brother and me while she was in class. I was four at the time, and after a while, when I started crying hysterically and clawing at my mother to hold me when it came time for her to leave for classes, she finally sat me down and asked why. I told her I didn't want to kiss Richard's peepee anymore.

My mother locked me in her bedroom and had the presence of mind to tape record me. When my father got home, she played the tape for him. He went wild, dragging Richard through the house into a bathroom where he beat him bloody. He gave him two choices—either jail or enlist in the morning. Richard chose the Army, and at first light my father took him to the recruiter's office.

When poor Ken showed up the next year, my mom later told me her heart broke for him. But in no way could she chance yet another son around me. After dinner, it was she, and not my father, who quietly dispatched Ken out the door and on his way. Ken told me many years later the interaction crushed him, and he could not understand why one son was allowed, yet he was not. That evening he chose to live in a friend's shed rather than return home. After about a week, he took the first job that came his way, so he could eat. He started doing residential construction clean-up and over time built a hugely successful construction company of his own.

Richard, on the other hand, had a long and lustrous career as a sexual deviant. He went AWOL from the Army, beat up a few wives, lied about being a Vietnam war vet, and later molested his other sister again, along with Ken's daughter and his own daughter. What astounds me to this day is the fact that my father, our father, knowing what he did to me at four years old, still chose to invite Richard and his wife and daughter to Christmas my second year of college. I was only nineteen at the time, struggling mightily with The Rage (as coined by my then boyfriend), and when my mother called me I was slightly confused.

"How do you feel about Richard, Ken, and Russ coming to Christmas?" she asked one day on the phone.

I really had no idea why she was asking. At the time, I had no real memories of any of them, but I would remember soon enough.

"Your father wants them to come," she explained. "He thinks now that they all have kids it would be a good idea."

"I don't care."

"You sure?"

I remember wondering why she was asking all of this. And why she was asking about Christmas when the semester had just begun.

"Yeah, I don't care, do whatever."

When I hung up the phone, I had an uneasy feeling, but I couldn't really identify it. I just knew something wasn't sitting right. Over the next few months that anxiety grew, along with my temper, and I began lashing out at my boy-friend, at one point even slapping him in an argument. When that happened, he told me flat out I needed help and I had better get over to the student counseling center if I ever wanted to talk to him again. I went.

I had never experienced counseling before, and when my counselor, Dr. Irving, started to peel back the layers, I think even he was aghast. What had started as a straightforward attempt to get back together with my boyfriend ended up exposing a void I did not know I had. When quizzed, I simply had no memories up until I was about ten. Dr. Irving found this to be unusual and said it indicated some sort of trauma. He decided to try hypnosis. And that was when the blue room and my half-brother Richard came distinctly into view.

Even now I shudder when I remember leaving his office that afternoon, the freshly found memory filling my veins like Ayahuasca, almost hallucinogenic with fear and loathing. I called my mom the minute I got back to my dorm room.

"Is it true?"

My hand gripped the receiver so hard I could see the veins coursing across my knuckles.

"Is what true?" she asked. I could hear dogs barking behind her.

"That Richard did *those things* to me when I was four?"

I could hear a sharp intake of breath. Her voice was lower, sadder. "Oh honey, I am so sorry, I thought you remembered. I thought you knew what I was talking about when I called."

"No, Mom, I didn't. I didn't remember. I didn't know. How could I? I was four. And we never talked about it."

So my mom and I talked about it. We talked about his cravenness, how utterly repulsive and vile a human being he was, and how I, as a toddler, could not have known or understood what he was doing. It was very important to my mom that I understood that none of this was my fault. She kept repeating over and over how she didn't know, how angry she was that my father's ex-wife didn't think it important to *warn* her, to let her know that a child molester was entering her halls, the very same child molester who had been thrown unceremoniously from his own home for equally aberrant behavior on an equally unsuspecting little girl.

But none of this mattered in the end. My father still insisted Richard come to Christmas, my mother never stood up on my behalf, and I was too traumatized by it all to do much other than watch my own emotional demise like a bystander.

When Richard's wife called me a few years later in tears asking me if the rumors were true and whether she should believe her nine-year-old daughter, I found myself much less an observer. This time I was pissed. At her request, I wrote a letter to the court outlining my experiences and exactly how much custody I thought he should get. His daughter does not speak to him to this day.

Upon the dissolution of his marriage to Ginny, and her remarriage to his brother, my father dropped off the grid for several years until he met my mother. He spent those years working in sales and living the bachelor life, skiing and drinking most weekends. It was on one of those weekends that he met my mother and searched for the infamous watch.

After our birth, my father told us he went to law school at the University of La Verne, taking night classes after working all day. He attempted to pass the bar twice. And failed. He claims he failed because he simply did not have the time to study with two small kids in the house. I believe he studied for the bar, as almost a third of that house on the hill is comprised of an enormous library full of books, and many of them are outdated law books. Perhaps once he realized he would not follow in the hallowed footsteps of his mother, he focused primarily on sales, ultimately landing on a hospital supply company as his career.

I first began to get suspicious about my father's claims: USC, football, decathlon, law school, all of it, when I caught him lying while my mom was recovering in the hospital from hip surgery. I had asked him where she was going to get physical therapy and how often she was supposed to go. He told me the doctor had written orders that my father could do the therapy and that my mother did not need to stay in the rehab center. I found this to be utterly ridiculous and a blatant lie. I could not imagine a doctor writing an order for an eighty-something-year-old man to do physical therapy on any patient.

When I challenged him on it, he hung up on me. This was about the time I was getting ready to move to Georgia and I had a lot to do to prepare for the move. Fighting with my father was not high on the list. Instead, I went to the hospital and spoke directly to the surgeon. While I did not ask him whether he had written orders to release her to the care of my insane father, I did ask what her release orders were, and as I suspected, he had her slotted for an ambulance ride to the local rehabilitation center for two weeks of hip therapy to learn to walk again.

On the day she was to be transferred, I made absolutely sure she went to the center and that she was not released to my father. I visited her every day in that place. He did not.

That interaction got me to wondering if he was willing to lie about that, wouldn't he be willing to lie about just about everything? For the first time in my life I actually questioned him. I had always just accepted his outlandish tales as factual, never once considering that they quite possibly could be made up. Over the next year and whenever I would think about it, I went online to research his athletic claims of glory, his education and his history. It was fairly easy—just time consuming—to match the timelines of his high school yearbook, his war years, his early marriages with public records, university and team rosters and albums full of photos.

I had always wondered about his university years and his claim that he was able to try out for the Olympic team as a decathlete, play on the USC football team and graduate. Having attended a university where I barely had time to brush my teeth, much less play two grueling sports, it seemed absurd. There is also the small fact that he played neither of these sports growing up. I started there. And what I found out stunned me.

He lied about it all. The only part that was true was the war. He did not graduate from USC nor did he play football or run track. He couldn't have. The years he claimed to be there were the years after the war, and those were the years he married his first wife Ginny and had three boys. And USC has no record of him. It turns out that it was his mother that attended USC and went to law school. Not him. He may or may not have attended college, but I could find no records nor any diplomas anywhere. He did not attend a law school that was not in existence during the years he claimed to be there. He may have attended some sort of school, but it was certainly not an accredited university nor one with any public records. In hindsight, I believe he did take the bar exam, but tried to do it on his own thinking that he was brighter than everyone else and he could outsmart the system.

What bothers me the most is the why of it. Why would anyone go to such lengths to weave a tale of such over-the-top unbelievability? Why create a false bar so high that not one of his children could ever attain it? Why the incessant need to feel superior to everyone around him? Why was it not enough that he had served admirably in a world war and had raised a family? I truly wondered what had happened to him that he felt a need to create a persona out of whole cloth that bore little to no resemblance to the person he really was.

Whether it was the war, genetics, mental illness, or a lethal combination of them all, I will never truly understand my father nor his incessant need for attention and adoration, his demand that all discussion center on him and his accomplishments, his hair-trigger temper and penchant to use his fists to draw blood. He was a man of tirades and brawls, equally as intent on beating a man half to death for stealing a mall parking spot as coaching a track team to national levels. Those who knew him socially saw a man of intensity and intelligence, a coach willing to spend hours with athletes, a salesman who could talk your ear off. Those of us who knew him behind closed doors knew otherwise: he was a shape shifter, a chameleon, a Zeus who could transform into a monster at will.

Throughout our lives, our father coached soccer and track, always finding a way to take over the teams altogether. Despite having never actually played any of the sports he coached, he was a decent coach, but sadly, many of my memories have nothing to do with my father as coach or mentor, but instead include flash images of midfield fist fights with opposing team fathers or referees. At his insistence, John and I ran track, not because it was our chosen sport, but because it was his. It became obvious that he was primarily interested in the outstanding athletes, ones for which he could receive accolades for their accomplishments. Luckily for my brother, he was an outstanding athlete both in track and basketball, so while he received little to no actual coaching or support from our father, at least he knew he was one of the chosen ones. That said, it is still very difficult to reconcile my brother's athletic prowess with the fact that my father refused to buy him the custom size fifteen shoes he needed in high school, instead forcing my brother to wear off-the-shelf size thirteens, since they were cheaper.

I, on the other hand, was definitively mediocre in track, and no longer registered on my father's radar. Girls soccer, the sport I was good at, was not offered at my high school, and my father refused to pay for club fees. His dismissal of me was glaringly obvious the year I started high school at a new school while he chose to remain at the rival high school to coach since his favorite local athletes went there. When "his" track girls finally graduated, he came over to my high school my junior year and immediately began to overshadow the existing coaches. It was always so strange for me to be at practice and watch my own father spend hours and hours with other students, timing them, encouraging them, pushing them, even buying them sweats when some of the local migrant kids couldn't afford them, all while I stared from a distance and waited for the next knock-down-drag-out fight at home.

To this day, some of our friends from high school remember him as such a great guy, such a dedicated coach, so energetic and cool, the guy who would do warm-ups to "Hells Bells" on loudspeaker and the coach who wore a ball cap embroidered with ACDC. We insiders knew better, we knew the cold-blooded fury and assaults, the fear that would grip your belly when you heard the car door slam, the look in your mother's eye when he began to snarl. But back then we said nothing, we nodded politely at those who told us we were lucky to have a father so *vested* in his kids, and we kept our mouths shut and our eyes wide open.

It was only when we both left our parents' house that John and I began to really talk about it, to put voice and words to it, to realize that we had missed out on so much by settling at Maslow's lowest hierarchy. For as long as I can remember, my brother and I scrambled on scabby knees and skinned elbows to attain his affection, his approval or his help only to receive rejection, disdain, disgust, and fury. For decades we tried to understand him, to love him, even to like him. Any part of him. Our efforts were futile and disregarded, and we were left to huddle in the pain of our dismissal. Over time, we both simply became adept at obscuring, deflecting and lying by omission, anything to eclipse the blood moon of our family.

A Fitting End

I got the call as I was driving back from Atlanta. The architect and I had been finalizing plans to remodel the house, and it was turning out even better than I had hoped. It was taking a bit longer than I had expected, and with the Northern Georgia weather to take into consideration, it looked as though construction would be delayed until the following spring. Even so, I was daydreaming about the view of the lake from my bedroom window as I drove and didn't really notice who was calling when the phone rang.

"Dorriah, this is your dad."

My stomach tightened, as it always did. It was as though he had a sixth sense, that no matter when I might have a moment of peace, he could sniff it out like a police dog and snap it away.

"It's your mom," he said. "They just took her to the hospital."

Wait, what? I had just talked to her two days ago. She sounded down, but not sick, only saying, "Oh honey, I'm not feeling too well," when I asked. And that was about it. The only thing I noted in that conversation was that she admitted she didn't feel well, something she rarely did. Over the last twelve months as we spoke on the phone, I knew she was not really improving and I was planning to go see her, *I was*, but the year had just gotten away from me, and with work and Delaney and living in an entirely new area, it had been difficult to find the time to fly across the country. *And truly, did I really want to? If I was entirely honest with myself, I had left for a reason, hadn't I? And underneath it all I knew she had already given up and that my presence would not never had made a difference.*

"What happened?" I asked. "Did she fall again?"

"No, she just wouldn't wake up this morning," he answered. "I had to call an ambulance. I couldn't get her up."

When he said that, I knew something was wrong. For my father to allow *other people* in that house meant something was terribly, horribly wrong.

Tears formed in tiny herds in the corners of my eyes before galloping down my cheeks. *My mom, my beautiful mom. I love you. I hate you. Please don't die.* I had to focus, and focus hard, on his next words.

"They just took her a little while ago. I'm leaving now."

I don't remember much about the next few hours other than the interminable drive down I-75 from Atlanta to Chattanooga, getting stuck behind trucks, unable to make a plane reservation as I drove, finally reaching the house and packing hastily, getting to the airport as quickly as I could. I didn't want Delaney to miss school, so I left her with a babysitter and caught the next flight to LAX. I suppose in my heart I knew this wasn't going to be good even before I got there, but dammit she wasn't that old, and maybe this was just a setback. But the thing was…I *knew* better. All our lives we didn't do doctors and we didn't do hospitals. My father was the self-anointed physician of the family and to have to go to the hospital *and by ambulance* meant very bad things.

While waiting for my flight, I called my brother.

"Hey," I said.

"Hey," he replied.

"It's happening, isn't it?" I asked.

"Yeah," he sighed, "it is."

We had discussed this our entire lives, this sequence of events, as inevitable as glacial erosion, that he would outlive her, that she would give up, and that it would be bad. We knew *and had always known* he would not be one of those guys who died within months of his fifty-year marriage, that he would live on and on, her memory a distant shadow as he continued to suck air into his lungs. How she would give up, never leaving that life, never escaping his jaws. So none of this was a surprise. This was a walk down a long dark hall that we had been anticipating for forty years. All of the brutality and pain had led us to this exact place, and it was time to sling the backpack of horrors over our shoulder and get on with it.

"What time do you land?" he asked.

"About five," I answered. "I'll head straight to the hospital."

"Okay, meet you there," he replied, his voice starting to waver. "This ain't gonna be easy."

"No. It is not."

As we talked, I realized I had not seen my brother in almost a year as well. In fact, we had barely spoken much at all. The last time we were together had not gone very well, and things were strained between us. I had asked him to come to Georgia to upgrade the flooring in my house from laminate to hardwood. He had done a really good job on the installation and the floors looked great, but when he left, despite being paid, he had helped himself to several of my belongings.

Soon after finishing the floors and returning to Oregon, I called him about it. He at first denied it, so I let it go, thinking maybe I had misplaced the missing gold coins or lost some of the jewelry. But as time wore on, I just knew he had taken them, and I wanted to know why. A few months later, I called again.

"Hey, I still can't find the coins. You know, the ones on the bookcase right by the arch?" I asked.

I could hear him inhale on the other end of the phone. A couple kids were yelling in the background and a door slammed. "Yeah, I know the coins," he answered.

"John, you know I am going to keep asking you. And you know, and I know, that you took them. I don't even want them back. I just want to know why."

He didn't even hesitate. "Yeah, I took them," he replied. "I wanted them, so I took them."

Even though I had already known the answer to my question, hearing him admit it still shocked me.

"But why?" I asked. "If you needed money, all you had to do was ask. You didn't have to steal from me."

"It wasn't the money," he answered. "I just felt like you were lucky. That you got breaks and I didn't. That you didn't deserve those coins and that I did."

Hearing him say those words felt like someone had spear-fished me, as though my insides had been depth-charged. I remember having to sit down when he said it.

"*Me*? The person you grew up with? That I was lucky?" I asked. The words felt like road tar as I pushed them out, that my mouth was hot pavement and the stench of the tar burned my lips as it passed.

"You've always been lucky," he replied. "You have the nice house, the nice job, the car, all of it. You don't just squeak by, like I do. You have shit, you go places. I don't have a pot to piss in."

"But, John, I've worked my whole life, none of this was free," I said. "I grew up in that house, too."

"Yeah, but you got away, you made something for yourself, you escaped." He took a deep breath. "I never could."

That conversation was both harsh and an ugly realization that he truly believed that I had made it out, that the fact he had lived in another state and far away from our parents for the last ten years, while I stayed behind, meant nothing, that my mental turmoil and untenable choices had little to no bearing on his outcome or beliefs, and that no matter how far both of us went or how hard we tried, the rotted twine still bound us all.

The memory of this conversation still lingered as I snapped back into our current discussion, how the fact that he had stolen from me *my own brother* had to be set aside, forgotten, so we could deal with our mom and her current situation.

John broke the silence. "Okay, just meet me at the hospital. I'll see you tonight."

By the time I got to Las Posas Hospital, visiting hours were long past. It didn't matter. I think there is a special hall pass for family members like me, people who are clearly hollowed out and are there for one reason, and one reason only, even if they don't know it yet.

The nurse at the unit desk was very kind. She showed me to her room, the curtains drawn around her bed, the lights dim. I don't know why I expected to see my father, but he was not there, his energy was not there. As I approached her bed, I thought they had shown me the wrong patient. This woman was not my mother. My mother was tall, six-foot, had dark hair with only tendrils of gray along the temple and beautiful skin. This person was tiny and thin, weighing maybe ninety pounds, her hair wispy and gray, almost nonexistent, her face a skull, its skin stretched taut across the bones. I had to look closer to believe it was really her.

"Oh, Mom," was all I could say. I could barely breathe. "What happened to you?"

Her eyes never focused on me, she did not know me, or perhaps she did, I didn't know. She was breathing, but not alive, and in that moment, I knew she was not only dying, but dead, and that I would never talk to her again.

The nurse came in to tell me that the doctor had left for the night but that he would come to see me in the morning. I was a little confused.

"Where is my father?" I asked her. He, the expert, the controller, the doctor over all doctors, he wasn't going to control every single last breath she had?

The nurse looked at me a little strangely. "I think it's best you wait to talk to the doctor," she answered. "For now, we have your mom on morphine and she is comfortable."

She patted my arm and asked if I wanted any water or food. I told her no and if it was okay I would just stay with my mom and wait for my brother. She nodded and left, closing the door slowly behind her.

For the next three hours, while I waited for my brother to arrive, I simply sat by the side of her bed. I couldn't stand to watch this broken, dying shard of a person imitate my mother, but I also could not leave. I just watched. Watched as she took a shallow, difficult breath. Watched as she shuddered, her eyes open and shutting, their deep blue recesses sinking slowly into her Catalina ocean. In between the tears and the snot, my heart screamed at her to read to me, tell me about the Owl and the Pussycat just one more time, to send me one more recipe, to be my mom just one more time, that I forgave her for everything, that it was okay that she never left him, that if she just stayed I would be there, that I would fix this mess and that I would make the right choice, I would move back and be close and I would help her be alive.

When my brother finally burst through the door, I practically screamed. He looked like shit. His t-shirt was rumpled with sweat, his eyes were bloodshot, and his now salt-and-pepper hair stood on end. The two of us stared at each other in confusion.

"How is she?" he asked, glancing at the bed, not really looking, but looking away as he asked.

I could only shake my head. There were no words, there was nothing I could say.

So we sat with her through that long night, not really talking, not really understanding, not really anything. Neither of us called our father, neither of us wondered why he was not by her side. We didn't want him there anyway. We were there for her, and her alone, and we wanted her to know that. We may have dozed, we may have stayed awake the entire evening, but we both knew it was our final bedtime story, and the last time the three of us would be together.

In the morning, the doctor came. He was young, tired-looking, and seemed agitated.

"Are you the family?" he asked, glancing down at the chart in his hands, and moving to the side of my mom's bed.

My brother and I said yes, my brother heaving his huge body out of the recliner in the corner, while I pulled my hair into a ponytail.

"Do you understand what is happening here?" he asked. "That your mother will not recover?"

I found it odd that he was talking to us that way. "What do you mean?" I replied. "What do you mean by 'what is happening here.'"

He finally looked away from the charts and at me. "Were you aware of her condition?"

I shook my head, confused. "I live in Georgia. My brother in Oregon. We haven't seen her for almost a year. We just got here last night. What do you mean by 'her condition'? We don't understand what is happening either."

He stared at both of us for a long minute, his jaw slowly clenching and unclenching. It was such a disjointed and odd moment, as though my brother and I had stepped through yet another looking glass.

"So your father, her husband, the man who registered her, is and was aware of her condition?" he asked. "And neither of you have seen her for the last year?"

We both nodded yes. I explained to him that when I had moved away a year ago, she was recovering from hip surgery but had been essentially healthy. That I had spoken with her on the phone every week, but I had no idea she was this ill.

The doctor then moved to her bed and pulled back the sheets. He asked the nurse to help him turn her. As he did, purple black sores appeared all along her underside, on her back and hips and buttocks, angry and seeping, her hip bones practically stabbing through her flesh, muscle and tendons showing through deep fissures and tears in her skin along her ribcage.

My brother lurched to the sink where he threw up. I could only stare.

"These are bed sores," said the doctor. "These are long-term, extremely painful, and the worst bed sores I have ever seen. These took months and months to form and never healed and were never treated. Do you understand what I am saying? How could you not know this? Your mother died of neglect. And abuse. She has pneumonia and her heart is failing. She has not been taken care of for months, if not the entire year. She has clearly not had any medical attention and she will die and it will be a relief from the pain. I have her on morphine and will keep her on morphine until that happens."

With that, he threw the sheets back over her and left the room. The nurse slowly covered my mom back up and looked at us.

She tried to smile but it slipped and fell from her face. "I need to know how much morphine to give her. This could take a while if we don't get her the right doses."

And so began the final chapter, the days and agonizing nights waiting for her to die, doctors and nurses constantly increasing the dosage of morphine because my father had lied to the hospital and said she did not drink heavily and the dosages were too low to accelerate her death, and my mom's brother and my cousins coming to say goodbye and the horror on their faces as they looked at her, and the fact that my father never once came to see her and how finally, when she did slip away at four a.m. that sixth day my brother and I could only stare at each other in shame and exhaustion.

I flew Delaney out for the funeral, and I made all the right motions and had the right ceremony and scattered my mom's ashes with the help of a friend over her beloved Catalina Island. When the detectives showed up and the Medical Examiner called to say they wanted to press criminal charges against our father for elder abuse and neglect, and when they told me that the ambulance personnel had been horrified by the house and had reported it to social services, my brother said he had to leave, that his job depended on it, and that it was up to me, that he would stay for the funeral, but the choice was mine.

And like so many of the choices I had been forced to make throughout my life, there was only one possible choice in all of this. Only one.

So I took her by the hand. "C'mon Delaney, let's go," I said. And I chose her.

Epilogue

2018

It is Christmas 2018—eight years after my mother's death—and I wake frantic in the knowledge that I have forgotten to buy her a present. It is minutes before it dawns on me that she is gone. And like so many times over the years, that knowledge is harsh, punches at my chest like a stubby knife. It seems I will never stop wishing that I had a mom. But interestingly, increasingly, time has been my redeemer, and I am able to move past, forward, beyond.

So much has changed since the day I spread her ashes over Catalina Island, my mind picturing her inscrutable expression at the bow of *The Seabird*, my hands releasing the bits of body now reduced to dust. Back then, I was convinced that I would never recover, that I was doomed to a guilt-ridden, untenable existence, forever linked to my deranged father, scrabbling to find some connection to my lost brother, and ultimately, alone.

In that, I was mostly wrong. After our mother's death, John and I decided to walk away from our father entirely. We knew, both overtly and intuitively, that to stay in his orbit was toxic, that neither of us could survive any further onslaught of his wrath or his lies. He had avoided criminal conviction by lying, which came as no surprise to either of us. He explained away our mother's condition and death to the authorities by convincing them that she had wanted it that way, that she, like her own mother, was a Christian Scientist, and that she had refused help, that he had begged and pleaded with her and at his frail age did the very best he could. We knew this to be an outright lie. The detectives did not.

He lived another five years. He continued to exist in that horrific house, surrounded by filth, until he died in 2016, alone, in bed, with a tray of tangerines beside him. By then, the trash and grime coated every surface, newspapers were strewn in piles across every inch of the bedroom, and the bathroom was caked in foulness. His body was found four days after he died, when some neighbors were unable to reach him by phone after noting that the mail was spilling out of the mailbox. John and I did not mourn. We did not cry. We did not host a memorial. He was gone, and we were glad.

Over the months it took to clean out that house, in the process of cremating our father's body, and disposing of our childhood, an astounding thing happened. John and I found each other, our true selves, and we were able to forgive each other's transgressions—to let go of envy and guilt, to talk through the absolute lunacy of our family. We finally accepted that we were victims, and not complicit. We did the right thing both for, and because of, each other. Today, he is gainfully employed, happily married, living in a beautiful home, and happy. We are as thick as thieves and I love him.

My daughter and I still go it alone, but I am, for the most part, happy. She is a teenager now and drives me crazy, as teenagers should, but she is my purpose. My crazy friends still make me laugh, my career is doing well, and while I cannot seem to bring myself to even attempt a relationship—*that part might be forever damaged*—my life is full. It was the telling of this story that allowed me to remove that backpack of horrors from my shoulders. It took years, many attempts, and at times, heaving, sobbing messy crying jags to the point I could not see the keyboard, before I could finish a chapter. But I did it. It was the writing of the words, the release of the shame, that was ultimately cathartic and healing. And for that, I am deeply grateful.

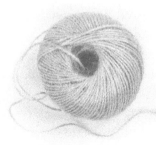

Acknowledgments

I owe many thanks to a long list of people. First, to Debra Englander for her continued support, time and insight into early drafts, the editing process and finally, just how to get it done. To my editors Heather King and Rachel Hoge for their unflagging support, keen insight, and invaluable assistance in making the manuscript the best it could be, and to the rest of the team at Permuted Press for well, everything.

To my dear friends of twenty years, Jon and Jane Swartzentruber, trusted readers, for reading and commenting on early drafts and constantly encouraging me to stay with it and never give up. Your words of support and encouragement rallied me to continue this journey and I owe you a lovely vintage bottle of something.

To Alexander and Rebecca Tseitlin, for your support of my writing dreams all the while helping me to raise a child. I will never forget your response to the story and how it inspired you to seek personal introspection on your end. That is a result I had never imagined.

To my friends, all of whom are represented liberally within these pages (life imitates life after all). Michelle, unwavering over thirty-plus years, Keeley and Brian, supportive and loving through every up and down, Jenny, my template for a fierce motherwarrior, Brandi, loyal and trusted confidante, Melissa, too many years and adventures to count, Bobbie Sue and Johnny, for always being there, and so many others—Sandy, Renee, Ron, Tom, Marlene, Brad, Ardean, Charlotte, Mary Margaret, Sharon, Greg, Mona, Alex, Scott, Garret, Dave, Glen, Mike, Rachael, and Travis.

To my family, John, Kevin, Keith, Mollie, Whitney, Dillon, Will, Cheryl, Gary, Christi, Josh, JJ, Chris, Craig, Mike, Jim, Rosalinda, Victoria, Nicole, Dave, and those we miss terribly, Carol, Joan, Ann, and Willy.

To my other kids, Arielle, Emily Rose, Sayde, James, Shelby, Rainer, and Ean. And finally, and most importantly, to my own child, Dennesy, apologies for the long hours in front of a computer, and the constant "hang on a second"s. It is my sincerest hope you think all of this was worth it. Sometimes moms aren't perfect, even though we certainly try to be. I love you and could not have survived this life of mine without you.

About the Author

Dorriah Rogers grew up in Southern California, in the rural pastures and orchards where the story of *Twine* is set. She earned her PhD from the University of California, Davis and still lives in California with her daughter, three horses, two cats, and a dog. This is her memoir.

PERMUTED PRESS

needs **you** to help

SPREAD (THE) INFECTION

FOLLOW US!

f | Facebook.com/PermutedPress
🐦 | Twitter.com/PermutedPress

REVIEW US!

Wherever you buy our book, they can be reviewed! We want to know what you like!

GET INFECTED!

Sign up for our mailing list at
PermutedPress.com

PERMUTED
PRESS

KING ARTHUR AND THE KNIGHTS OF THE ROUND TABLE HAVE BEEN REBORN TO SAVE THE WORLD FROM THE CLUTCHES OF MORGANA WHILE SHE PROPELS OUR MODERN WORLD INTO THE MIDDLE AGES.

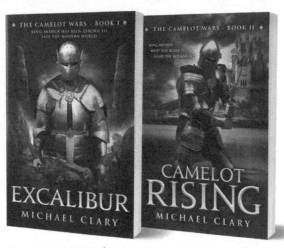

EAN 9781618685018 $15.99   **EAN** 9781682611562 $15.99

Morgana's first attack came in a red fog that wiped out all modern technology. The entire planet was pushed back into the middle ages. The world descended into chaos.

But hope is not yet lost— King Arthur, Merlin, and the Knights of the Round Table have been reborn.

THE ULTIMATE PREPPER'S ADVENTURE.
THE JOURNEY BEGINS HERE!

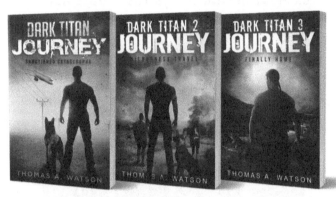

EAN 9781682611654 $9.99   **EAN** 9781618687371 $9.99   **EAN** 9781618687395 $9.99

The long-predicted Coronal Mass Ejection has finally hit the Earth, virtually destroying civilization. Nathan Owens has been prepping for a disaster like this for years, but now he's a thousand miles away from his family and his refuge. He'll have to employ all his hard-won survivalist skills to save his current community, before he begins his long journey through doomsday to get back home.

PERMUTED
PRESS

THE MORNINGSTAR STRAIN HAS BEEN LET LOOSE—IS THERE ANY WAY TO STOP IT?

An industrial accident unleashes some of the Morningstar Strain. The

EAN 9781618686497 **$16.00**

doctor who discovered the strain and her assistant will have to fight their way through Sprinters and Shamblers to save themselves, the vaccine, and the base. Then they discover that it wasn't an accident at all—somebody inside the facility did it on purpose. The war with the RSA and the infected is far from over.

This is the fourth book in Z.A. Recht's The Morningstar Strain series, written by Brad Munson.

PERMUTED
PRESS

GATHERED TOGETHER AT LAST, THREE TALES OF FANTASY CENTERING AROUND THE MYSTERIOUS CITY OF SHADOWS...ALSO KNOWN AS CHICAGO.

EAN 9781682612286 $9.99   EAN 9781618684639 $5.99   EAN 9781618684899 $5.99

From *The New York Times* and *USA Today* bestselling author Richard A. Knaak comes three tales from Chicago, the City of Shadows. Enter the world of the Grey–the creatures that live at the edge of our imagination and seek to be real. Follow the quest of a wizard seeking escape from the centuries-long haunting of a gargoyle. Behold the coming of the end of the world as the Dutchman arrives.

Enter the City of Shadows.

PERMUTED
PRESS

WE CAN'T GUARANTEE THIS GUIDE WILL SAVE YOUR LIFE. BUT WE CAN GUARANTEE IT WILL KEEP YOU SMILING WHILE THE LIVING DEAD ARE CHOWING DOWN ON YOU.

EAN 9781618686695 $9.99

This is the only tool you need to survive the zombie apocalypse.

OK, that's not really true. But when the SHTF, you're going to want a survival guide that's not just geared toward day-to-day survival. You'll need one that addresses the essential skills for true nourishment of the human spirit. Living through the end of the world isn't worth a damn unless you can enjoy yourself in any way you want. (Except, of course, for anything having to do with abuse. We could never condone such things. At least the publisher's lawyers say we can't.)

PERMUTED
PRESS